CW00497623

THE RAZOR G[

By Simon McCleave

A DC Ruth Hunter Murder File
Book 2

No part of this publication may be reproduced, stored, or transmitted in any form or by any means, electronic, mechanical, photocopying, recording, scanning, or otherwise without written permission from the publisher. It is illegal to copy this book, post it to a website, or distribute it by any other means without permission.

Names, characters, businesses, places, events, and incidents are either the products of the author's imagination or used in a purely fictitious manner. Any resemblance to actual persons, living or dead, or actual events is purely coincidental.

First published by Stamford Publishing Ltd in 2021
Copyright © Simon McCleave, 2021
All rights reserved

Your FREE book is waiting for you now

Get your FREE copy of the prequel to
the DI Ruth Hunter Series NOW
at www.simonmccleave.com[1]
and join my VIP Email Club

For my friend Gordon Baker
A kind, generous and wonderful man
(1960-2021)

PROLOGUE

Balham High Street, South London
Tuesday 13th November 1956

Alfie Wise pulled up the black velvet collar on his long neo-Edwardian coat against the icy wind that swirled around the bottom of Balham Hill, South London. His older brother Charlie'd had the coat made to measure for Alfie at Henry London Tailors on Battersea Rise the year before. That was Charlie. Flashy but generous. Alfie, who had just turned seventeen, ran his fingers through his greasy black quiff. He thought his hairstyle made him look just like Tony Curtis, especially when Curtis had played a boxer in the film *The Square Jungle*. Alfie's dad said he looked like a tart and spent more time on his bloody hair than his sister Evelyn. Alfie didn't care what his dad said. He was old, grumpy and boring.

Trevor Walsh, or just 'Walshy' to his mates, sat next to him at the bus stop carefully rolling up a ciggie. He tried to shield it from the wind which picked up tiny flakes of tobacco and whisked them away.

It had been close to ten o'clock by the time they left Balham Odeon. They had watched the new rock'n'roll film, *The Blackboard Jungle*. Everyone was talking about it. When Bill Haley and His Comets appeared up on the screen singing *Rock Around The Clock*, some local Teddy Boys jived with their birds in the aisles until the ushers told them to sit down. Alfie thought there might have been a scrap but they settled down. Watching a trailer for the film *Love Me Tender* with the new American singer Elvis Presley, Alfie found himself totally mesmerised. He had never told anyone, not even Walshy, but he had a bit of a crush on Elvis the Pelvis.

Normally, Alfie and Walshy would have travelled by bus, or got a lift from Charlie, to the Coronet at Elephant and Castle if they were going to the pictures. Last month they'd seen a boring Western called *Giant* starring James Dean. However, two weeks ago, a gang of Teds called the Elephant Boys had ripped the cinema to pieces during the film, then had a dust up with the local coppers and now the film was banned from the Coronet. Some newspapers said the film was going to be banned everywhere. His brother had read to him from the paper that it was '... *a symbol of Britain's delinquent teenagers and declining standards.*' Alfie didn't know what either of those things meant. And he didn't care.

Alfie and Walshy hoped it was going to kick off in the Balham Odeon too, but it never did. Instead, Walshy threw popcorn at some other teenagers hoping to get a rise out of them. They ignored him, which was just as well as Walshy was a bit of a nutter and handy with his fists. Now he and Walshy were shivering at the bus stop, waiting to travel the five miles back to Peckham where they lived.

Alfie looked at Walshy's freckled, handsome face, blue eyes, and his gingery quiff that was curled and so long that it rested on his forehead. He reached out slowly to touch Walshy's hand. For a moment, Walshy responded as they looked at each other. His fingers were icy. Then Walshy withdrew his hand and looked embarrassed as his eyes darted around furtively. 'Not 'ere, eh?'

Alfie nodded uncomfortably. They didn't want to get nicked. Alfie had heard that coppers enjoyed beating up queers. He rubbed his hands together to keep warm as the wind picked up a bit and said through chattering teeth, 'It's brass monkeys.'

Walshy gestured up the street to three teenage Teddy Boys sauntering in their direction. 'Who the fuck are this lot? Plough Boys?'

Alfie wasn't in the mood for yet another fight. Walshy loved getting into scraps but it was too cold. Alfie wanted to go home, have a cup of tea and a jam sandwich, and chat with his brother Charlie. 'I bloody hope not.'

The Plough Boys were a notorious Teddy Boy gang who hung around near the Plough Pub up by Clapham Common. They had stabbed and murdered some kid a few years ago after a knife fight on Clapham High Street. It had made the front page of all the national papers. They caught the boy that had done the stabbing but they didn't hang him. Not like that kid, Derek Bentley. He hadn't even shot the copper down in Croydon, but they hanged him anyway. Alfie's dad thought they should hang the bloody lot of them. He said he didn't fight Rommel in the desert for a load of fucking hooligans to roam the streets of London and scare everyone.

Walshy sneered as he glared at the approaching gang. 'Just fucking cosh boys, that's all.'

That was Walshy. He wasn't scared of anyone.

'Cosh boys' referred to Teddy Boy gangs' weapon of choice. A 'cosh' was made from a small leather handle and a lead weight covered in leather at the end. A quick blow of a cosh to the head would knock most blokes to the ground.

As the Teddy Boys got closer, Walshy stretched out his legs across the pavement, gave an audible sigh and grinned at Alfie.

Alfie rolled his eyes. *Oh, here we go.* It was a deliberately provocative move.

'Walshy?' he groaned.

Walshy shrugged. 'What?'

The gang slowed as they were forced to walk around Walshy's outstretched legs. Alfie could feel his heart racing. They were outnumbered. He could smell the Teddy Boys' aftershave and cigarette smoke.

'Evening lads,' Walshy said with a smirk.

The Teddy Boys stopped about ten yards away, looked back at them and talked in hushed voices.

Alfie's stomach was now knotted.

I don't fancy our odds here. We're gonna get our heads kicked in.

Glancing around, Alfie looked for the best escape route if they were set upon. Maybe jump on a train from Balham tube station?

The tallest member of the gang looked about eighteen or nineteen. He had olive skin and let a cigarette droop from his mouth like he was bloody James Dean. His drape jacket had a thin black collar and long sleeves, and his tapered trousers exposed his light-coloured socks and thick-soled brogues. He burst into laughter at something one boy had said – a comment clearly referring to Alfie and Walshy.

Walshy glared at the older boy. 'Something funny, you flash cunt?'

Alfie took a deep breath. He knew they weren't getting out of this without a fight, in which case he might have to get stuck in.

The older boy laughed, cupped his ear and smirked at Walshy. 'You say something?'

Another boy, whose quiff came down to the bridge of his nose, frowned sarcastically. 'Frank, I think he called you a cunt!'

Frank snorted with ironic laughter. 'Did he?'

'Walshy? Come on, let's leave it tonight,' Alfie said quietly, but he knew it was no use.

Standing up, Walshy turned to face them and yelled, 'You deaf? I called you a *cunt*!'

Frank flicked his cigarette so that it hit Walshy in the chest and showered his waistcoat in red embers. 'Oops, careful.' The other boys laughed.

Suddenly, Walshy was up and he pounced on Frank, punching him to the pavement before another Teddy Boy jumped on his back.

Alfie stood up and was preparing to get stuck in when he saw that the third member of the gang - a short, overweight boy with acne - was heading for him with his fists clenched.

'Come on then, let's have it!' the boy growled.

Alfie reached into his trouser pocket and felt the cold brass knuckle duster that Charlie had given him. He slipped it over the back of his hand. He knew how to handle himself and used to practise boxing with his older brother.

The short boy bounced around in front of him with his fists up. 'Come on, you nonce. What you waiting for?'

I'm going to knock you out, you little prick.

Alfie pretended he wasn't going to put up a fight. But then, in one swift move, he withdrew his hand with the knuckle duster from his pocket and threw an almighty punch across the boy's jaw. It knocked him flying.

'Have that, you fucker!' he yelled as the boy crumpled and fell in a heap on the pavement.

Alfie felt the rush of adrenaline surge through his body.

Out of the corner of his eye, he saw Frank was coming his way.

I'm taking out this big fucker now, Alfie thought. His blood was up.

In Frank's hand he saw a large flick knife with a black handle.

Shit! I'm gonna get stabbed.

'I've done your mate. Now it's your turn, you little wanker,' Frank snarled.

I'm not bloody fighting someone with a knife.

Turning on his heels, Alfie sprinted off down the pavement, out onto the icy road and headed down Balham High Street towards the underground station. He could hear the clatter of feet behind him and some shouting.

As he headed into the station lobby, Alfie's winklepicker shoes skidded on the black and white tiled floor. He barged past the ticket collector and turned right down the stone steps that led to the trains. He was running so fast he thought he was going to lose his balance and tumble down the stairs.

As he looked ahead at the deserted platform, he saw the last carriages of a Northern Line train pulling out. He turned back and saw Frank at the top of the stairs.

Shit! Now what? And what happened to Walshy? I hope he's all right.

Scanning up and down the empty platform, Alfie realised he was trapped. The only way out was up the staircase or over the tracks.

Frank had stopped at the top of the steps and glared down at him. 'Stay there, you tosser.'

Alfie had two choices. Jump down onto the electric tracks and cross over to the other platform while avoiding the trains, or stand his ground and fight. He thought of his brother, Charlie. What would he do? Charlie was a hard man and never backed down.

I'll do him, even if he's got a fucking knife.

Taking a deep breath, Alfie gripped the knuckle duster and readied himself.

Let's do this! Let's have this fucker.

Frank walked slowly down the steps with a smirk. 'Oh dear. What's your old lady gonna say when she sees your dead body with shit in your pants?'

Alfie smiled and then gestured to the knife. 'Very brave using that. Why don't you put it down and we'll have a proper scrap, eh?'

Frank held up the flick knife, which Alfie could see had blood on it. 'This? I can't do that. I need this to cut your little bollocks off.'

'Well, you'd better come and do it, big man.'

Alfie's heart was thumping hard against his chest. He was trying to get his breath.

Moving quickly, Frank lunged at him with the knife but Alfie knocked his arm away.

They circled around each other for a few seconds.

Alfie feigned to swing a punch.

Frank ducked back and lashed out wildly with the knife.

Throwing out jabs, Alfie kept mobile on his feet like Charlie had shown him.

Frank came again, slashing the knife towards his face. 'Come here, you fucker! I'm gonna cut you up.'

Spotting that Frank was off balance each time he swung, Alfie waited for him to make another move.

Frank sprang forward, jabbing the knife towards Alfie's neck.

Instantly, Alfie swung his fist. The knuckle duster connected with Frank's temple with a loud crack, splitting open the skin and knocking him to the floor.

The flick knife dropped from his hand and skidded away on the concrete platform.

Alfie scurried forward, picked up the knife, and turned around to face Frank who was trying to get to his feet.

Blinking the blood from his eye, Frank shook his head and steadied himself. He pulled a leather cosh from the inside of his jacket.

'It's a fair fight now!' he growled.

Moving forward, Alfie could see that Frank was still reeling from the punch, and the blood from the gash in his head was making it difficult for him to see.

With the odds now in his favour, Alfie went in to finish the job. Distracting Frank with a swift kick to the shins, he plunged the knife into his chest before he saw it coming.

Wincing with pain, Frank clutched at the knife that was now sticking out of his bloodied waistcoat.

He staggered sideways.

Alfie moved backwards and watched in shock as Frank's feet shuffled under him and he lost his balance. He fell off the platform edge and disappeared out of sight.

Oh shit. This is not good.

Taking a breath, Alfie looked down at his shaking hands that were now splattered in blood. He couldn't believe what had just happened.

Before he had time to go over to the platform edge, there was a powerful gust of wind against his face. Then a rumble of noise which grew louder as a tube train came thundering into the platform.

If Frank hadn't died from the knife wound, he was going to die now.

There was a terrible metallic squeal of brakes as the tube driver spotted the body on the tracks but it was too late.

Alfie turned and ran up the stone steps and out of the station.

CHAPTER 1

eckham, South London, August 1997

P   Detective Constable Ruth Hunter and Detective Constable Lucy Henry were stuck in the stationary traffic on Peckham High Street on their way back to Peckham CID. It was a scorching hot day and a heat haze rose and shimmered above the road ahead. Teenagers in basketball vests and shorts sat on the pavement outside the Chicken Shack and squinted in the sunlight.

Bloody hell, it's too hot to be sitting here like this, Ruth thought.

She put the car into neutral, pushed her sunglasses up onto her head and changed the radio station. When she heard *Closer Than Close* by Rosie Gaines, she turned the volume up and said in a silly voice, 'Tuuuuuune!'

Lucy rolled her eyes. 'Aren't you too old to like this music?'

'All right, grandma. I'm driving so I'm the DJ,' Ruth responded.

Lucy puffed out her cheeks and looked to see if the car's AC would go any higher. 'Jesus, I'm sweltering here.'

A gang of older teens outside the Chicken Shack looked over at them. They were smoking a spliff and had already clocked they were coppers. They weren't remotely concerned. Peckham was that kind of place.

Ruth ignored them, pulled her sunglasses back down, took a ciggie from the packet on the dashboard and lit it. She wasn't about to jump out of the car in the middle of traffic to book the lads for possession. It wasn't worth the time spent on paperwork.

There was a sudden waft of marijuana smoke inside the car. Ruth shook her head as she looked over at the gang. 'Very subtle.'

Lucy raised an eyebrow. 'I thought you used to like a bit of the old wacky backy?'

Ruth snorted. 'Wacky backy? Bloody hell, Lucy. My nan is more streetwise than you.'

Lucy laughed and then wagged a finger at Ruth's cigarette. 'And I thought you were going to quit?'

Ruth shrugged defensively. 'Was I? When did I say that?'

'I thought Lady Shiori had quit and suggested that you join her?'

Lucy was referring to Ruth's Japanese girlfriend, whom Ruth had been seeing for about three months.

Ruth sighed, 'Yeah, she *suggests* a lot of things.'

'Honeymoon period over is it?'

'Definitely. I think what she actually wants is a maid and a nanny, not a girlfriend,' Ruth muttered.

The Tetra radio in their car crackled. 'Alpha three zero from Dispatch, do you read, over?'

Lucy picked up the radio, 'Alpha three zero receiving. Go ahead, over.'

'Report from a uniformed patrol at Dixon's Timber Yard on Thread Street. Possible discovery of human remains, over.'

'Alpha three zero to Dispatch, show us attending, over.' Lucy looked over at Ruth and pulled a face. 'Human remains? I'm glad I've already had my lunch.'

Ruth pointed to the dashboard. 'Blues and twos then?'

'Definitely. I'm not sitting in this bloody traffic.'

Ruth hit the button and the siren and blue lights burst into life, making everyone on the pavement turn to see what was going on.

Pulling the car out of the traffic, Ruth hit the accelerator and sped down the waiting line of cars towards the timber yard. She could feel a rush of adrenaline as she sped through the traffic lights and turned right.

BY THE TIME RUTH AND Lucy arrived at Dixon's Timber Yard, the SOCO team, which stood for Scene of Crime Officer, had arrived. Uniformed police had taped off an area to the rear of the yard. The air smelled of hot wood and chemical treatments such as creosote.

A constable stood by the blue and white tape that read POLICE LINE DO NOT CROSS. As Ruth and Lucy approached, they flashed their warrant cards and he lifted the tape for them to pass under.

Ruth lifted her sunglasses and looked at him. She was trying to establish how gruesome the discovery had been by the look on his face. 'What have we got over there, Constable?'

He gestured to some workmen sitting on stacks of wood to their right. 'Workmen were breaking up the ground to lay foundations. They found bones and a skull and called us.'

'Have we got all their details?' Ruth asked.

He hesitated for a second and then tapped his shirt pocket where he kept his notebook. 'All in here, boss.' Ruth wondered if the question had annoyed him, as if she had somehow questioned his ability to do his job. She had met plenty of uniformed officers who were defensive around CID. She couldn't blame them as many CID officers were incredibly arrogant and treated those in uniform with disdain.

Lucy put away her warrant card. 'Anyone set up a scene log, Constable?'

He pointed to a small huddle of SOCOs in white forensic suits, and two more uniformed officers. 'Not yet. My sarge is over there with the Chief SOCO.'

Lucy gestured to the yard. 'Can we set one up before someone treads their gigantic size bloody tens all over what might be a crime scene?'

The constable bristled but said, 'Yes. Right away.'

They turned and made their way towards the small group near where the ground had been excavated.

Lucy looked back at the constable and then at Ruth. 'He was a bit frosty.'

'I used to be like that when CID used to swan into a crime scene like they owned the bloody place.'

They took out their IDs and identified themselves.

An area of ground about twenty feet by ten feet had been dug down by about four feet to reveal dry brown earth and rocks. Two SOCOs crouched down inside the excavated area. As Ruth peered inside, she saw several long bones and a skull.

As the SOCO nearest to them turned and looked up, Ruth recognised him as Chief Forensic Officer Martin Hill, whom she and Lucy had worked with before. He was late 50s, blonde and thin, with a faint Cornish accent. He didn't suffer fools, but Ruth trusted his work implicitly.

'Afternoon ladies.' Hill squinted at the sun and smiled. 'My heart always sinks when we get called to look at human remains. But at least these are old enough that they don't smell, eh?'

Lucy raised her eyebrow sardonically at Ruth. 'Erm, I guess that's one way of looking at it.'

That's SOCOs for you, Ruth thought. *Clinical and detached, with a strangely dark sense of humour.*

'What can you tell us?' Ruth asked.

'It's a *he.* Looking at the slightly underdeveloped femur, I would guess that he was young, maybe adolescent.'

Lucy peered down. 'Any obvious cause of death?'

Hill shook his head. 'No, not yet. I'll know a lot more when I get him back to the lab.'

'What about timescale?' Ruth asked.

Hill pulled a face. 'Sorry. It's really difficult to say.'

Ruth was surprised that he couldn't give them anything to go on. 'Okay, but are we talking medieval peasant or a Peckham drug dealer from five years ago?'

Hill pulled his mask down a little and wiped his brow. 'You could probably rule out five years ago but I'm sorry, ladies. The soil around here is chalky, which makes it very alkaline. It creates a perfect environment for bones to survive. These could be the bones of a Roman teenager from two thousand years ago.'

Ruth looked at Lucy – that wasn't what they were expecting when they first arrived.

'Boss?' said a voice with some sense of urgency. It was the female SOCO at the other end of where they had been digging.

Hill moved forward to see what she was gesturing to. 'What is it?'

The female SOCO turned the skull to reveal the back. About four inches from the top was a neat, circular hole about the size of a ten pence piece. Hill crouched down to have a look at it for a moment.

'What is it?' Lucy asked.

Hill hesitated as he inspected it and then glanced back at them. 'It's a bullet hole.'

Ruth's eyes widened in surprise. 'I guess that rules out our Roman teenagers and medieval peasants then?'

CHAPTER 2

Standing in the small garden of her ground floor Balham flat, Ruth took the dry clothes from the clothes horse as her daughter Ella played noisily nearby with her best friend Koyuki. She couldn't believe that Ella would be three years old by the end of the year. How did that happen? The girls were happily throwing coloured balls at skittles as she went inside to pour herself a well-earned glass of wine.

Opening an envelope, she saw that it was a cheque for £45 from her ex-husband Dan, Ella's father.

Are you bloody joking? she thought angrily. It was only the third time that Dan had sent any money to help with Ella's keep since he'd walked out in April. It was after Dan had left that Ruth discovered he had been having an affair with an Australian woman called Angela. Even though Dan had promised to stay in Ella's life, he had failed to pick her up to take her out on many occasions. Ruth was furious with him because he just didn't seem bothered whether or not he saw Ella.

Ruth poured herself a glass of white wine and took out a cigarette. They went together so perfectly. When Ella had been born, she promised herself that she would stop smoking. When she realised she couldn't do that, she told herself she would never smoke in front of her. Now that she was a single parent, that was no longer an option, but she felt guilty every time she did.

The sound of a key in the front door broke her train of thought. It was Shiori, Ruth's girlfriend. She was a Japanese-American journalist, recently divorced, who lived nearby in Clapham. Ruth had met her because Ella and her daughter Koyuki had become best friends at nursery. Even though they'd both had previous encounters with women, it was the first time either of them had been in a proper gay relationship. However, Ruth was finding Shiori increasingly irritating. Her demands upon Ruth's time, and the expectation that she would take care of Koyuki, were starting to grate.

Shiori swept into the kitchen and plonked her bag down onto the sofa. 'Christ, what a day! If I meet another privileged, middle-aged man with an attitude problem today I'm going to stab them.' She frowned and looked at Ruth. 'Have you been smoking?'

Ruth just wasn't in the mood. 'Yes.'

And how was your day, Ruth? I found the remains of a man's body who had been shot in the head. Thanks for asking, Ruth thought sardonically to herself.

Shiori looked at Ruth. 'I thought you weren't going ... Never mind. I need a drink. Is there wine in the fridge?'

Ruth bristled. 'Yes. I bought some on the way home.'

Shiori grabbed a glass, marched over to the fridge, pulled out the bottle and poured herself a glass. She waved the bottle. 'Want some?'

Ruth shook her head. 'I'm fine thanks.'

Shiori took two mouthfuls of wine and gave an audible sigh. 'Better. I need a massive favour tonight, honey.'

Ruth could feel herself tense. *Here we go.*

Shiori leant against the kitchen counter. 'I need to meet another journalist for drinks in town. It won't be a late one, but could Koyuki stay here?'

Ruth wouldn't have minded, but it was becoming a regular request at least once or twice a week. And Shiori had very quickly gone from being incredibly grateful and buying Ruth flowers or wine, to fully expecting her to say yes with little word of thanks.

I'm seriously not in the mood for this tonight, Ruth thought.

'Sorry but I can't,' Ruth said firmly.

Shiori frowned. 'What?'

Ruth shrugged. 'I'm tired and I want an early night. I don't want to feed and bath Koyuki again and then wait up for you to get back and tell me all about your night.'

Shiori glared at her. 'What am I meant to do then?'

'Go home and arrange a babysitter.'

'I probably won't get one now.'

Ruth could feel her pulse quicken. 'Not my problem. I didn't get into this relationship so that you could have free childcare on tap. And I'm fed up with people taking the piss. So, I'm sorry if you don't like it but I'm not in the mood.'

Shiori shook her head. 'I don't know why you're being such a bitch about it.'

I'll let that go before I really explode, Ruth thought.

Shiori went over to the patio doors. 'Koyuki, we're going now darling.'

Ruth could feel the tension, but she wasn't going to back down now.

Taking Koyuki by the hand, they headed towards the hall-way. Shiori turned, scowled, and then waved the keys to Ruth's front door. 'Do you want these back then?'

'It's up to you, Shiori,' Ruth said with a shrug.

Shiori went over to the table, slammed the keys down, grabbed Koyuki's hand and left.

As the front door closed with a bang, Ruth breathed a sigh of relief. Maybe she just needed some time on her own.

IT WAS EARLY EVENING as Lucy walked out of her patio doors and felt the warm wind against her face. It smelled of the lavender plants that she had recently bought and placed in two huge azure blue pots at the far end of the garden by the fence.

A figure appeared behind her with a smile. The man was carrying a bottle of beer and a glass of white wine which he handed to her. It was Brooks. He leant in and gave her a kiss which turned into a snog.

Lucy laughed. 'Easy tiger.'

Brooks smiled. 'I can't help myself.'

'Anyway, I thought we were having a night off the booze?'

Brooks gestured to the setting sun that was turning the sky tangerine and flamingo pink. 'It's too hot not to drink.'

'Cheers to that. It was a crap idea in the first place.' Lucy clinked his glass.

Brooks gestured to his bottle. 'Probably best if I get a bottle opener. I would use my teeth but they cost me a fortune.'

Lucy laughed and watched him walk away. Even though he was fifteen years older than her, he was fit, handsome and the kind of man she knew would take care of her. It had only been three months since Harry had left his wife and moved in. And it would have been perfect except for one minor detail.

Brooks was Harry by night. However, during the day he was Detective Chief Inspector Harry Brooks, Head of Peckham CID and her guv'nor. Only Ruth knew about their relationship and she wasn't going to say anything. But if anyone discovered it, the Met's top brass would probably force Lucy to transfer to another station.

Glancing down the side passage of the house, Lucy spotted the rubbish bin and remembered that tomorrow was collection day. She put her glass of wine down on the circular patio table, walked down the passageway and grabbed the bin. Opening the side gate, she wheeled it to the front of the house where it would be collected at about 6 am the following morning.

The sound of a car engine drew her attention. As she glanced left, her stomach tensed. It was the third time she had seen the same blue Renault Clio outside her house in the last two weeks. The Clio pulled away from the curb and sped off – far too quickly not to be suspicious.

What the bloody hell is that all about?

Lucy hadn't told Brooks as she thought he might think she was being paranoid. This time she was convinced there was something to be concerned about. Squinting, she caught the beginning of the number plate - *H274.*

Locking up the side gate, she returned to the patio where Brooks stood drinking his beer.

He smiled at her. 'I was going to do that.'

'Remember H274,' Lucy said as she headed inside to grab a pen.

Brooks followed her inside. 'Everything okay, Luce?'

Lucy found a pen and a scrap of paper and said, 'H274. It's the beginning of a number plate.'

'And you're writing it down because ...?

Lucy glanced up at him. 'I've seen a car sitting outside here twice in the last two weeks. I've just seen it again, and they drove off when I came out with the bin.'

'H274?' Brooks asked with a frown.

'Yeah.'

He pursed his lips. 'A dark blue Renault Clio?'

Lucy looked at him in surprise. 'Yeah? How do you know that?'

'It's Karen's car,' he said despondently.

Karen was Harry's ex-wife.

CHAPTER 3

A s Ruth entered Peckham CID, she could see that it was full as detectives prepared themselves for DCI Brooks' morning briefing. She was late as she had been trying to track down the history of Dixon's Timber Yard. Scanning around the room, she noticed that the only available chair was next to Detective Sergeant Tim Gaughran.

Sod it, Ruth thought.

She had Gaughran's number as soon as she'd joined Peckham CID. Young, arrogant and misogynistic. He came from a family of coppers, which meant that he thought he knew everything and everyone.

With a forced smile, Ruth gestured to the empty chair. Gaughran had sprawled himself out, and she needed him to sit up and move. 'Okay if I sit here?'

Gaughran gave her his trademark smirk. 'Here? Yeah. Be my guest.'

Ruth saw Lucy giving her a look of amused condolence as she sat down. 'Thanks.'

Gaughran looked at her. 'I thought you didn't like me, Ruth?'

Ruth met his gaze head on. 'I don't. It's the only chair left.'

'Fair enough. I will grow on you, eventually.'

Ruth smiled. 'What - like bacteria?'

'That's funny.'

'Come back to me when you've had a personality bypass.'

'Bit harsh,' Gaughran laughed as he sat back and crossed his chubby thighs.

The murmur of conversation dwindled as Brooks made his way to the middle of the CID office. 'Morning everyone. First things first. I know it's bloody hot in here at the moment, so I've put in an order for some fans to see if that makes it at all bearable.'

'Except they won't get here until Christmas, guv,' Gaughran quipped. There were a few laughs.

'Thanks for your optimism, Tim. If it gets too much, you can always 'borrow' a fan from uniform downstairs. They're out most of the day.' There were a few more laughs at Brooks' suggestion to steal fans from uniform. There was little love lost between CID and uniform, so it was an amusing idea. 'Okay, Tim and Syed, how are we doing with the robberies on the high street?'

Ruth looked over at Detective Constable Syed Hassan, Gaughran's awkward partner in CID.

The next ten minutes were taken up with Hassan and Gaughran's investigation into a poorly-run protection racket on various shops and businesses in the Peckham High Street area. Gaughran was convinced it was just a bunch of kids from the local estates trying their luck.

When they had finished, Brooks looked over at Lucy. For a split second, there was a furtive glance between them that no one except Ruth would spot. She wondered how long Brooks and Lucy could keep their relationship a secret.

'Lucy, what's happening with the remains that were found over at Dixon's Timber Yard?' Brooks asked.

'Waiting for forensics to see if they can date them. There's a bullet hole in the skull, which we assume narrows it down a bit. Maybe post-war. Ruth and I are looking at the history of the site.'

'Remember, there is no statute of limitations on murder,' Brooks said with an air of gravity. 'And if this is a murder case, there might still be relatives that were affected by what happened to whoever has been found. I know I don't need to tell you, but we have to give it our best work.'

Lucy nodded. 'Yes, guv.'

As the briefing ended, a uniformed officer from reception approached Ruth. 'DC Hunter?'

Ruth smiled at him. 'How can I help?'

'Message from forensics. They've found something they want you and DC Henry to go and look at. It sounded urgent.'

EVEN THOUGH IT WAS less than four miles from Peckham nick, it was going to take twenty minutes to get to the Metropolitan Police Forensic Science Laboratory. Built in the late 60s, the building was a commanding concrete building with enormous glass windows, external concrete stairways and a fifty-foot concrete ventilator shaft.

As Ruth got out of the car and headed for reception, she gestured to the building. 'I wonder how long before we start going to some private lab?'

There were rumblings that the Met was going to use private forensic laboratories to drive down costs.

Lucy shrugged. 'If they're cheaper, then what's the problem?'

Ruth shook her head as they flashed their warrant cards and signed in. 'We don't need them to be cheaper. They need to be precise, accurate and reliable.'

As they walked to the allocated forensic lab, Lucy pulled a face. 'From what I hear, there's a lot of money being wasted in places like this.'

Ruth sighed out loud. 'Bloody hell, Lucy. You really are a Tory girl. And at the first sign of a private lab buggering up results and some expensive miscarriage of justice, the Met will take them all back in-house.'

Lucy smirked, opened the door and beckoned Ruth to go into Laboratory 4. 'We'll see. It's not our job to stand in the way of progress or modernisation.'

Ruth sneered at her. 'Lucy?'

'Yeah?'

'Shut up,' Ruth said with a forced laugh.

On the other side of the large laboratory was Martin Hill. He gestured for them to come over. 'Ladies. Twice in two days,' he said as he handed them a mask each.

Putting on her mask, Ruth remembered that she didn't like them – they made her feel claustrophobic. 'We got your message. Something interesting.'

Hill rubbed his chin and said, 'Well, there's good news and bad news.'

'Bad news first,' Lucy said immediately.

'There was no DNA match on the bones we recovered. That means the only way of getting any idea of date is to have them carbon dated,' he explained.

'How long does that take?' Lucy asked.

'Could take a week, I'm afraid.'

Ruth shrugged. It wasn't as if the case was particularly time sensitive. 'What's the good news?'

'Two bits of good news actually,' Hill said as he turned, took a clear evidence bag from a nearby counter top and held it up. To Ruth it looked like a small locker key of some sort. 'We found this under the hip bones. My guess is that it was in a trouser pocket. We've had a go at cleaning it up.'

Lucy moved a step closer and peered at the key. 'What is it exactly?'

'I've asked around. I think it's a car key,' he explained.

But it doesn't remotely look like a car key, Ruth thought.

'Really. Are you sure? It's tiny,' she said, hoping she didn't sound rude.

Hill nodded. 'I asked one of the older sergeants earlier. He thought it looked like a car key from the 50s. Apparently they were much smaller. There was a serial number on it, but it's been rusted away. However, if you turn it around you can see this symbol on the other side.'

Ruth looked carefully. There was an image of wings cut into the metal. 'Any idea what car make that is?'

Hill shook his head. 'Sorry. No one seems to know.' He grabbed another small evidence bag. 'We also found this signet ring as well.' He held it up. 'We cleaned it up but there's nothing engraved on it. I was hoping for some initials or something.'

Ruth looked a little closer. The ring was gold with a black rectangle in the middle. 'What's that?'

'Onyx. Very fashionable in rings of that type in the 50s.'

Ruth nodded – the two bits of evidence meant they could start to narrow down when the murder had been committed.

RUTH AND LUCY PARKED up outside Marson's, the scruffy old garage at the far end of Peckham High Street which had been there for decades. Getting out of the car, Ruth put on her sunglasses and puffed out her cheeks. It was unbearably hot and the air was thick with heat and oil fumes from the garage.

Lucy looked at her and raised an eyebrow. 'Shall we just go and drink cider in the park?'

Ruth snorted. 'If only.'

A man in his 40s, shaved head, in grease-stained overalls came out of a Portakabin wiping his hands with a cloth. 'Can I help, ladies?'

Ruth pushed her sunglasses up, pulled out her warrant card and showed it to him. 'We're from Peckham CID. Wonder if you can help us?'

The man chortled and put his hands up. 'Whatever it is, darling, I didn't do it. Honest.'

Lucy rolled her eyes at Ruth and then showed the man the key inside the evidence bag. 'Wonder if you can help us and have a look at this key?'

'I'll do my best, love,' the man said as he studied it.

'Is there anything you can tell us about it?' Ruth asked.

He scratched his chin thoughtfully. 'It's old. Could be forties ... actually, more like the 50s.'

Lucy turned the key to show him the sign. 'Do you know what that is?'

'Yeah. It's the old Chrysler sign. Before they changed it,' the man explained.

Lucy looked at Ruth and pulled a face. Neither of them were particularly well-informed about cars.

'And when you say Chrysler, what type of car is that?' Ruth asked.

The man gave a condescending laugh. 'A big, bloody American car. Like you see in the films. V8 engine, great big wings at the back.'

'We're trying to track down the owner of the car that matches that key,' Lucy explained.

'You looking around this area?' the man asked.

Lucy nodded. 'Yeah, why?'

'You won't have much problem finding out who owned it then,' he said.

Ruth frowned. 'Why's that then?'

The man shook his head. 'Hardly anyone had a car in Peckham in the 1950s. If you had a car, it meant you had money. And if you were driving around in a bloody Chrysler, then everyone would know who you are. There were probably only a handful in London. You're looking for someone who used to be a right flash bastard with a decent amount of dough.'

'Thanks,' Ruth said. 'That's very helpful.'

'This bloke still alive is he? The fella who owns that key?'

Ruth put her sunglasses back on. 'We're not sure yet.'

CHAPTER 4

Opening the file in front of her, Ruth looked at the HM Land Registry file that had been sent over that morning. It was a record of who had owned Dixon's Timber Yard and if there had been any change of use. The first record of the property that Ruth could find was December 1863 where the word *Warehouse* had been handwritten to describe the building. In 1903, the premises had been bought and expanded by the London Milk Supply Company, who developed the site as a small bottling plant and creamery. Finally, in 1948, Mr Arnold Dixon had purchased the site and created Dixon's Timber Yard.

Scribbling down notes, Ruth wondered if Arnold Dixon was still alive. It was likely that the site had been Dixon's Timber Yard when the body had been buried there. Even though it was nearly fifty years ago, she wondered if Arnold Dixon remembered anything. If they could identify the remains they might get a clearer idea of when the murder had taken place and, possibly, why.

Noticing that Gaughran was heading her way, Ruth prepared herself for an inane comment or insult.

Here we go, she thought.

As he reached her desk, she noticed the large sweat patches developing on his blue shirt. *Lovely.*

Ruth gave him a forced smile. 'How can I help, Tim?'

'The guv told me you'd found a car key with those remains that dates back to the 50s,' he said.

Ruth gave him a suspicious frown. It was rare for Gaughran to say anything that didn't involve a dig or an infantile double entendre. 'Erm, yes. The key belongs to a Chrysler, which would have been pretty rare round here back then.'

Gaughran nodded. 'Yeah, it would. My old man was on the beat in Peckham in the 50s. Do you want me to mention it to him? You never know.'

Ruth looked at him. 'What's the catch?'

Gaughran shrugged. 'There is no catch. He took early retirement and does a bit of security work. But he loves talking about the old days. He might remember something.'

Ruth was curious. 'That would be helpful, Tim. But you haven't made a stupid homophobic joke or been sarcastic yet?'

'I'm trying to turn over a new leaf.'

Ruth snorted. 'Bloody hell. How long is that going to last?'

'No idea,' Gaughran said. 'Let me know if you want the old man to come in though.'

'Will do,' Ruth said.

What the hell just happened?

Sitting back for a second, she sipped her coffee and stretched her back. The office was baking hot and she could feel sweat on her top lip. The fan that was spinning on a nearby table just seemed to blow hot air around the office. She needed to get outside hoping there would be some kind of breeze. She spotted Lucy striding purposefully into CID holding a fax, and hoped she had something that would get them out of the building.

Lucy waved the fax at her as she arrived at Ruth's desk. 'Bingo.'

Ruth gave her a quizzical look. 'What have we got?'

'Spoke to the DVLA in Cardiff,' Lucy said as she handed her the fax to look at. 'This is the only Chrysler registered in South East London in the 50s. It was bought by a Charlie Wise in 1954, and the registered address at that time was in Marmont Road.'

'Brilliant. Let's go.' Ruth got up from her chair and grabbed her jacket. Marmont Road was less than ten minutes away.

NUMBER 81 MARMONT ROAD was in the middle of a long row of small terraced houses that were in relatively good condition. As Lucy got out of the car, she felt a warm breeze against her face mixed with Ruth's cigarette smoke. A hundred yards opposite the houses in Marmont Road was one of Peckham's dilapidated housing estates. Built in the 1970s, it was five floors high with concrete stairwells. The litter-strewn grass area at the front had a large black patch where there had clearly been a fire, and two abandoned wheel-less cars that were now resting on bricks. The loud bass of some music vibrated from high up and filled the air.

Ruth spotted Lucy looking over at the estate. 'Remember when we found that weed factory on the fifth floor?'

Lucy pulled a face. 'It stank. I don't know how the neighbours put up with it.'

'Free weed,' Ruth said sardonically.

'Is that ragga or reggae?' Lucy asked.

Ruth shook her head with a smile. 'Oh my god, you are so white.'

Lucy laughed. She had got used to being patronised by Ruth for being unfashionable and uncool. 'And you're not?'

Lucy approached number 81, which had a smart new door, and knocked.

They waited for a minute before Lucy knocked again. They weren't counting on Charlie Wise, or a relative of his, still living in the same house forty years later, but it might give them a lead. Otherwise, they were going to have to track down every Charlie Wise in London and find out if he once owned a Chrysler. Of course, there was also a strong possibility that the bones they had found in Dixon's Timber Yard belonged to Charlie Wise – why else would he have the car key in his pocket?

Moving over to a ground floor window, Lucy cupped her hands to look inside. The sunlight was too bright on the glass and all she could make out were the shapes of furniture.

'Anything?' Ruth asked.

Lucy shook her head. 'Nope.'

Now Ruth tried knocking on the door, but louder.

The noise had clearly alerted the next door neighbour to their presence. A tall Afro-Caribbean woman in her 60s came out of her front door and looked over at them with a smile. 'They've gone to work, dear. Won't be back until six.'

Lucy got out her warrant card and showed it to her. 'Can you tell me who lives in this property?'

'Fiona and Patrick,' the woman said. 'Houston. Young couple.'

'Have they lived here long?' Lucy asked.

The woman shook her head. 'No, no. Couple of years, that's all. Do you want me to pass them a message?'

Lucy shook her head. 'No, thank you. Can I ask how long you've lived here, Mrs ...?'

'Jenkins.' The woman thought for a moment and gave a little laugh. 'I've lived here for forty three years now.'

Lucy moved a few steps closer so they didn't have to speak in raised voices. 'I wonder if you can help us then. We're trying to track down a Charlie Wise who used to live at this property.'

Mrs Jenkins' face lit up at the name and she shook her head. 'Charlie, Charlie. Long time ago. But yes, Charlie lived here. Lovely Charlie.'

Ruth looked over. 'Could you tell us when he moved out?'

Mrs Jenkins shrugged. 'Maybe it was thirty years ago? 1970s? Something like that.'

'I don't suppose you kept in touch, did you? Or do you know where he went?' Lucy asked hopefully.

'Yeah, he comes back here every once in a while. Does a lot for the local community. Of course, I don't call him Charlie anymore. He doesn't like that.' Mrs Jenkins put on her best upper class accent. 'It's Sir Charles ... That boy done good. I saw him on the television last week.'

Sir Charles Wise?

Lucy frowned at Ruth. She knew the name from somewhere.

Ruth's eyes widened. 'Sir Charles Wise. Bloody hell.'

Mrs Jenkins went back to her front door with a beaming smile. 'You won't have a problem finding him. Someone told me he's got a big house that overlooks Wimbledon Common now. Ten bedrooms, swimming pool. He got the lot and good luck to him.' She went inside and closed the door.

Going over to Ruth, Lucy was still none the wiser. 'Why do I know the name Sir Charles Wise?'

'Multi-millionaire businessman. Made his money in retail. Owned all those department stores for a while.'

Lucy nodded slowly as the penny dropped. 'He did that programme about young entrepreneurs on the telly?'

'Exactly ... I wasn't expecting that.'

Lucy turned towards the car. 'Neither was I. Looks like we're going to Wimbledon.'

CHAPTER 5

Turning right along West Side, Ruth gazed over at Wimbledon Common which was full of people walking dogs, picnicking or playing games in the sunshine. An aeroplane flew low overhead as it descended west towards Heathrow. It seemed to glide effortlessly above the clouds, with a graceful ease that contradicted its size and speed. She wondered where it had been, and imagined an exotic location such as Barbados or the Maldives. It's where she assumed the residents of SW19 went for their summer breaks.

Glancing left, she saw a series of large mansions that were set back behind fences and neatly trimmed hedges. Gravel driveways were populated with expensive 4x4s or gleaming sports cars.

They were less than ten miles away from Peckham, but it might as well have been a thousand miles. It was a different world.

'Wonder what it costs to live around here?' Lucy asked no one in particular.

'Millions.'

'So, The Wombles were loaded were they?' she said with a laugh. She was referring to the BBC children's television series set on Wimbledon Common.

'I guess they must have been.'

'And tree hugging environmentalists long before anyone else.'

Ruth frowned. 'What?'

'The Wombles roamed undetected across Wimbledon Common picking up litter out of the goodness of their own hearts,' Lucy said, and then made the peace sign. 'They were eco-warriors before their time, man.'

Ruth laughed. 'Fair point. But you are aware they're not real, aren't you, Luce? There aren't actually furry little animals roaming around litter picking just over there.'

Lucy shook her head ironically. 'That's it Ruth. Shatter all my childhood memories, why don't you? You're such a bitch ... My favourite Womble was Tobermory.'

'Oh no. Uncle Bulgaria was mine.'

Lucy pulled a face. 'Really? Uncle Bulgaria? I thought there was always something creepy about him. You know, like he was a kiddy fiddler or something.'

Ruth rolled her eyes. 'Did you actually just say the phrase 'kiddy fiddler'? You're a police officer.'

Lucy shrugged. 'Okay. I thought that Uncle Bulgaria might have been a paedophile. Is that better?'

Ruth sighed. 'Really not.'

Slowing down, she spotted the address that Brooks had been given by the Wimbledon police and pulled onto a large gravel drive. Parked to one side was a dark blue Bentley and a black Range Rover.

Ruth and Lucy got out of the car and gazed up at the enormous house that had recently been painted and repointed. There were white shutters at every window, and the brickwork was shrouded in orderly swathes of dark ivy. As Ruth reached the imposing front door, she saw there was an entry phone. She supposed that if you lived in a house like this, you wouldn't answer the door to just anyone.

Pressing the buzzer, she immediately heard the deep sound of a barking dog from inside.

Bloody hell, that made me jump!

Lucy, who was holding a case folder, looked at her and pulled a face. 'It sounds friendly.'

'And very big.'

'Hello?' said a man's voice from the entry phone. His accent was distinctly London.

'Hi there. It's DC Hunter and DC Henry from Peckham CID. We're looking for a Mr Charlie or Charles Wise?' Ruth said.

'Yeah, hold on a sec. I'll just get rid of the dog,' he said in a friendly tone.

A few seconds later, the door opened and a man looked out at them and frowned. He was in his early 60s, handsome, slim, with silver swept-back hair. His face was tanned, teeth white, and he wore a pressed pink Ralph Lauren shirt, jeans, and a gold Rolex and bracelet.

'Peckham, eh? Bloody hell,' he said with a wry smile. 'How can I help?'

Ruth showed her warrant card and said, 'We're looking for a Charlie or a Charles Wise?'

'Yeah, that's me. You'd better come in,' Charlie responded with a cheeky grin. He gestured for them to come inside. 'Do I need my brief?'

Ruth looked over at Lucy and frowned.

'I'm only joking. Come through and I'll put the kettle on,' he said in a confident, warm tone.

The house was refreshingly cool inside. It was fashionably decorated with antique furniture and large oil paintings on every wall. They came to a vast kitchen and dining area that had floor to ceiling windows which led out to an immaculate garden.

Wow. This is nice, Ruth thought with a slight touch of envy.

Charlie gestured for them to sit at the large oak dining table. 'Have a seat. Coffee or tea? Although you'll have to bear with me as my better half is out and she usually does all that stuff.'

Lucy smiled at him. 'We're fine actually, Mr Wise.'

'It's Charlie. Well, it's Charlie if you're south of the river. People north of the river call me Sir Charles, but you know what they're like,' he said with a knowing laugh as he came over and sat down opposite them. 'Sure I can't get you anything?'

Ruth and Lucy nodded.

'Fair enough. Saves me making a complete tit of myself when you realise that I can't make a decent cuppa.' Charlie gave them a winning smile as he sat with his elbows on the table and his fingers interlocked. 'So, detectives, how can I help?'

Christ, he's incredibly calm and confident for someone who has just had two CID detectives knocking on the door.

Ruth looked over at him. 'DVLA records show that you purchased a Chrysler Imperial back in 1954. Is that right?'

Charlie smiled and nodded. 'Yeah. Christ, the Chrysler Imperial. It was a lovely ice blue. That takes me back. Yeah, beautiful car. I was a bit of a flash git when I was younger.'

'Do you still have it?' Lucy asked.

Charlie frowned and snorted. 'God, no ... Sold it in the early 60s. Can't remember who to though.'

Lucy took a photograph of the key from the case folder and pushed it over the table towards him. 'Does this look like the key for that car?'

He took a pair of reading glasses from the pocket of his shirt, put them on, and peered at the photograph. 'Yeah. Looks about right. Long time ago though.'

Lucy took the photograph back and said, 'Did you have two keys for the car when you bought it?'

Charlie thought for a moment. 'Yeah, but I lost one somewhere along the line. I was pretty sure that my younger brother had it, but that's a very long story. When I sold the car, I told the bloke I only had one.' He then smiled. 'You haven't come all this way to tell me you found my old spare car key, have you?'

Ruth shook her head. 'No ... we found the key along with some human remains at Dixon's Timber Yard. We were wondering if you could shed any light on why it might have been there?'

The colour drained visibly from Charlie's face. He smoothed his hand over his chin as he stared into space. The news had clearly distressed him. He cleared his throat, then said in a virtual whisper, 'Oh god ... I think you've found him then.'

Ruth looked over at Lucy for a second. 'Found who, Charlie?'

He took a deep breath and blinked as tears came into his eyes. 'My brother, Alfie.'

'Could you tell us why you think it might be your brother?' Lucy asked gently.

Charlie closed his eyes for a few seconds. He took a hand-kerchief from his pocket, dabbed his tears and then looked over at them. 'Sorry. I never thought he'd ...' He wept and then took a deep breath. 'Sorry ... I ...'

Ruth's heart went out to him as he pressed his thumb and forefinger against the bridge of his nose. 'You don't need to apologise, Charlie.'

He wiped another tear with the back of his hand. 'You find anything else?'

Lucy took the photograph of the signet ring from the folder and showed it to him.

More tears came as Charlie nodded imperceptibly and pursed his lips. 'Yeah ... That's Alfie's ring. It's him. Bloody hell. I never thought we'd find him. Poor sod.'

Ruth gave him a compassionate look. 'I'm so sorry to hear that.'

He sniffed as he gazed at the photograph. 'I bought him that ring for his sixteenth birthday.'

'Could you tell us what happened to your brother?' Lucy asked.

Charlie sat back in his chair. 'The 27th of November 1956. That was the day Alfie went missing. It was a Tuesday. He'd borrowed the motor to do a few things for me. Then he dropped it back and went out. That was the last time I saw him. He just vanished off the face of the earth. No one knew what had happened to him ... I assumed he must have kept the key in his pocket and forgotten all about it.'

'Did you report it to the police at the time?' Ruth asked.

'Yeah, course. They searched all the parks. They even went up to New Cross and the banks of the Thames at Deptford. A few posters. But we couldn't find him,' Charlie said and then wiped his face again. 'Sorry ...'

'Please don't apologise. This must be very difficult for you,' Lucy said.

Charlie looked up at them. 'Yeah ... Do you know what happened to him yet?'

Ruth said quietly, 'I'm really sorry but we suspect your brother was murdered.'

'Jesus!' Charlie's face looked pained. 'Really? ... Bloody hell, I thought this day might come ... but I wondered if we'd lost him forever. It's a bit of a shock.'

Lucy gave him a sympathetic smile. 'Of course it is.'

'Do you know why anyone would have wanted to harm your brother, Charlie?' Ruth asked.

He nodded. 'Yeah. I've got a fair idea.'

Ruth and Lucy exchanged a look – that wasn't the answer they were expecting.

'Really? Why do you say that?' Lucy asked.

Charlie got up from the table and wandered over to a cupboard where he grabbed a bottle of Irish whiskey. 'Alfie was involved in some kind of gang fight in Balham two weeks before he went missing. Teddy Boys from Clapham Common. Alfie and this bloke Frank Weller ended up fighting down on the underground. Frank Weller got stabbed, fell under a train and died.'

Ruth watched as Charlie found a heavy glass tumbler, took ice from the enormous American fridge, and poured himself three fingers of whiskey. 'I would offer you ladies a drink, but I know you're on duty. Not like the old days.'

'What happened to Alfie?' Lucy asked.

'He came home and told me what had happened. I cleaned him up. He was in a right old state. He laid low with me for a few days. I wasn't about to hand him over to the Old Bill. It was all over the papers but it looked like your lot didn't have a suspect for it. After a couple of weeks, I assumed somehow he'd got away with it. So, like I said, he went out in my car to run a few errands. Came back. Went out again, and that was the last I saw of him.' Charlie took a gulp of the whiskey, puffed out his cheeks and shook his head. 'I still can't believe you've found him after all this time. Dixon's Timber Yard, did you say?'

'That's right.'

'It's been there donkey's years. Arnold Dixon used to own it.'

'That's right,' Ruth said.

'Is he still alive?' Charlie asked.

'We're not sure,' Ruth replied.

'How did you find Alfie then?'

'Workmen were digging foundations for a new building,' Lucy explained.

'I see,' Charlie said as he swigged his drink and stared into space.

Ruth gestured to her notepad. 'Going back again, Charlie. So, you told the police all about Alfie being responsible for this stabbing at Balham Station when you reported him missing?' Ruth asked.

'I had to. Wouldn't have made any sense not to,' Charlie explained. 'They charged me with conspiracy and I got a two year suspended sentence.'

Ruth looked at Charlie. 'What did you think had happened to Alfie?'

Charlie's manner had gone from what looked like shock and grief, to some kind of anger. He moved the glass of whiskey around on the coaster for a second. 'Word was that Frank Weller's family and his mates knew it was Alfie that had killed him. They weren't going to tell the Old Bill so they could hunt him down themselves and get their revenge. Two of the boys that were in the fight that night belonged to a local gang. They'd stabbed and killed a boy on Clapham High Street in '53. They called themselves The Plough Boys.' He took another swig, drained the glass and then looked at them. 'I assumed they found Alfie that day and killed him.'

CHAPTER 6

Having checked that Ella had fallen asleep, Ruth wandered back to the large room at the back of the flat that was a kitchen and living area. The patio doors were open and the warm summer air was filled with the smell of someone barbequing. A few doors down, children were playing and shouting. She went over to the stereo, took out the Portishead album *Dummy* and put it on. She had read somewhere that music like Portishead's was rather cleverly labelled 'trip hop'. She could see why. The redolent smells of a balmy summer evening combined with the music made her hanker after a spliff. She dug around in the drawers and small wooden boxes to see if Dan had left any weed behind. Opening a patterned wooden box that he'd bought on one of his many trips to India, she spotted a small plastic bag with enough grass to have a smoke.

Bingo! Just what I need tonight, she thought as she took cigarette papers and tobacco from the box. She sat down on the sofa and constructed a neat spliff. *Bloody hell. It's been a while since I've done this,* she thought as she lit it and took a deep drag. She felt her head instantly become fuzzy and her body more relaxed.

Standing up, Ruth wandered over to the table where she had spread out some photocopies. She'd dug them out of the Peckham police station archives that were stored in the basement of the building, comically referred to as 'the salt mines'.

The photocopies were from a mix of local and national newspapers dated November 1956. She wanted as much background information as she could get on the knife fight and murder that Alfie Wise had been involved in. It was a little chilling to think that it had happened only a mile down the road from where she was standing now.

The Daily Mail headline read – *South London Gang War – Youth Stabbed To Death.* The Daily Express carried an equally dramatic front page – *Teddy Boy murdered in Balham.* The Daily Mirror had an inside article about the growing dangers of teenage gangs and delinquency – *Flick Knives, Dance Music and Edwardian Suits.*

Scanning another paper, Ruth saw the headline:

WAR ON THE TEDDY BOYS

Menace On The Streets Of Britain's Cities Is Being Tackled At Last!

The menace of the Teddy Boys is being challenged by the concerted action of police, and dance hall and cinema managers, who are taking a firm stand against the delinquent gangs. In some places, groups of 'vigilantes' have been formed to combat the thugs in Edwardian dress who are often armed with razors, bicycle chains and knuckle dusters and have been terrorising the peace-loving people of Britain for several years now.

Ruth's train of thought was interrupted by a knock on the door. Now panicking a little, she stubbed out the spliff and tried to waft away the smell. Straightening her hair and composing herself, she went to the door and opened it. It was Dan, looking a little awkward and sheepish.

Ruth frowned. 'You're not meant to pick up Ella until Saturday and she's in bed.'

'Actually, it's you I wanted to talk to. Can I come in?' he asked, avoiding any eye contact.

'Do you have to?'

'It's important.'

Ruth looked at him for a second. *Just slam the door in his face and tell him to fuck off!*

She gave a deliberate audible sigh and ushered him inside. 'Why not? Come in ...'

As she followed him to the back of the flat, she was aware that it smelled of weed. She didn't care.

'Have you been smoking gear?' he asked with a frown.

'None of your business.'

'You used to tell me off for smoking gear when Ella was in the flat.'

Are you joking?

She glared at him and raised an eyebrow. 'Really? You're going to bloody lecture me about what I do in this flat?'

'No, of course not,' he said. 'Can I sit down?'

Ruth shook her head. 'No ... Why? How long are you planning on bloody staying?'

He looked at her and she gestured to the sofa. 'Go on then.'

She wondered why he had come to see her. It wasn't going to be anything good. It never was.

Avoiding eye contact, Dan talked quietly. 'I need to talk to you about me and Angela.'

'Oh good.' Ruth pulled a face. 'If I'm honest, I'd rather not know anything about you and Angela.'

He continued as if she hadn't spoken. 'We've been talking. She's struggling to settle in London and ...'

The penny dropped. Ruth knew exactly what was coming next. It had crossed her mind before.

She interrupted him. 'Bloody hell, Dan! Really?'

'What?' he said with an innocent shrug. 'I haven't said anything yet.'

'You and Angela are moving to Australia where you're going to play happy families,' she snapped loudly.

Dan couldn't hide his awkwardness as he waited a few seconds before responding. 'Yeah. I'm sorry. She's just not happy here anymore.'

'It's not her happiness that I care about, Dan.'

'Sorry.'

Ruth yelled, 'Don't apologise to me! What about Ella? You're her father!'

There were a few seconds of silence. Dan said nothing.

Ruth took a deep breath. She was furious. 'What, and that's it? Sorry darling, I'm off to Australia. Have a nice life. I'll try to pop back for your eighteenth if I can.'

'It's not like that. What am I meant to do?' he asked.

Ruth shook her head. She really wished him physical harm. 'Dan, you're a spineless wanker. You always have been. And I want you to go.'

He got up slowly from the sofa and glanced at her. 'I'll come back when you've calmed down.'

'Fuck off!'

Oh my God! I want to kill you!

Grabbing a glass, she went to throw it at him and then managed to stop herself.

He walked towards the door and left.

Sitting on the sofa, Ruth closed her eyes and then tears ran down her face. They were tears of both frustration and of terrible sadness. She thought of Ella sleeping innocently in her bed, unaware of what was going on. Ruth knew that her beautiful daughter would grow up knowing that her daddy didn't love her enough to stick around and had instead moved to the other side of the world.

LUCY AND HER MOTHER, Pauline, were sitting out on the patio as the sun set behind the trees. It was a balmy evening, but it was that time of year when Lucy noticed the days shortening with the promise of autumn and then winter. With the chirps and calls of the robin, blackbird and song thrush, it was hard to imagine that they were only four miles south of Big Ben, the Houses of Parliament, and Central London.

Lucy sat forward in the garden chair and gestured to her mother's empty glass. 'Do you want anything else, Mum?'

'No, darling. I'm driving.' Pauline looked at her. 'I need to ask you a favour.'

Lucy shrugged. 'Go on. Unless it's a speeding ticket again which, as I explained, I can't make disappear.'

Pauline laughed. 'I just asked. It was the first time I ever got stopped in forty years of driving.'

Typical Mum. We're going round the houses, Lucy thought.

'Mum?'

'What, darling?'

'You need to ask me a favour.'

Pauline giggled. 'Oh yes. Bloody hell, I'm losing my marbles. It would have been me and your dad's thirtieth wedding anniversary on Sunday.'

Lucy nodded. Her father had died in traumatic circumstances a few years ago and she and her mum had both found it difficult to deal with. 'You want me to come with you to his grave?'

'Would you mind? I mean if you and Harry are busy ...'

'Mum?'

'What?'

'Of course we'll come!'

Pauline laughed. 'Oh, okay then.'

'In fact, Harry can drive us and then we'll take you out for a pub lunch. How does that sound?'

Pauline's face broke into a beaming smile. 'You know what, that would be lovely, darling. As long as he doesn't mind?'

Lucy grinned. 'He'll do as he's bloody told.'

'Oh, right. Well, don't scare him off, dear.' Pauline looked at her watch. 'Where is he anyway?'

'Strategic policy meeting.'

'What the hell does that mean?'

Lucy shrugged. 'No idea. And frankly, I don't care.'

A metallic noise came from inside. Lucy recognised it as the clatter of the letterbox. *Definitely not the postman.*

Getting up from the table, Lucy gestured to the kitchen. 'Sure you don't want another drink, Mum? You've had one gin in three hours so I think you'll be all right.'

'Yeah, go on then. One for the road, eh? If I get stopped again, you can get me off.'

Lucy rolled her eyes, took their glasses and headed inside. Spotting a brown padded envelope on the floor by the door, she went over and picked it up. Her name and address were on a typed label and there was a red *Confidential* stamp at the top of the envelope. She assumed it was work related. There had been rare occasions when documents had been sent to her home by mistake.

She headed back into the kitchen with the envelope, poured two gin and tonics, and made her way back to the patio.

'Here you go, Mum,' she said, as she put the glasses down on the table.

Pauline gestured to the padded envelope. 'Is that work stuff?'

Lucy sat down and tore it open. 'Must be.'

Pauline shook her head. 'They work you too hard, don't they?'

Now that the envelope was open, Lucy could feel that there was something stuck inside. She gave it a shake, and three small objects fell out and landed in her lap.

It was dog excrement.

'Jesus Christ!' she yelled as she flicked the excrement off her lap.

Pauline gasped. 'Oh my God!'

'For fuck's sake!' Lucy said getting up from the table.

Pauline got out of her chair. 'Come on, love. I'll help you clean up. Who the hell would send you that?'

Lucy didn't say anything, but she had a good idea.

CHAPTER 7

Ruth's day in CID began just after seven as she set about creating a scene board for the investigation into the remains found at Dixon's Timber Yard. There were dates and times of the events of November 1956, along with photographs.

She was now on her second coffee. Even though she had smoked the rest of her spliff and finished a bottle of wine after Dan had left, she hadn't slept well. She wasn't sure how and when to break the news to Ella. Was it better once he had gone, or should she prepare her so she could say goodbye knowing that he was moving away?

A tabloid newspaper dropped onto her desk, which broke her train of thought and startled her.

'What is she doing with that man? Balding, hairy, and butt ugly?' Lucy said loudly, pointing to the front page.

'Christ, Lucy! You made me jump.'

'Sorry!' Lucy pointed to a paparazzi photograph of Princess Diana on a yacht with Dodi Fayed, son of Mohammed Al-Fahed - the famous business tycoon and owner of London's most famous department store, Harrods. 'But what is Diana doing? Did you see her on the front of Vanity Fair last month? She's completely beautiful.'

Ruth shrugged. 'No, I didn't.' If she was honest, she couldn't care less who Princess Diana was or wasn't dating.

'And yes, what does she see in a multi-millionaire with an enormous yacht in the Mediterranean?'

Lucy rolled her eyes and took her paper back.

Ruth sniggered. 'Well, there's a word for women who sleep with men for money.'

As Brooks walked into CID for the morning briefing, Lucy scuttled back to her desk and the volume of conversation waned as detectives turned their chairs to face the front of the room.

'Right everyone, if we can settle down, let's get cracking for the day, shall we?' Brooks said. He was already in shirtsleeves with his tie loosened. It was hot and stuffy, and it wasn't even nine o'clock.

There was a brief discussion of the ongoing robbery investigation before Brooks looked in Ruth and Lucy's direction. 'I understand that yesterday you had afternoon tea with Sir Charles Wise?'

There were mutterings and piss-taking from some of the detectives.

Ruth gave a wry smile. 'Sort of, guv.'

'Slumming it was he?' Gaughran joked to more laughter.

Ruth grinned and gave him the finger.

Brooks gestured to the front of the room. 'Can you bring us up to speed, Ruth?'

Getting up from her desk, Ruth knew that she wasn't really in the mood to address the whole of CID. Her head was fuzzy from tiredness, wine and weed. She went over to the scene board, composed herself and pointed to a forensic photograph of the skeletal remains that had been found. 'As most of you know, two days ago human remains were discovered by builders at Dixon's Timber Yard. The skull that was found had what looks like a bullet hole at the base. Our forensic team believe it was the cause of death but are waiting for the Coroner to carry out a full post mortem.'

'Which means this is effectively now a murder investigation?' Brooks asked.

'Yes, guv.'

'Any way of dating the remains?' he asked.

'We ran a DNA sample through our database but there wasn't a hit. The lab is going to send a sample for carbon dating but it may take some time,' Ruth explained.

She then pointed to photographs of the car key and the signet ring. 'However, this car key and signet ring were found with the remains. We traced the key to a Chrysler Imperial car that was owned by Sir Charles Wise in the 1950s.' She indicated a photograph of him. 'Yesterday, Lucy and I visited Sir Charles at his home. He confirmed the car belonged to him and that he bought it in 1954 and sold it sometime in the 1960s. The DVLA confirmed it was sold in 1966.' Gesturing to a black and white photograph of a teenage boy with a black quiff, Ruth said, 'Sir Charles told us that he believes his brother, Alfie Wise, had the spare car key to the Chrysler when he disappeared on the afternoon of the 27th November 1956. He has never been seen since. I've checked the Met's missing persons file, and he's still on there. We will ask Sir Charles for a DNA sample in the next few days, but he was very upset by the discovery so we should hold off on that for at least today and tomorrow.'

'Any other blood relatives we could ask to speed up that process?'

Ruth shook her head. 'No, guv. Mother and father died quite some time back, and his sister was killed in a car crash five years ago.'

'Any idea who the last person to see Alfie Wise alive was?' Brooks asked.

Ruth shook her head. 'No, guv. At the moment, we're assuming it's his brother Charlie.'

'Oh, Charlie now is it?' Gaughran asked, taking the piss.

Ruth rolled her eyes. 'He likes people to call him Charlie, unless they're complete tossers ... Looks like you'll be calling him Sir Charles, doesn't it Tim?'

There was laughter as Gaughran mimed being shot and injured. Lucy grinned at her – they loved to get their own back on Gaughran.

Ruth looked back at Brooks. 'Until we check if there's an actual missing persons file somewhere here in the basement, we're going to assume that Charlie was the last person to see Alfie alive. We showed him the gold signet ring that was also found with the remains. He confirmed the ring belonged to his brother, so there is a very strong possibility that the bones that were found were Alfie Wise.'

There were a few more murmurs from the team.

Brooks shook his head. 'I never knew that Sir Charles Wise had a brother that mysteriously disappeared.'

Ruth nodded. 'He was very emotional yesterday, as you can imagine, guv. His seventeen-year-old brother went out one afternoon in November 1956 and just never came back. It's taken forty-one years to find him.'

Gaughran looked up from his desk and frowned. 'Any idea why Alfie Wise might have been shot and killed?'

Ruth moved closer to the board and indicated a photograph of another teenager with a quiff who looked a little older than Alfie. 'This is where it gets interesting. Two weeks before his disappearance, Alfie was involved in a fight with this young man, Frank Weller. They ended up on a platform in Balham underground station where Frank Weller was stabbed and fell under a train. It was all over the papers the next day. There had been a spate of stabbings and fights between Teddy Boy gangs in South London in the mid-50s. Alfie Wise went home and laid low for a few days, but the police never came to interview him. For whatever reason, the local police didn't have him down as a suspect. On the day he disappeared, Alfie took Charlie's car to run some errands, dropped it back home and then went out again. That was the last time anyone saw him.'

'Did Alfie say where he was going?' Hassan asked.

Ruth shook her head. 'No. Just that he was popping out.'

Gaughran looked up from writing in his notepad. 'Do we think that Alfie Wise was murdered as revenge for Frank Weller?'

'That was Charlie's theory,' Ruth said. 'He always assumed that's why Alfie had gone missing. He said he guessed that Frank Weller's friends had tracked Alfie down and killed him.'

'Do we know who these friends were that were involved in the fight?' Brooks asked.

Ruth pointed to some names that she had written on the scene board. 'Alfie was with a mate of his called Trevor Walsh. They'd been to the cinema in Balham and were waiting for the bus home when the fight broke out. Frank Weller was with two mates who were part of a Teddy Boy gang, based up by Clapham Common, called The Plough Boys.'

Gaughran nodded. 'Yeah, I've heard of them. Used to carry razors, coshes, and bicycle chains.'

Ruth indicated the other two names. 'Terry Droy and Eddie Bannerman were the two other teenagers that were with Frank when the fight broke out at a bus stop on Balham High Street.'

'Any idea where they are now?' Hassan asked.

Lucy shifted in her seat and looked over. 'Terry Droy is serving time in Wandsworth for assault and theft. Nothing for Eddie Bannerman.'

Ruth looked at her notepad. 'We do have an address for Frank Weller's sister, Jackie.'

'Trevor Walsh?' Brooks asked.

Ruth shook her head. 'Nothing yet, guv.'

Brooks rubbed his chin. 'Right, Ruth and Lucy, go and have a chat with Jackie Weller. Tim and Syed, get yourselves over to Wandsworth and see what this Terry Droy has to say for himself ... That's great work everyone.'

CHAPTER 8

Ruth and Lucy parked under the railway bridge at Clapham North underground station, and headed round the corner to Jackie Weller's flat in Landor Road. The sun was burning down on them as they passed a large beer garden that was full of young people drinking in the sun.

As they reached the door of number 8, Lucy saw the name *J Weller* scribbled beside the bottom buzzer. Pushing it, she heard the sound inside. A few seconds later, the front door opened and a woman in her late 50s appeared. She was diminutive with neat but old-fashioned clothes and haircut.

'We're looking for a Jackie Weller?' Lucy asked as she showed her warrant card.

The woman smiled. 'Yes. That's me. Am I in trouble?'

Lucy smiled back but wasn't sure if she was serious or making a joke. It was hard to tell. 'No, no. We're hoping that you can help us with an investigation.'

'Yes, okay,' Jackie said. 'Would you like to come in?'

'Thanks,' Lucy said as they followed her into her ground-floor flat.

It was clean and tidy, and had high ceilings. The smell of baking made it feel warm and welcoming. The décor was a little tired and didn't look like it had been updated since the 1970s. Lucy spotted a few religious posters on the wall advertising a local church. Although it was guesswork, it looked like Jackie lived alone as there were no signs of anyone else.

Jackie motioned to the sofa. 'Please, sit down. Can I get you anything? Tea or a glass of water, perhaps?'

Lucy now noticed that Jackie had the faintest trace of an Irish accent.

Ruth smiled at her. 'We're fine thank you.'

Leaning forward, Lucy composed herself. Bringing up her brother's murder from over forty years ago might be difficult for her. 'Jackie, we want to talk to you about your brother, Frank.'

Jackie's brow furrowed for a few seconds as though she hadn't understood what Lucy had said. Then she gave a slight nod and murmured, 'Yes. What do you want to know?'

Ruth took out her notepad before giving Jackie a compassionate smile. 'I know this is difficult for you, but we want to talk to you about the time when Frank was killed.'

'I see. Yes.' Jackie looked visibly upset and her eyes began to water.

'What can you tell us about your brother?' Ruth asked.

'My brother was a lovely young man. Very generous and funny. And handsome. That's what my mother used to say ...' Jackie said, her voice breaking from emotion.

Ruth took out a handkerchief and passed it over to her. 'Here you go.'

Jackie took it, and dabbed her cheeks. 'Thank you. I'm so sorry. I haven't spoken about Frank for a long time, you see.'

Lucy nodded. She noticed that Jackie wasn't wearing a wedding ring. 'Take your time, Jackie. We're in no rush,' she said empathetically.

'All I know is that Frank went out with some of his friends one evening. The police told us he got into a fight of some kind ... They took my mother to St George's hospital to identify his body. Then I think she cried for a week after that.'

Ruth looked up from her notepad. 'Was your father around at that time?'

Jackie shook her head sadly. 'My father never came back from the war. He was killed in Burma.'

'I'm sorry to hear that,' Lucy said. 'And was it just you and Frank, or did you have any other siblings?'

'No. It was just us.'

Shifting forward on her seat, Ruth looked at her. 'Does the name Alfie Wise mean anything to you?'

Jackie couldn't hide her reaction. She looked away and shook her head almost imperceptibly. 'No, I don't think so.'

Lucy glanced over at Ruth - it was clearly a lie.

'Jackie, I know it was a long time ago,' Ruth said gently, as if talking to a child. 'Are you sure you don't know the name Alfie Wise?'

Jackie blinked as tears came, and she wiped her cheeks again. She was finding it all too much. 'No. I just told you that, didn't I?'

'Do you remember Terry Droy?' Lucy asked.

Jackie frowned and then said, 'Yeah. One of Frank's friends. I went to school with his sister, Pauline.'

'And Eddie Bannerman?'

'Yeah. Eddie knocked about with Frank and Terry.' Jackie gave a half smile. 'The Three Musketeers they used to call them-selves. Always getting into bloody trouble.'

Lucy waited for a few seconds, then sat forward and looked directly at Jackie with a kind smile. 'And you're sure that Terry and Eddie never mentioned the name Alfie Wise?'

Jackie took a breath – she was clearly debating whether or not to continue the lie. Then she whispered, 'Yeah ... they did.'

'What did they say about him, Jackie?' Lucy asked.

'They said they was gonna find him.' Jackie pursed her lips and sniffed. 'They said he was the one that had ... you know ... attacked Frank at Balham station.'

'Did they say what they were going to do when they did find Alfie Wise?'

Jackie closed her eyes and nodded, 'Yeah. They said they were gonna sort him out for good.'

'What did you think they meant by that?' Lucy asked.

Jackie thought for a second and then said quietly, 'I suppose I thought they were gonna kill him.'

GAUGHRAN AND HASSAN made their way along the long corridor towards one of the interview rooms on the ground floor of Wandsworth Prison. Built in the 1850s, Wandsworth was one of the largest prisons from the Victorian era. Gaughran had been there lots of times since he joined the force. The high, echoing corridors were painted a vanilla cream colour and the doors and metalwork were all dark blue.

'You watch Match of the Day?' he asked Hassan. Gaughran was from a family of Chelsea supporters that went back generations. His great, great grandfather had even been to the club's first ever game in 1905.

'Yeah. Saw your lot battering Barnsley,' Hassan groaned. He was a fair-weather QPR fan.

Gaughran grinned. 'What did you say last week about Vialli? Over the hill? Waste of money?'

Hassan shook his head. 'Yeah, all right. Rub it in.'

Chelsea's Italian striker, Gianluca Vialli, had scored four goals against Barnsley at the weekend.

Gaughran had worked with Hassan as his partner for two years. Although Hassan was too cautious for his liking, they performed well as a team. Wanting to be a copper was all Gaughran could ever remember. His old man, uncle, and brother had all been in the Met. He knew that some officers in CID thought he was arrogant. As far as he was concerned, he had been surrounded by coppers since he could walk and the job was part of his DNA. That gave him a knowledge and an edge above those he worked with.

Pointing to the old-fashioned brass sign *No. 12,* Gaughran said, 'We're in here.'

Entering the sparse interview room, Gaughran saw that Terry Droy was already sitting at the desk. A prison officer stood nearby.

Gaughran looked at the screw. 'Thanks. We can take it from here.'

Droy was in his early 60s. His greying hair was short and brushed forward from the back. He was overweight, with a rounded jaw and was clean shaven.

'Terry Droy?' Gaughran asked as he and Hassan sat down at the desk opposite him.

Droy sat back in his chair with a smirk and took a cigarette from the pocket of his blue regulation prison shirt. 'Yeah. Who are you two then?'

Gaughran pulled his chair closer to the table and looked directly at him.

I'm not having this fucker think he can intimidate me. I'm in charge in here.

'DS Gaughran and DC Hassan, Peckham CID,' Gaughran said, not taking his eyes from Droy's. If he wanted a staring competition, bring it on.

Droy snorted as if something was funny. 'Bloody hell. Peckham? What you doing over here?'

'We'd like to talk to you about Frank Weller,' Hassan said.

Droy frowned as he lit his cigarette. 'Frank? Jesus, that's ancient history. What do you want to know?'

Gaughran put his arms on the table. 'You were with Frank on the night he was killed in November 1956, is that right?'

Droy blew smoke across the table. 'Yeah. I was there. So what?'

Gaughran studied Droy's face carefully as he asked, 'The name Alfie Wise mean anything to you?'

Got you!

Droy reacted, leant forward and tapped his ash into the ashtray. 'Nope.'

'Don't lie to us, Terry,' Gaughran growled.

'Piss off. I've never heard that name before.'

Hassan raised an eyebrow. 'We've got a witness that says otherwise, Terry.'

Sitting back in his seat, Terry ran his hand over his short hair. 'You been talking to Jackie Weller, have you?'

Gaughran leant forward aggressively. 'Don't dick us about. We know that you and Eddie Bannerman were looking for Alfie Wise. We know you thought he killed Frank.'

Droy said nothing for a few seconds. 'Why you asking me about this now, eh? It was forty years ago. Unless something's changed or you found something.'

Hassan sighed. 'Just answer the question.'

Droy ignored Hassan and looked at Gaughran. 'What is it, eh? What are you not telling me?'

'You know where Eddie Bannerman is?' Hassan asked.

'Nope. I haven't seen Eddie for about thirty years. You wanna tell me what's going on?'

'You see, Terry, you've got a bit of a problem,' Gaughran said.

Droy smirked. 'Have I?'

'You know what DNA is Terry?' Gaughran asked.

Droy snorted. 'Yeah, I read the papers. I'm not a fucking caveman.'

'You know that they can now get the DNA from the tiniest fragment of skin, clothing, blood, anything?'

Droy stubbed out his cigarette. 'Fascinating.'

'You know how long DNA survives on a body?' Gaughran asked.

'Enlighten me.'

'Millions of years. It doesn't go away. It stays there. Forty years ago, no one had even heard of DNA had they? Unless you left a fingerprint, footprint, or a decent piece of clothing fibre, you could pretty much get away with anything,' Gaughran explained in a menacing tone. 'But if I took a tiny strand of your hair, or a sample of your blood or saliva, I could match it to something from decades ago. It would be as good as having your fingerprint.'

Droy stared at Gaughran for a few seconds as he bit his lip. 'You found a body then have you?'

'Maybe. If we did find a body, Terry, would you be nervous about that?' Hassan asked.

Droy continued to stare at Gaughran, who assumed that Droy wouldn't speak to Hassan because he was Asian. That's what blokes like Terry Droy were like.

Droy smiled and shook his head. 'No. You're definitely barking up the wrong tree.'

Gaughran shrugged. 'Then you won't mind us taking a DNA sample from you?'

Terry smiled. 'Knock yourself out. I've got nothing to hide.'

Droy's confidence concerned Gaughran. *Why's he so bloody confident? Either he's very good at bluffing, or he's got nothing to hide.*

Gaughran knew it was time to hit Droy with the discovery of Alfie Wise's body and see if that rattled him.

Waiting a good ten seconds, Gaughran glowered across at Droy and said, 'We've found a body which we believe is Alfie Wise. Is there anything you can tell us about that Terry?'

Droy seemed unflustered as he shook his head. 'Nothing to do with me, but I'm not gonna pretend I'm not happy that he's dead.'

'What happened, Terry? You and Eddie Bannerman found out it was Alfie Wise that had killed Frank. You tracked him down, put a bullet in his head and then buried him?'

Droy snorted. 'Wish I had. But you're on the wrong track. Alfie Wise's murder didn't have anything to do with Frank.'

Gaughran glanced over at Hassan for a second. *What's he talking about?*

'How do you know that?'

'After Frank was killed, me and Eddie *did* try to track Alfie Wise down. We never found him. But the word was that Alfie was going to get hurt because he was a poof.'

Gaughran frowned. 'Alfie Wise was gay?'

Droy laughed. 'Yeah. Had a boyfriend. Some bloke called Trevor Walsh. We found him and he shat his pants. Thought we were Old Bill.'

Gaughran knew that in the 1950s, you could be arrested and face a fine or imprisonment for being gay.

'Rumour had it that Alfie put it about with every bloke he could get his hands on. Really rubbed this bloke Walshy's face in it.'

Gaughran wondered if Droy was telling the truth or just muddying the water.

Droy raised his eyebrow and sat forward. 'You might wanna have a look at his brother too. Charlie. Sir Charles or whatever he calls himself these days.'

'Why's that?'

'Someone told me he hated poofs. Charlie was humiliated because his brother was queer. Maybe one day he decided Alfie was just too much of an embarrassment and got rid of him.'

CHAPTER 9

It was the middle of the afternoon when Ruth finally found an address for Trevor Walsh. She had contacted the main secondary school in Peckham, who consulted their records and confirmed that Trevor Andrew Walsh had attended the school between 1950 and 1956. His date of birth was 12th July 1939. Now that she had a name *and* date of birth, Ruth knew she was far closer to tracking him down. Having contacted the electoral register, main utility and mobile phone providers, she had drawn a blank. However, a phone call to the DVLA allowed her to check for a driving licence for any person named Trevor Andrew Walsh born in 1939. There was only one, and his full date of birth matched the one Ruth had been given by the school. The DVLA gave her the registered address in Catford, South East London.

Looking up from her desk in CID, Ruth saw Brooks had come in. Across from her, Gaughran and Hassan were both on the phone, chasing leads. They had described their meeting with Terry Droy - his denial of any involvement with Alfie Wise's death and his disclosure that Alfie was gay. It had brought home to Ruth how horrendous it must have been to be gay only thirty years earlier. It wasn't until the Sexual Offences Act of 1967 that homosexuality had been made legal. That was only two years before Ruth was born. Given her current relationship with Shiori, she was shocked at the thought that not that long ago it would have been illegal.

Brooks scanned the room. 'Can you guys tell me where we're at with the Alfie Wise investigation? I've had a phone call from the Commissioner. He wants us to tread very carefully as Sir Charles Wise is high profile.'

Gaughran looked up. 'Terry Droy told us he and Eddie Bannerman tried to find Alfie Wise but they never found him before he disappeared.'

Brooks raised an eyebrow. 'What do you think?'

'Droy told us that Alfie Wise was a promiscuous homosexual. He implied that Trevor Walsh was a jealous lover. He also said that rumours were that Charlie Wise wasn't pleased that his brother was gay.'

Ruth was dubious. She frowned and asked, 'What, so he just put a bullet in his brother's head?'

Brooks shrugged. 'I've heard worse. Very different world in the 50s. If you were working class from round here, and gay, you kept it very quiet.'

Ruth nodded. 'That might well be true, but Charlie was genuinely upset when he realised we might have found his brother. I really don't think he had anything to do with it.'

'We'll keep that hypothesis on the back burner,' Brooks said, and then looked at Hassan. 'Syed, what did you think about what Droy said?'

Hassan sat back in his chair. 'He seemed very confident that there would be nothing at the crime scene that might implicate him. But he would say that, wouldn't he?'

'Well, yeah. He's not going to confess just because you've told him a body's been found,' Brooks said. 'What about the old boy who owns Dixon's Timber Yard?'

Gaughran looked over, 'Yeah, Arnold Dixon. Me and Syed are going to have a chat with him at the yard in an hour.'

'Good. See if he remembers anything. Someone buried Alfie Wise in his yard forty years ago. He must have seen or heard something.'

The door opened and Lucy came in. She waved a fax at them. 'I've got an address for Eddie Bannerman.'

Brooks looked at his watch before glancing back at Gaughran. 'Tim and Syed. First thing tomorrow, go and see what you can get out of Eddie Bannerman.' Brooks looked over at Ruth and Lucy, who had now returned to their desks. 'Ruth and Lucy. Go and pay Sir Charles Wise another visit now on the pretence that you are keeping him in the loop with the investigation. Stress that we are doing everything we can to find out what happened to his brother. And then, with the utmost tact, ask about Alfie Wise's sexuality.'

Ruth gestured to her notepad. 'Yes, guv. I've now got an address for Trevor Walsh.'

'Right, go and see him first thing tomorrow.' Brooks looked at them. 'Good work, guys.'

CHAPTER 10

Gazing out of the window of the impressive seventeenth floor office, Lucy watched as a Thames River cruise boat moved slowly east down the river. Charlie had agreed to meet her and Ruth at the offices of his company, *Stanmore,* that were on the 16th and 17th floors of a huge office block on the south side of the Thames, a mile east of the Southbank Centre and National Theatre. From where she stood in the large reception and waiting area, Lucy could see for miles. To the north, the towering television mast at Alexander Palace, and to the east the high rise towers of Canary Wharf, which had been open since the early 90s.

'It's quite a view,' said a man's voice. It was Charlie Wise. He smiled and joined Lucy and Ruth at the window.

Lucy was still transfixed by what she could see. 'It's incredible.'

'Over two thousand years of history stretched out before us,' Charlie said. 'Makes you think. You should see how the Yanks react when they look out there.'

'I can imagine,' Lucy said as she gazed at the dome of St Paul's down to the right.

'Of course, I had to have my offices south of the Thames. I find they're a funny lot once you get on the other side of the river,' Charlie said sardonically.

Ruth laughed. 'That's what my dad always said.'

'Then your dad's a wise man.'

He gestured for them to follow him into his office. It was top spec, with designer furniture and an enormous window with a similar view over London. At the far end, there were a couple of framed Crystal Palace FC shirts.

'Come and sit down. You want tea or coffee?' Charlie asked as they sat down at a large glass boardroom table with black and chrome chairs.

Lucy shook her head. 'We're fine. Thanks.'

Ruth smiled over at him. 'It's really just a courtesy call to update you on the case. And to assure you that we're going to do everything in our power to find out what happened to your brother.'

Lucy could tell from Ruth's manner, and from several comments she'd made, that she had a soft spot for Charlie. It wasn't a surprise. He was charismatic and charming, but also genuinely self-effacing.

'I'm glad to hear that. It's been quite emotional since you told me the news,' Charlie admitted. 'Sounds strange, but I wish my sister Evelyn had been around to find out what had happened to Alfie. She talked about him a lot in the last few days of her life. It really got to her not knowing what had happened to him or where he was.'

'Of course. We've been speaking to various people who knew Alfie at the time he disappeared. Trying to build up a picture of what he was like and what was going on in his life,' Ruth explained. 'And obviously we are treating those seeking revenge for Frank Weller's death as the primary focus of our investigation.'

Charlie nodded. 'Yeah, obviously.'

Lucy caught Ruth's eye and could see that she felt awkward. On the journey to the South Bank, they had agreed that talking to Charlie about the possibility that Alfie was gay was going to be tricky.

'However, there is something that has come to our attention that we need to talk to you about, Charlie. And it's delicate,' Lucy said gently.

Charlie shrugged. 'I've been around the block a few times. And if it's going to help get justice for Alfie, then I'm more than happy to discuss anything.'

'Did you ever have any doubts about Alfie's sexuality?'

Charlie frowned and ran his hand over his chin. 'Alfie? No, I don't think so.'

That was a very calm, considered reaction, Lucy thought.

'Did you ever know Alfie to have a girlfriend?' Lucy asked.

Charlie sat back in his seat and took a sip of water. 'Now that you mention it, not really. He made comments about birds that he fancied. But I don't remember a proper girlfriend. Not that it would have mattered to me either way. I don't care about that sort of thing.'

Either Charlie was an excellent liar, or he genuinely had no idea that Alfie might have been gay and wouldn't have cared if he had been.

Lucy looked over at him. 'It's something that came up in an interview. And we're trying to corroborate the information.'

Charlie thought for a few seconds. 'No ... I would have noticed something. But maybe I didn't. It was a long time ago.'

'The boy he was with the night that Frank Weller was killed ...' Ruth said.

'Trevor Walsh? Everyone round there called him Walshy.'

'We believe that he might have been Alfie's boyfriend?'

'Really? I mean, everyone thought Walshy was a bit light on his feet.' Charlie then pulled a face. 'Sorry, that's not the right thing to say these days is it?'

'You suspected Trevor Walsh was gay?' Ruth asked.

Charlie nodded emphatically. 'Yeah. Well, everyone did.'

'Could they have fallen out about something?' Ruth asked.

'I dunno.' Charlie was clearly deep in thought, as if the penny had dropped about something. 'Christ, I never thought that Alfie could have disappeared because he was gay … It's hard for me to get my head around. But if you're looking at Walshy, that would make sense.'

'How do you mean?'

'Trevor Walsh wasn't the full shilling, if you know what I mean. He had a real temper on him. I told Alfie to stop knocking about with him. I knew it was gonna land them in trouble one day. But I never thought he would ever hurt Alfie.'

Lucy looked over at Charlie. 'And you wouldn't have minded if Alfie was gay?'

'No,' Charlie snorted. 'Wouldn't have bothered me one bit.'

Lucy frowned. 'Not even in 1956?'

Charlie shook his head and gave them a meaningful look. 'There's this myth that being gay makes you less of a man or makes you weak. The hardest, most frightening man I ever met was Ronnie Kray, and he was as bent as a nine bob note. Some bloke called Ronnie a fat poof, and Ronnie walked into a pub and put a bullet in his head. So, no. I never had a problem with gay men.'

THE HEAT OF THE DAY had subsided a little by the time Gaughran and Hassan drew up in the customer car park at Dixon's Timber Yard. As he got out of the car, Gaughran took off his sunglasses and was hit by the smell of chemicals and wood that had built up over the day. The yard was busy, and he watched as a noisy forklift truck whizzed by with wooden pallets piled up and strapped down.

A young man approached and, before he had chance to say anything, Gaughran had pulled out and flashed his warrant card. 'DS Gaughran and DC Hassan, Peckham CID. We're here to see Arnold Dixon.'

Gaughran would never get tired of the thrill of pulling out and flashing his warrant card and seeing people's reactions. Most of the time, they were frightened or respectful. There were a few morons who immediately became hostile or argumentative, but he knew how to deal with scrotes like that. He remembered the pride he'd felt watching his old man pulling out his warrant card when he'd spotted a kid in Tesco pushing joints of meat into the arms of his coat. The look on the kid's face was priceless, and Gaughran had given him a smirk as the security guard had carted him away.

'He's over in the Portakabin,' the young man said, gesturing to the right of the car park.

As they made their way across the car park, Gaughran looked over at the police tape and the mounds of earth where Alfie Wise's remains had been found.

Staring intently at the area, he stopped.

'Something wrong, Sarge?' Hassan asked.

'If this was your yard, even if it was forty years ago, you'd know what it looked like wouldn't you?'

'I guess.'

'I mean you come here every day. Serving customers, helping pile up the wood.'

Hassan nodded, but Gaughran could see that they weren't on the same page.

'So, if someone came here, dug a bloody great hole, buried a body and filled it in again, you would think that someone would have noticed, wouldn't you?'

Hassan gave a wry smile. 'Now that you've put it like that, yeah.'

'I mean it's got to be difficult to do that and not leave any mess or trace that shows what you've done.' Gaughran gestured over to the Portakabin. 'Let's have a word, shall we?'

A few seconds later, he knocked on the flimsy-looking door and an elderly man answered it. He was around seventy, bald, with a barrel chest and thick forearms that were decorated with faded naval tattoos.

'Hello?' he said with a puzzled look on his face.

Gaughran waved his warrant card again. 'Looking for an Arnold Dixon.'

The man gave a wry smile. 'Well then, it's your lucky day. I was expecting you. Why don't you come in?'

As they entered the Portakabin, a wave of cigarette smoke hit Gaughran. The office was untidy with bills and shabby old adverts stuck to the wall. There was a Millwall FC calendar by the door.

Gaughran rolled his eyes. 'You lot Millwall fans, are you?'

Dixon nodded. 'Yeah. I take it you're not then?'

'Chelsea,' Gaughran said puffing out his chest a little. He was proud of his football team and Millwall were the enemy. Their fans were made up of tough dockers from places like Deptford in the South East of London. When the two teams played, there was always a guarantee of trouble and fighting.

Dixon snorted. 'Chelsea? Fucking Chelsea.'

'Yeah, well we'll see you next time we drop down a division,' Gaughran said, mocking him.

Dixon sat down, gestured to some seats and smiled. 'Well, I was gonna offer you a cuppa, but not anymore!'

Gaughran laughed as he and Hassan sat down on some plastic chairs. 'As you're aware, we found the remains of a body here a couple of days ago.'

'Yeah. Bit of a shock, that was,' Dixon said.

Hassan fished out his notebook. 'We believe that the remains have been there for over forty years.'

'It said something about that on the news the other day.'

'Does the name Alfie Wise mean anything to you?'

Dixon thought for second and nodded. 'Yeah. Alfie Wise. I remember when he went missing all those years ago. You think that's who you found here?'

'We're not sure yet.' Gaughran sat forward on his chair. 'Did you know Alfie Wise then?'

Dixon shook his head. 'Not really. I'd seen him around a few times. I knew his brother Charlie a bit. We'd knock about together when we was kids up at the park.'

'We believe that Alfie Wise's body might have been buried in your yard around the 27th November 1956,' Hassan said.

Dixon shrugged. 'You're not expecting me to remember what I was doing that day, are you? I can't remember what I had for fucking breakfast yesterday.'

Gaughran gave a wry smile. 'No ... But you do remember hearing that Alfie Wise had gone missing in the area?'

Dixon nodded. 'Oh yeah. There were posters up on the High Street. People were talking about it in the boozer.'

'If you can think back to that time, do you ever remember seeing anything suspicious in your yard?' Hassan asked.

Dixon shook his head. 'The thing is, it didn't look like it does now. Where those builders found the body was all over-grown. There was rubble from where the old warehouse had been. It was a right mess.'

Gaughran frowned. 'It just struck me that if someone came into your yard one night, dug a hole, buried a body and then filled it in, someone would have noticed?'

Dixon snorted. 'Yeah, I can see why you would think that. But believe me it was a right shithole over that side. You could have come in and buried a bloody tank and no one would have noticed. Anyway, if I'd suspected anything I would have called your lot. Having a dead body buried in your yard isn't good for business, is it?'

'No, I don't suppose it is,' Gaughran said dryly. He was more convinced now that Dixon wasn't hiding anything.

'Did anyone ever say what they thought had happened to Alfie Wise?' Hassan asked.

'It had to be something to do with Charlie, didn't it?' Dixon said.

'Why's that?' Gaughran asked, raising an eyebrow.

'Charlie Wise. Jesus, he was a right spiv, poncing about in that bloody car. Charlie knew some very serious people in South London. In fact, I'm surprised it wasn't Charlie that got topped and stuck in a hole.'

CHAPTER 11

It was the following morning and, twenty minutes after briefing, Ruth and Lucy were making their way over to Catford to talk to Trevor Walsh. Heading east on the A205, they had hit morning traffic and were crawling along slowly. As a double-decker bus pulled away from its stop, Ruth gazed out at the busy pavements. Catford was a deprived area of South East London, at the heart of the Borough of Lewisham. It had the predictable array of fast food outlets, newsagents, and bookmakers along its high street.

Ruth glanced at Lucy who was still thumbing through a tabloid newspaper.

Lucy pointed to the paper. 'Apparently Diana and Dodi are going to Paris to stay in the Hotel Ritz, which his dad owns.'

Ruth gave a sardonic smile. 'Why do you care?'

'I wish Harry's dad owned a posh hotel in Paris we could stay in.'

'Yeah, that would be nice.' Ruth raised an eyebrow. 'You guys all okay?'

'Slight problem,' Lucy said and pulled a face. 'I haven't said anything to you, but his wife isn't taking their breakup lying down.'

Ruth looked mystified. 'But you've been together for months now.'

Lucy shrugged. 'A woman scorned and all that.'

'Why, what's she doing?'

'I caught her sitting outside my house the other night. And it wasn't the first time.'

'Bit creepy.'

'Night before last, she posted an envelope full of dog shit through my letterbox.'

'Bloody hell, Luce. You can't have that going on. What's Harry said?'

Lucy pursed her lips. 'He said he'll talk to her. But I'm not sure that's going to work.'

'If there's anything you want me to do ...'

Lucy smiled over at her. 'Thanks. Not sure I want to escalate it at the moment.'

Ruth laughed. 'Yeah, you don't want to come home to a domestic pet cooking on the hob.'

Lucy gave a twisted smile. 'No, that wouldn't be the best.'

Spotting Doggett Road, Ruth indicated and turned left out of the traffic. A few seconds later, she spotted a house marked number 68. Walsh lived in Flat B. They parked up and got out.

Ruth pushed her sunglasses up onto her head and looked up at the tall, scruffy, Victorian house that had been converted into three flats. Two young boys riding mountain bikes sped past them on the pavement.

'Little sods!' Lucy grumbled.

'You could tell them they should be on the road and wearing helmets?'

Ruth watched as the two boys circled around and then came back to where her and Lucy were standing on the pavement.

They couldn't have been more than ten or eleven-years-old.

'That your car, Miss?' said the one with curly hair.

Ruth shared a look with Lucy – *What the bloody hell are they up to?*

'Might be. Why do you want to know?' Ruth asked with a quizzical smile.

'Bit rough around here, Miss,' said the other boy who was wearing a red baseball cap.

'Is it?'

The curly-haired boy nodded. 'Yeah. Cars get scratched all the time. Or people take windscreen wipers or wing mirrors.'

'That doesn't sound good,' Ruth said as she looked over at Lucy who seemed tickled by the boys' antics.

'Tell you what, Miss. You give us a pound and we'll protect your car for you. Make sure no one damages it,' the boy said.

Ruth reached for her warrant card. 'That does sound like a good deal.' She then flashed her ID at them. 'But if anything happens to my car, then I'm going to be banging on your mum's door.'

The boy's eyes widened. 'Oh, shit!'

'Come on, let's go!' the other boy yelled.

The two of them turned and cycled away as fast as they could.

Lucy laughed and shook her head. 'A life of crime starts early round here!'

Ruth smiled. 'Bloody hell. My dad used to give me ten pence for cleaning his car, and that took me and my brother an hour.'

They walked up the stone steps to the house and rang the buzzer for Walsh's flat.

TEN MINUTES LATER, Lucy shifted uncomfortably on Trevor Walsh's threadbare brown sofa. His flat was definitely a health hazard. It smelled of cigarette smoke, alcohol, and wet dogs. The walls were stained and there was beige lino rather than carpet on the floor.

Walsh was small and weathered looking. Even though he was only about sixty, he looked ten years older. Given the empty cans and the smell, Lucy assumed he had some sort of alcohol problem.

Leaning forward, Walsh licked a paper as he rolled himself a cigarette. 'Bloody hell. I never thought I'd have to talk about Alfie Wise again. Ancient bloody history, that is.'

Lucy took out her notepad. 'You were there the night that Frank Weller was killed. Is that right?'

'Yeah.' Walsh nodded. 'But he bloody deserved it.'

Ruth frowned. 'Why do you say that?'

Walsh lit his cigarette and blew a plume of bluish smoke up into the air.

Great. Now I'm getting second-hand cancer to go with my scabies, Lucy thought.

'Frank and those other two tossers started on us. Me and Alfie were just sitting on the bench waiting for a bus, minding our own business,' he explained.

'But Alfie was carrying a knife, wasn't he?' Lucy asked.

Walsh shook his head. 'Nah. Alfie never carried a knife. It was Frank Weller's knife. He stabbed me in the leg with it. Alfie must have got it off him. I told your lot at the time but they weren't interested.' He tapped some ash and frowned. 'What's all this about then?'

'You know the names Terry Droy and Eddie Bannerman?' Ruth asked.

'Of course. The other kids that were there that night. Fucking Plough Boys giving it large. Well Alfie showed them. Weren't so fucking cocky after that were they?' Walsh said in an aggressive tone that implied he was proud that Frank Weller had been killed.

Lucy looked up from her notepad. 'Did you ever have your suspicions about what happened to Alfie?'

'A few.' Walsh blew smoke out of his nostrils and sat forward. 'Have you found him then?'

'We have found a body that we believe to be Alfie Wise.'

Walsh blinked as he took in the news. 'That's sad, that is ... I thought I'd go to my grave and never know what happened to him.'

'We believe he was murdered,' Ruth said.

'Really?' Walsh shook his head. 'Poor bastard. Not a big surprise, but at least Alfie can be put to rest now, eh?'

'How would you describe your relationship with Alfie?'

Walsh pulled a face. 'Relationship? What does that mean?'

'Am I right in thinking that you're a homosexual, Mr Walsh?'

'Not that it's any of your business, but yeah I am.' Walsh rubbed his nose and then looked at Lucy. 'Oh right. You think me and Alfie ...'

Lucy shrugged. 'Well ... were you in a relationship with him?'

Walsh snorted. 'Leave off. Alfie was what we called AC/DC.'

'You mean bi-sexual?' Ruth asked.

'Yeah. We were just mates. Nothing more than that.'

'You sure about that? We've been told that you were in a relationship with him.'

'No. No way,' Walsh grunted. 'He wasn't my type anyway.'

'We heard that you might have been jealous or angry because of Alfie's behaviour with other men?'

'Bloody hell! Where are you getting all this crap from? Jackanory?' Walsh leaned forward and stubbed his cigarette out. 'You think I killed Alfie in some kind of lover's tiff. Jesus, you're way off, love.'

Lucy looked over at Ruth – they weren't going to get any further with this line of enquiry.

'He did send me a letter,' Walsh said.

'Alfie?'

'Yeah,' Walsh nodded. 'Just before he went missing. Said he was going away for a while and wouldn't be around.'

Ruth frowned. 'What did you think he meant by that?'

Walsh shrugged. 'No idea. I thought he might have been talking about prison.'

'But you never saw him after the night Frank Weller was killed?'

'No. I was too frightened.'

'Have you still got that letter?'

'Yeah, somewhere,' Walsh said. 'I can dig it out if you want?'

Ruth nodded. 'That would be helpful.'

Lucy looked up from her notepad. 'Do you think that Terry Droy and Eddie Bannerman were responsible for Alfie's death then?'

Walsh shook his head as he reached to the floor for a can of super-strength lager. 'No. They were definitely looking for him. I know that much. They found me and gave me a good kicking. And they would have killed him, if they'd found him.'

Lucy frowned. 'Then who do you think killed Alfie?'

Walsh rolled his eyes. 'It was to do with Charlie, wasn't it? It had to be.'

'Why do you say that?'

Walsh laughed. 'Not really doing your job, ladies, are you? Charlie Wise, or Sir Charles fucking Wise as he is now, was involved in all sorts of shady stuff. Drove around in a big American car, suits made up in the West End. Right flash wanker.'

'When you say *shady stuff*, what exactly do you mean?'

Walsh shook his head in disbelief. 'He was a gangster, love. It's the world's worst kept secret. There was a club over on Balham High Road. The 211 Club. Big place with a casino upstairs. Charlie used to work there. Place was owned by that Freddie Foreman.'

Lucy frowned – she knew the name.

'Freddie Foreman?'

'He was an enforcer for the Krays in the late 50s and 60s. Brown Bread Fred they called him,' Walsh explained.

Lucy and Ruth looked at each other – they weren't expecting that.

Walsh gave a wry grin. 'Fucking funny when you think about it now. Technically, Sir Charles Wise once worked for the Kray twins. And when Charlie boy didn't do as he was told, or pissed someone off, they murdered Alfie as a warning.'

'Do you have any idea who that person might be?' Lucy asked.

'I've got a few ideas,' Walsh said.

'Can you tell us who you think might have killed Alfie?'

Walsh looked nervous as he shook his head. 'No chance. If I give you names, and you start poking around, you're going to find me dead and buried in a hole.'

CHAPTER 12

Gaughran and Hassan had soon found the address they had been given for Eddie Bannerman in Brockley, which was about two miles south east of Peckham. The road was residential, with small, semi-detached houses that had been built in the 1930s.

Gaughran parked outside No. 23, turned off the ignition and unclipped his seatbelt.

'Don't think I've been out to Brockley before,' Hassan admitted.

'It's nice. Well, nicer than Peckham. But then again, so is Beruit,' Gaughran joked and pointed to the right. 'My old man used to take us for walks on Blythe Hill, which is just over there. Used to fly kites when it was windy enough.'

Getting out of the car, Gaughran took his sunglasses from the top pocket of his short-sleeved shirt and put them on. Even though it was hot, there was a decent breeze. He spotted an old Renault 5 on the drive – *looks like someone's in.*

Walking up to the front door, Hassan knocked and stepped back. Gaughran joined him and they waited for a few seconds.

Nothing.

A dog barked from somewhere inside.

'Pint after work?' Gaughran asked. He had a bit of a thirst on and a cold pint or two of lager would go down a treat.

'Sounds good,' Hassan said as he knocked on the door again, this time a lot harder.

There was no doubting that anyone inside would hear them now.

Gaughran snorted. 'Bloody hell, Syed! We're not the drugs squad doing a raid, mate. You'll give the poor bloke a heart attack.'

'He's old. He might be deaf,' Hassan laughed as he cupped his hands and tried to peer through the thick frosted glass panel on the front door.

'Anything?' Gaughran asked.

Hassan turned and shook his head. 'Nothing, Sarge.'

Then they heard a bang from somewhere inside the house. It sounded like a door closing.

Gaughran exchanged a look with Hassan. 'Well, someone's definitely in.'

Stepping over a small rockery wall, Gaughran went to a large downstairs window and gazed inside. There was an old-fashioned three-piece suite, a television and a large coffee table.

The front door then opened about six inches and a man in his 60s looked out. A Rottweiler was barking and snarling at his feet.

Hassan showed him his warrant card. 'Eddie Bannerman?'

Bannerman frowned. 'Yeah?'

'We're from Peckham CID. We wondered if we could ask you a few questions to help with an ongoing investigation?' Hassan said.

'You got a warrant?' Bannerman sneered.

Gaughran stepped forward and glared at him. 'We don't need a warrant. We just want to ask a couple of questions.'

'About what?'

What a prick, Gaughran thought.

Gaughran sighed. 'You really want us to go and get a warrant?'

'Is this about that body you found in Peckham? I saw it on the news this morning?'

Hassan nodded. 'We're investigating what we think was a historic murder and we just want to ask you a couple of questions.'

Bannerman blinked as the dog continued to bark. 'LBC said the body might be someone called Alfie Wise?'

Gaughran raised his eyebrows. 'Why don't you let us in and we can talk about it.'

Bannerman gestured to the dog. 'I'll just get rid of him. Hang on a sec.' He then closed the front door.

'He looked rattled,' Hassan said.

'He looked bloody guilty.'

'Wasn't your old man a copper at Peckham?' Hassan asked.

Gaughran nodded. His father, Arthur Gaughran, had been a serving police officer for over thirty-five years in the Met and had only retired at the end of the 80s. Even though he would never admit it, Gaughran worshipped the ground his father walked on and he was proud to have followed in his footsteps. 'Yeah. I'm pretty sure he was a bobby on the beat when all this happened. I should ask him about it.'

'Yeah, he might remember something.'

Gaughran then frowned at Hassan. 'He's taking his time, isn't he?

Suddenly, he spotted Bannerman dashing from the side of the house towards the Renault 5. For a second, Gaughran couldn't quite believe what he was witnessing. *What the bloody hell does he think he's doing?*

Bannerman jumped into the car and started the engine.

'Oi! Stay there!' Gaughran yelled as he ran across the paved front garden towards the car.

Hearing the gearbox clunk, he realised it was too late. Bannerman was in no mood to talk and was fully intent on doing a runner.

Cheeky bastard!

The Renault sped forward, hitting the back end of their navy coloured BMW 3 Series. The back light and indicator smashed and glass fell onto the road.

The car turned sharp left and accelerated away.

'Are you fucking joking?' Gaughran growled.

Running to look at the damage, Hassan glanced over. 'It's okay, Sarge. It's driveable.'

'I don't give a shit about that. We've only had that car for two months and it's police property.' Gaughran grabbed his Tetra radio. 'Control from Delta three eight. We have a possible suspect, an Edward Bannerman, in a blue Renault 5, plate unknown, heading south on St James' Terrace. Requesting assistance, over,' Gaughran hollered into the radio as he jumped into the BMW.

The Tetra radio crackled. 'Delta three eight, received. Will advise, stand by,' said the female voice of the Computer Aided Dispatch controller.

Gaughran could feel the anger surge through his body as he stamped on the accelerator. 'What a wanker! Wait 'til I get my hands on him.'

The car roared up the road in pursuit. Gaughran worked through the gears quickly, pushing the car's acceleration as fast as he could. Forty miles per hour. Fifty.

A car nosed out of a side road. Gaughran swerved and hit the horn. 'Get out of my fucking way! Twat!'

Hassan glanced over, looking concerned. He always got like this when Gaughran lost his shit. 'Sarge?'

'What?' he barked. 'You wanna fucking drive?'

Hassan held his hands up defensively. 'No, Sarge. But I'd like to get home to see my kids tonight.'

Gaughran ignored him. That was the problem with Hassan. He lacked the bottle to be a top detective.

Eddie Bannerman had a one minute start on them. Gaughran knew they needed him to have been held up at a junction or traffic lights.

Scanning left and right as they reached the main road, there was no sign of the Renault. *Where the bloody hell is he?*

Hassan clicked his radio. 'Control from Delta three eight. We are still in pursuit but have lost visual contact, over.'

'Delta three eight, received. We have Alpha five seven en-route to assist, will advise, out.'

Then suddenly, Gaughran saw the blur of red brake lights further down the main road to the right. The cars had stopped for a temporary traffic light by some roadworks.

Gaughran pointed. 'Isn't that him?'

Hassan squinted. 'Yes, Sarge.'

Gaughran hit the siren and the blue lights that were embedded in the radiator grill. He knew he had a short temper, but Bannerman doing a runner and hitting their car had really got to him.

I'm coming for you, you fucker!

With an abrupt jolt, they sped out onto the main road and down the outside of the line of waiting traffic. Gaughran could feel the adrenaline starting to pump through his body.

The Renault pulled out of the line of traffic, zipped straight through the red light and narrowly missed a cyclist coming the other way.

Hassan shook his head. 'What an idiot!' He then grabbed the radio again. 'Control from Delta three eight. We have visual contact with suspect. Travelling north on the B2142. A blue Renault 5. Plate foxtrot seven zero, sierra, delta, yankee, over.'

'Three eight received.'

The Renault pulled out onto the other side of the road to overtake a lorry. Gaughran followed. Fifty miles per hour, fifty five miles per hour, sixty.

Suddenly, the Renault had a tyre blow out. Bits of the wheel went flying into the air. Gaughran could smell the burnt rubber coming in through the air conditioning unit and started to brake.

The Renault lurched left and then right as Bannerman fought to control the car. It was no use. The car clipped a lamppost, spun a full 180 degrees and then came to a stop in the middle of the road.

'Jesus!' Gaughran said.

Hassan shook his head. 'Christ, he was lucky. A foot either way and he'd be dead.'

Gaughran unclipped his seatbelt and opened the car door. 'He'll wish he was dead by the time I finish with him.'

Marching quickly over to the damaged Renault, he saw the driver's door open slowly. Reaching the car, he looked at the man who had a nasty gash in his forehead – his face was now covered in blood.

The man squinted up at him.

'Take the keys out of the ignition,' Gaughran snapped angrily, taking the cuffs from his belt.

'Why don't you fuck off!' Bannerman said wiping the blood from his face.

Taking a cursory glance to make sure no one was around, Gaughran kicked the man hard in the leg.

'Oi, you can't do that!'

'Give me the keys!' Gaughran growled.

Bannerman took the keys from the ignition and handed them over.

'Dickhead,' Gaughran muttered as he held his wrists and cuffed him. 'Eddie Bannerman, you're under arrest for dangerous driving and criminal damage.'

CHAPTER 13

Sipping her hot coffee, Lucy pushed open the doors to the CID office to allow Ruth to enter ahead of her. Inside, she could see that Gaughran, Hassan, and several other detectives had assembled for the afternoon briefing that Brooks had called. When they had mentioned to him what Walsh had told them about Charlie, Brooks had been understandably concerned.

Going over to the scene board, Brooks looked out at them. Lucy loved it when Brooks was in full DCI mode. He was really sexy. 'Right guys. We seem to have various lines of enquiry in this investigation. I need everyone to be up to speed as to where we are. Lucy?'

For a moment, Lucy was still thinking how sexy Brooks was when she realised that he needed her to feedback to CID what she and Ruth had learnt from their visit to Trevor Walsh. She got up from her desk, went over to the scene board and pointed to an old photo of Walsh from the 50s. 'This morning, Ruth and I spoke to Trevor Walsh. He was the boy who was with Alfie Wise the night that Frank Weller was stabbed and killed at Balham underground station. We followed up on Terry Droy's claim that Walsh and Alfie were in a homosexual relationship, and that Walsh was jealous. He admitted he was homosexual. He denied ever being in a relationship with Alfie and said that Alfie was bi-sexual. He then told us that Sir Charles

Wise was heavily involved in the South London criminal underworld in the 1950s and early 1960s. Sir Charles, or Charlie
as he was then, worked in the 211 Club in Balham, which was
owned by Freddie Foreman. Foreman had links to the Kray
twins.'

Several detectives exchanged looks – it was surprising
news.

Brooks let out an audible sigh. 'The bloody Krays yet
again.'

Ruth gave Brooks a quizzical look – she didn't know exactly what he meant. 'Sorry, guv. What do you mean?'

'Ever since I joined the Met, the Kray twins seem to pop up
in the conversation far too often for my liking. I once heard a
joke headline from a London newspaper – *Shocking Revelation.
Man in East of London found who <u>didn't</u> know the Krays!*'

There was ironic laughter in the room.

Brooks continued. 'Let's just get it straight. The Kray twins
were not working class heroes. They didn't keep law and order
in the East End. They were two nasty little thugs who hurt innocent people and took their money.'

Ruth could see that Brooks was getting wound up by the
mention of the notorious gangster brothers.

Lucy picked up some photocopied newspaper articles.
'Guv, I did some digging around. The *News of the World* tried
to run an exposé on Wise's alleged criminal background in the
80s when it was first suggested that he might get a knighthood.
He took out a libel suit against the paper and the story never
actually ran in its entirety.'

'Any details of what they were going to print?' Brooks
asked.

Lucy shook her head. 'No, guv. It was all buried in litigation. But it sounds as if Charlie was keen that his past didn't come out.'

'Maybe we can talk to the journalist who wrote the article?' Hassan suggested.

'He died last year,' Lucy said. 'We could go and talk to the editor, or his widow, but I'm not sure how much they'll give us.'

Brooks nodded. 'Yeah, that might end up being a bit of a rabbit hole. We'll come back to that if we need to, Luce.'

Ruth then pointed to a photo of Charlie Wise on the scene board. 'Walsh claimed that Charlie had fallen out with someone in the criminal underworld. Alfie was murdered to send a message or as some kind of revenge.'

Gaughran frowned. 'Did he give you a name?'

Ruth shook her head. 'No. He said he was still too scared.'

Brooks rubbed his chin and took a sip of his coffee. 'The one person who would know about this is Sir Charles Wise. But I don't suppose he's going to admit to any of it ... Tim, what have you guys got?'

As Ruth went back to her desk, Gaughran looked up. 'Guv. Me and Syed went for a chat with Arnold Dixon at Dixon's Timber Yard yesterday. It was a timber yard, even back in 1956. Dixon remembered when Alfie Wise had gone missing and said he knew him by sight. He claimed that the yard was a mess and if someone had come and buried a body over by the back, no one would have noticed.'

Brooks frowned dubiously. 'What did you think?'

'Hard to say, guv. He didn't seem to be hiding anything. And he pointed out that if he'd thought something or someone had been buried in his yard, he would have called the police.'

'Unless he had something to do with it?' Hassan suggested.

'My instinct was that he was telling us the truth,' Gaughran said. 'He also confirmed this idea that Charlie Wise was some kind of gangster back then and was hanging around with some very dangerous people. In fact, Dixon said that he was surprised it wasn't Charlie who ended up being murdered.'

'Okay. What about Eddie Bannerman?' Brooks asked.

Hassan looked over. 'We went to talk to Bannerman this morning. He was the other boy who was with Frank Weller the night he was killed.'

Gaughran snorted and said, 'And when we arrived, Bannerman did a runner. We pursued him for a couple of miles before he drove into a lamppost. He's been seen by the police doctor and is having a little lie down in a holding cell downstairs.'

Brooks walked slowly over to the scene board. 'At the moment, we seem to have three lines of enquiry. Alfie Wise was killed in revenge for the death of Frank Weller. Or he had a lover's tiff with Trevor Walsh. Or he was killed because his brother was heavily involved in criminal activities ... However, we don't seem to have a front runner, do we?'

Ruth shrugged. 'They all seem viable, guv. It was forty years ago, so we don't have any CCTV, up-to-date witness statements, or a decent crime scene.'

Gaughran nodded. 'Agreed. We've also got the problem that some of the people we might need to talk to just aren't around anymore.'

Brooks sat on the table. 'Tim and Syed. I want you to go and interview Bannerman. We need to know why he ran at the mention of Alfie Wise's name. If we know that Droy and Bannerman were looking for Alfie Wise, they have to be our prime suspects. However, if they never found Alfie, they'll have a good idea of who did find him.'

Hassan got up from his desk. 'Yes, guv.'

Brooks looked at Ruth and Lucy. 'I'm afraid you're going to have to go and talk to Charlie. Obviously I don't need to say it, but tread very, very carefully. This man has lunch with the PM. But if there is something in his past that will allow us to find out who killed Alfie Wise, then I need him to tell us.'

By the time Gaughran and Hassan had got to Interview Room 2 on the ground floor, Bannerman had been brought up from the holding cell. He was sitting next to the duty solicitor, a tall man with a pointed nose and thin-rimmed glasses.

Gaughran strolled over, took a chair and sat down opposite them. The room was stark with very little light. There had been a police station on the site since the late 1800s and not many improvements had been made. Hassan put a case folder down on the table, pulled his trousers up a little at the knees to stop them creasing, and sat down quietly.

Gaughran indicated the cut on Bannerman's temple that now had two butterfly stitches. 'Looks nasty, Eddie. But then again, if you drive like a lunatic, things like that will happen.'

Bannerman sat with his arms folded and avoided eye contact. His double chin and cheeks were covered in stubble and he looked like he hadn't washed for a week.

'We asked you if we could speak to you about Alfie Wise and then you decided to do a runner. Why is that Eddie?' Hassan asked.

Bannerman sighed. 'Why do you think?'

Hassan shrugged. 'I haven't got a clue. You tell me.'

'You gonna charge me with something so I can get out of this shithole and go home?'

'I don't think so,' Gaughran snorted as he leant forward and fixed Bannerman with a stare. 'You're going nowhere until you tell us about Alfie Wise.'

The duty solicitor frowned. 'You have to disclose to me and my client why he has been arrested and held.'

'I'm not sure where to start.' Gaughran smiled, leant over and tapped the folder that sat in front of Hassan. 'For starters, according to the DVLA, Eddie, you're in the middle of a one-year ban for drink driving. Is that right?'

Bannerman looked at him. 'No comment.'

Gaughran sighed heavily. 'Oh, we're going down that route, are we? Not very clever on your part, Eddie.'

'Why don't you want to talk to us about Alfie Wise?' Hassan asked.

'Bloody hell. You two should know why more than anyone.'

Gaughran exchanged a confused look with Hassan. *What the hell is he talking about?*

'Let's start at the beginning. You were with Frank Weller and Terry Droy when you got into a fight with Alfie Wise and Trevor Walsh on Balham High Street on the 13th November 1956. Correct?' Gaughran asked, sitting back in his chair. He wanted to get Bannerman talking and so getting him to confirm what was already on record was a decent start.

'Yeah, I was there.'

'What had you been doing that night, Eddie?' Hassan asked.

'Me and Terry had been called up to do our National Service. We went out with Frank for a few drinks before we went off to do our basic training,' Bannerman explained.

'And then what?' Gaughran asked.

'We headed down to Balham where Terry lived. He had a bottle of whiskey stashed somewhere and we were gonna have a few more drinks.'

'Except that's not what happened, is it?'

'No. There were a couple of kids sitting at the bus stop. One of them got into a row with Frank and called him a cunt. Next thing it kicked off. I saw Frank chasing that Alfie down to Balham station.'

'Did you follow them down there?'

Bannerman shook his head. 'No. I saw a couple of coppers coming towards us so me and Terry did a runner.'

'So when did you know that Frank Weller had been stabbed and killed by Alfie Wise?' Hassan asked.

'When I saw a paper the next day. My old man showed me it because he knew Frank was my mate.'

'Alfie Wise stabbed and killed your mate.' Gaughran raised an eyebrow. 'How did that make you feel, Eddie?'

Bannerman pulled a face. 'How d'you think it made me feel? I'd known Frank all my life.'

'So, you were bloody angry. And you and Terry Droy tried to track down Alfie Wise to get revenge? Is that correct?'

'No comment.'

Hassan gestured to his notebook. 'Terry told us you tried to find Alfie, but you never found him. And then he disappeared. Is that right?'

Bannerman snarled. 'Yeah. Me and Terry were doing our National Service by the time all the missing posters went up. We weren't even in London, we were in Kent.'

Gaughran looked over at Hassan. *So now they've magically got an alibi.*

'Funny that you and Terry haven't mentioned that before,' Gaughran said sarcastically.

Bannerman shrugged. 'Long time ago. My memory is shocking.'

Hassan glared at him. 'We can check that, Eddie.'

'Check all you like. Anyway, we'd stopped looking for Alfie before we even left for basic training.'

'Why's that?'

'We were warned not to look for him. We didn't have much of a choice.'

'How do you mean?' Gaughran asked.

'Alfie and Charlie were into some pretty heavy stuff. Hanging around with some very dangerous people. We were warned to keep our noses out by one of your lot,' Bannerman explained.

Hassan shifted forward in his chair and furrowed his brow. 'You mean a police officer?'

'Yeah, of course. The word was that there were a couple of detectives from the South London Murder Squad looking for a regular backhander from the 211 Club in exchange for turning a blind eye to the after-hours drinking, gambling and drugs. Plus, they had a few brasses knocking around,' Bannerman explained. 'Except Charlie and the other blokes around the club told them to piss off. There was a fight, and some detective got thrown down the stairs and broke his leg. Three days later Alfie Wise disappeared off the face of the earth.'

Gaughran felt his stomach turn. He didn't like what Bannerman was implying. 'Are you trying to say that bent coppers were responsible for whatever happened to Alfie Wise?'

Bannerman gave him an ironic smile. 'I'm sitting in a South London police station, so I'm not saying anything. But Charlie Wise had a fight with a copper. Then his brother disappeared and you've only just found him. You can draw your own conclusions.'

CHAPTER 14

Ruth and Lucy had been looking out at the view from Charlie's seventeenth floor company reception window for about ten minutes now. They had come to ask him a few questions, and this time they had arrived unannounced. It was a tactic designed to catch him a little off guard. Since their last meeting, they had learned of Charlie's nefarious past and his involvement in South London's gangland. The receptionist said that she wasn't sure where Sir Charles was. He had been in earlier, so she was going to talk to his PA and track him down.

It was late afternoon and Ruth gazed out at the magnificent view of the capital below. The sun was beginning to set to the west. The hazy sky above the capital was turning tangerine and there were strands of pink clouds, like pulled candyfloss, where the horizon was visible in the distance.

Lucy pointed down towards the Thames below them. 'When my grandad, my mum's dad, got back from the war, he used to be a lamplighter. My family lived on an estate over in Pimlico. Every evening, just before dusk, he'd jump on his bike and cycle down the embankment from Pimlico right down to St Paul's. He had to stop at every gas streetlamp, reach up with a long lighting pole and light it. Took him nearly three hours. And then, at dawn, he'd go out again and turn them all off. And you know how much he got a week for doing that?'

Ruth shrugged. 'Not a lot.'

'Five pounds and twelve shillings a week.'

Charlie's glamorous PA arrived in a fluster. 'Hi there. I'm afraid Sir Charles has gone to Belfast this afternoon for a meeting. I could make an appointment later in the week if you like?'

Ruth glanced at Lucy and raised a brow. 'Erm, that's fine. We'll try to catch up with him in the next few days.'

The PA smiled and left them.

Ruth waited until she was out of earshot and then said, 'Doesn't that strike you as odd?'

'A little bit, yeah.' Lucy gestured to the double doors, and they headed out to the state-of-the-art lifts. 'Your brother has been missing for forty years. His body is discovered two days ago. And you decide to go and pop off to Ireland on a business trip.'

The lift arrived, and they got in. Ruth pushed the button for the ground floor.

'Maybe he wants to keep busy?' Ruth suggested.

'If he's not in the office, you'd think he'd be at home with his wife, waiting for any news of the investigation.'

The doors opened on the ground floor and they headed for the sleek glass exit to the building. As they came out, they descended the stone steps to the pavement that was now bustling with commuters heading to Waterloo Station. The air was warm and smelled of cigarette smoke and the diesel fumes from two buses that were waiting at a busy bus stop.

Spotting their black BMW car up on the right, Ruth reached inside her jacket to get the keys. Both her and Lucy were clearly deep in thought about Charlie's trip to Belfast.

Ruth checked her watch. 'We'd better head back to base if I'm going to get Ella on time.'

'Are you on Koyuki duty tonight as well?' Lucy asked sardonically as she got into the car.

'No. If I'm honest, that's not really going very well at the moment. Shiori gave me my flat keys back and stormed out the other night,' Ruth explained as she started the car.

'Oh dear. What did you do?'

Ruth pulled out into waiting traffic. 'I refused to bath, feed and babysit her child again.'

'Good for you. You're a single parent and a full-time copper. You don't need someone taking the piss, do you?'

Ruth shook her head. 'It's a bit of a relief if I'm honest. Me and Ella haven't had any time to ourselves since Dan left. Which brings me to my other news. Dan announced the other night that he's moving to Australia with Angela.'

For a few seconds, Lucy said nothing. Ruth could sense that she wasn't listening.

Oh well, that's charming.

Instead, Lucy was focussed intently on something else going on outside the car.

'Everything all right?' Ruth asked as she edged forward in the traffic.

Lucy pointed to a large black Jaguar that was parked about a hundred yards ahead of them in a layby with its hazard lights flashing. 'Not really.'

Ruth looked at the stationary car and couldn't see anything remotely wrong. Then she glanced at the pavement and her jaw dropped. Charlie, dressed in a navy pinstripe suit, was striding over to the car with an attractive woman. Opening the back door to the Jaguar, the woman got in and Charlie followed. He clearly had a chauffeur.

Ruth's eyes widened. 'Bloody hell!'

'Well, he's not in bloody Belfast, is he?' Lucy growled.

Ruth shook her head. 'Cheeky bastard.'

'And that's not his wife.'

'How do you know that?'

'While I was digging around, I saw some photos of Charlie and his wife in the papers. She's a mousy little thing,' Lucy said. 'Why's he avoiding us?'

'I don't know.'

'Until now, Charlie has been acting as if he's devastated that we've found Alfie's

body and he'll do anything to help with the investigation,' Lucy said. 'What's changed?'

'Maybe he knows that we've been digging around in his past?' Ruth suggested.

'How would he know that?'

'Walsh? Although that doesn't seem likely,' Ruth said.

They watched as the Jaguar indicated and pulled out into the traffic three cars ahead of them.

Ruth glanced over at Lucy. 'Follow him?'

Lucy nodded. 'Definitely.'

Within five minutes, they were driving across Waterloo Bridge. The Thames was cluttered with river cruisers and smaller boats making the most of the beautiful summer's day. Ruth glanced left and spotted Big Ben and the Houses of Parliament in the distance.

'Do we think Charlie had something to do with Alfie's murder?' Lucy asked as they passed Somerset House and then turned left along the Strand. They were heading towards Trafalgar Square and the centre of London.

Ruth pursed her lips. 'I'm not sure. I don't think so. He seemed genuinely upset when we broke the news to him, didn't he?'

'Yeah, he was crushed.'

'That would be very hard to fake if you knew your brother was buried there all along.'

'But if Alfie was murdered because of something Charlie had done, then he wouldn't have known,' Lucy said. 'And he would therefore be truly upset when we told him he had been found.'

'I think we need to know more about what Charlie was up to around the time of Alfie's disappearance,' Ruth said as they left Trafalgar Square. 'My money is still on Terry Droy and Eddie Bannerman.'

Ruth slowed down as they began to weave through the back streets of Soho. 'Alfie Wise gets into a fight with three blokes. He kills Frank Weller. We know that Droy and Bannerman were looking for him. Two weeks after the murder, Alfie disappears off the face of the earth. There's no way that can be a coincidence.'

'I don't like coincidences either,' Lucy said. 'But Alfie was working for Charlie. And they were mixed up with some very nasty thugs.'

Looking up, Ruth could see that they had turned into New Bond Street. They were now in the heart of Mayfair, one of London's most affluent and exclusive areas.

Lucy peered out at the large white Georgian buildings and designer shops. 'Bloody hell. Now I know why Mayfair is £500 in Monopoly.'

Ruth laughed. 'It's a long way from the Old Kent Road. Although I do always enjoy buying the Old Kent Road and Whitechapel Road and whacking a cheap hotel on them both.'

Lucy raised an eyebrow. 'Which makes you an exploitative slum landlord.'

Ruth smiled and then saw that the Jaguar had pulled up outside a shop called Cavendish Travel, which had a sign promising *Bespoke Global Travel Packages.*

Ruth pulled over on the opposite side of the road, and watched as Charlie got out of the car and went into the shop. About a minute later he came out holding a folder and some documents, got back into the car and pulled away.

'Looks like Charlie is taking a trip,' Lucy said.

Indicating left, Ruth attempted to pull out from where she was parked. However, a dustcart lorry pulled alongside them.

'Shit!' Ruth thundered.

Lucy groaned. 'Get out of the bloody way!'

Jumping from the car, Lucy waved her warrant card and gestured for the refuse lorry to move out of the way. There were nods and gestures from the refuse collectors.

Come on! Come on!

Any longer and Charlie's Jaguar would be lost in the maze of roads in Mayfair.

After another minute, the lorry pulled forward.

Ruth groaned. 'Too late, you idiot.'

Lucy gestured over to Cavendish Travel. 'Fancy finding out where he's going now we've lost him?'

Ruth shrugged. 'Might as well.'

They got out of the car, crossed the road, and entered the boutique travel shop. It smelled of new carpets and expensive perfume.

A woman in her 30s, dressed in a designer suit, gave them a quizzical look as she approached.

Clearly we don't look like her usual clientele, Ruth thought. *What a snob!*

Ruth got out her warrant card. 'DC Hunter and DC Henry, CID.'

The woman pulled a face. 'Oh gosh. Can I help you with something?'

'A man just came in here and picked up some travel documents,' Ruth said.

The woman looked uncomfortable. 'I'm not sure that I can discuss that with you.'

'We'd like to know where he is travelling to and when,' Lucy said, ignoring her.

'As I said, it's not something I could discuss with you.'

Lucy raised an eyebrow as she looked at Ruth and then back at the woman. 'Look, you're a travel agent. Not a doctor or a solicitor. You don't have a legal right to keep client confidentiality. Sir Charles Wise came in here a minute ago and picked up some documents. We need to know where he is travelling to and when.'

The woman bristled at Lucy's no-nonsense tone. 'And as I've explained very clearly to you, I couldn't possibly release that kind of information.'

Ruth gave her a forced smile. 'We're investigating a murder. So, we are going to need that information right now.'

The woman shook her head. 'I will have to ring the owner before I do anything.'

Lucy let out a sigh of exasperation, which Ruth knew meant that she was about to get seriously pissed off.

'I'm going to make this really easy for you ...' Lucy leant forward to read her name badge. '... *Felicity*. Either you give us the information right now or we can go away, contact a magistrate and get a Section 18 Search Warrant. When I come back with that warrant, I'm going to make sure that my team of officers take every computer and every file in this shop back to Peckham. We're going to take a good week, or longer if I feel like it, looking through all that while you try to keep this shop up and running with nothing in it. I'll also let the owner of Cavendish Travel know that this has all happened because of your lack of co-operation.'

Ruth looked at Felicity. 'Yeah, she will. I've seen her do it before. And it's never pretty.'

Lucy raised her eyebrows. 'Or you can just tell us what we need to know.'

'This is utterly ridiculous.' Felicity was completely flustered. 'Sir Charles is travelling to Malaga in Spain in a few days' time.'

'On his own?' Lucy asked.

Felicity shook her head. 'No, with a business associate of his. Leslie Harlow.'

The woman he was in the car with, who is probably his mistress, Ruth thought.

Lucy smiled. 'Thank you, Felicity. You've been incredibly helpful.'

CHAPTER 15

It was early evening, and Lucy had offered to cook for Ruth and Ella. Lucy hadn't seen Ella for a few weeks and it was always lovely to have her over. She hadn't ever mentioned it, but watching Ella toddle around the garden and play made her broody.

Bringing over a glass of wine, Lucy handed it to Ruth and slumped down on the armchair next to her. 'Right, pasta is on. I know Ella's a bit fussy so she can have cheesy pasta. I'm trying a new recipe for us.'

'Which is?'

Lucy's mouth curved into a smile as she walked over to the open cookbook and read, 'Pan fried cod, with roasted vegetables on a bed of couscous.'

Ruth nearly choked on her wine as she laughed. 'Oh my god, did you actually just say *bed of couscous?*'

Lucy grinned. 'That's what it says in the book!'

'Bloody hell. Last time I came here I got beans on toast.'

'I'm trying to improve myself.'

'Well be careful,' Ruth laughed. 'You'll start calling dinner supper and then it'll be downhill from there.' She took a sip of her wine. 'I spotted you watching Ella earlier. You'd make a good mum, you know that?'

'Except for the swearing, the drinking and the excessively dangerous job, I'd be perfect,' Lucy said sardonically. She felt uncomfortable talking about the subject, but she didn't know why.

'Hey, that's the same as me and I've got Ella.'

'Yeah and I don't know how you do it all.'

'Not for you then, motherhood?' Ruth asked.

Lucy took a few seconds to answer, even though she knew that deep down she was dying to have a child. 'No, it's not that.'

'Sorry, it's not even my business.'

'Don't be daft. I tell you everything. It's just me and Harry …'

Ruth looked at her quizzically. 'You and Harry haven't had a conversation about kids yet?'

'That's about the long and short of it.'

'But you do want kids?'

'Definitely.' Lucy surprised herself with the certainty of her answer.

Ruth sipped from her wine. 'But … Harry doesn't?'

Lucy pulled a face. 'Not sure. I think he does, but we never seem to get the time to sit down and actually talk about it properly.'

Ruth gazed over at her. 'Are you scared that Harry is going to say he doesn't want kids and that will throw a whopping great big spanner in the works?'

Lucy smiled and bit her lip. 'Ooh, you can read me like a book, you sod. You should be a detective or something.'

Ruth laughed. 'Give it time. You're not even thirty yet.'

'I know, but Harry's kicking on a bit. I don't want his swimmers getting old, knackered and not able to do their job.'

Ruth almost choked again as she swallowed her wine. 'Lucy! Swimmers? Jesus! Where do you get this stuff from?'

'God knows. But you get my point?'

'Yeah, I definitely got the point you made so graphically. I wouldn't worry. I read an article the other day that said men could father children in their 60s and even their 70s.'

Lucy grimaced. 'Yeah well fathering a child when you're seventy is plain wrong.'

Instead of laughing, Ruth looked panicked as she put her wine down, jumped up from the sofa and sprinted into the garden.

'What's wrong?' Lucy asked as she got up and ran outside with her.

Ruth had picked up Ella in her arms, and the blood had drained from her face. 'Someone was in your garden. They went down there.' She pointed to the passageway at the side of the house.

Without hesitating, Lucy took off at a sprint.

There was the clattering noise of a gate being opened forcefully.

As she thundered into the side passage, a figure in a black t-shirt, grey Adidas trousers and a black baseball cap, was already through the gate and heading for the road.

Bastard! How dare he come into my garden in broad daylight.

'Stop! Police!' Lucy bellowed as she raced left down the hill.

The figure turned left to where Lucy knew there were some old garages.

Lucy followed, sprinting down the rickety, overgrown driveway.

The figure climbed nimbly up onto one of the garage roofs.

Lucy already had it in her head that she was probably chasing a teenage boy who might have been trying to fund a drug habit, or just looking to snatch a handbag, or cash, and run.

As she reached the garage and began to climb, she saw the figure had a dark brown ponytail. It was a girl or a woman. She wasn't expecting that!

'Stop, police!' she yelled, but the girl had already headed to the other side of the garage roof and disappeared out of sight.

'Shit!' Lucy growled. She had no choice but to follow. Her heart was already thudding.

She jumped and pulled herself up the side of the garage. At first, she thought she wouldn't make it. It had been a long time since she'd pulled up her own bodyweight with just her arms. She shook with the sheer effort.

Bloody hell! This reminds of doing PE at school. I hated PE!

She clambered onto the garage roof, grazing the skin from the palms of her hands on the rough asphalt. It stung, but she had no time to think about it.

Lucy went to the other side of the roof. Below was an open area of grass and the local children's playground. There were two young boys on a swing being pushed by their mother.

The escapee dashed across the playground, through an opening in a brick wall, and disappeared down Channing Street.

Lucy hesitated. It was high enough for her to break her bloody neck.

Bollocks, she thought as she leapt, hit the concrete and felt a pain shoot up the outside of her knee.

'For fuck's sake!' she said out loud, much to the annoyance of the mum by the swings.

Sprinting flat out, Lucy gritted her teeth and turned to follow the girl. Her knee was throbbing. Then she had a thought as she got out onto Channing Street. What if that's not a teenage girl looking for drug money? What if it's Harry's ex, Karen? Didn't he say she ran marathons or triathlons? If it is her, I'm going to kill her!

As Lucy turned, she saw the girl, or whoever it actually was, nearly a hundred yards away. If it was Karen, then Lucy was determined to catch her and arrest her for trespass. That would teach the bitch.

How dare she come into my garden!

With anger now raging, she broke into a full sprint, pumping her fists as she went. She'd managed to run off the pain in her knee. To her left, the lurid orange of the local Kebabs, Pizzas & Burgers shop. On the right, the bright green of a bookmakers. That said it all. Two mums pushing prams gave her a curious look as she pounded past them.

The figure went left into Duke's Road and out of sight.

As she slowed for a second, her phone rang in her pocket. It was Ruth.

'Hello?' Lucy gasped into her phone.

'Where the bloody hell are you?' Ruth sounded concerned.

Lucy glanced around. 'Erm, on the corner of Duke's Road.'

'That doesn't help me! What are you doing?' Ruth asked, getting frustrated.

'I think it was Karen,' Lucy said, now aware that her feet were numb and the sweat was running down her back and dropping from her forehead.

'Harry's ex?'

'Yeah. It could have been,' Lucy panted as she wiped her forehead on her t-shirt sleeve and glanced down the street.

The figure had gone.

Lucy was feeling dizzy as she jogged up Prince's Road, and shook her head to try and stabilise herself.

'Bloody hell, Luce. What if it's not? What if it's some psycho crackhead with a knife?'

'I'm pretty sure it's not. They seem pretty fit as psycho crackheads go!'

'Get yourself back here now.'

'Right, I will do. See you in a minute,' Lucy said as she ended the call.

I'll just have a quick check around though.

Between houses were abandoned garages, alleyways, flat pieces of concrete peppered with weeds. It was quiet except for the distant noise of children playing. There were various side streets all the way up Duke's Road. It was basically a maze from here on and the fugitive could have gone anywhere.

A noise came from the side of an old boarded-up house. Slowing down cautiously, Lucy jogged across the weeds to take a look.

Then a clatter. Metallic, maybe.

Lucy moved slowly and put her back against the wall. The brickwork felt rough through her sweaty shirt.

Another click. What the bloody hell was happening? Was that a weapon?

Lucy took a slow, quiet breath as her pulse thudded in her eardrum. She didn't want to peer down the side of the house only to get a blade shoved into her throat. The noise stopped.

Lucy moved her shoulder round, face touching the brick-work, and inched across to see.

Suddenly, out of nowhere, a cat sprang off an old, stained mattress, yowled and bounded past her towards the fence.

'Shit!' Lucy blurted, jumping out of her skin. 'You little fucking ...'

With a resigned sigh, Lucy knew that whoever she had been chasing was now gone.

She turned back, wondering if it really had been Harry's ex-wife and what they were going to do if it was. She began to hob-ble – her knee hurt like hell.

Something metallic glinted on the road by her feet. It was a set of keys. Picking them up, she saw they were a set of house keys. She wondered if the fugitive had dropped them when running away. If she gave them to Brooks, then maybe he could confirm whether it had been Karen whom she had been chas-ing.

GAUGHRAN, HIS FATHER Arthur, and his Uncle Les were on the green of the 18th hole at the Dulwich and Sydenham Hill Golf Club. Gaughran was having a nightmare round as usual. If he was honest, he didn't like playing golf mainly be-cause, unlike his father and uncle, he wasn't very good.

Arthur, in his mid-60s, was a retired South London copper who had worked in the Murder Squad in the 60s and 70s. Tall and thin, with a long face and curious eyes behind thin-rimmed spectacles, he looked more like a science teacher than a hard-ened detective. He walked with a limp which, Gaughran knew, came from a car crash while pursuing a suspect. Uncle Les had followed a similar career path but ended up in Robbery for most of his working life.

Gaughran took the ten-foot putt and his ball picked up speed across the perfectly trimmed green. It went sailing past the hole and ended up about twelve foot the other side. 'Bollocks!'

Arthur shook his head and laughed. 'I think you should just give up, son.'

'Yeah, well, you two live on this bloody golf course,' Gaughran groaned. 'You should be good at it.'

As Arthur went to putt his ball, Les looked over. 'What's all this about a body being found off the High Street?'

'Yeah, it was found at Dixon's Timber Yard,' Gaughran replied.

'Dixon's? That's been there for donkeys years,' Arthur said as he took his putt and the ball stopped about an inch from the hole. 'You can give me that.'

'Go on then.' Les went over to his ball and grinned at Gaughran. 'Watch and learn old son, watch and learn.'

Arthur picked up his ball by the hole and looked at Gaughran. 'Someone said it was Alfie Wise you found there?'

Gaughran nodded. 'Yeah. Weren't you on the beat in Peckham in 1956?'

'Must have been. I remember him going missing,' Arthur said. 'There were a couple of missing posters up in the station.'

'I thought you might come and have a chat with two of the female DCs that are working the case,' Gaughran suggested.

'Plonks?' Les snorted. It was an old-fashioned, derogatory term for female police officers.

'It's all right, thanks,' Arthur said. 'I can talk to you, can't I?'

Gaughran shook his head. 'If you speak to me, it might prejudice the case.'

'Fair enough. If you want me to come in, I can do that. I forgot that it's all about dotting the i's and crossing the t's these days.'

'You got a suspect yet?' Les asked.

'Nothing concrete,' Gaughran said as he tried to line up another putt. 'We've been talking to his brother.'

Arthur hissed, 'Charlie fucking Wise.'

Gaughran frowned. It was unusual to see his father react like that. 'Did you know him?'

'*Everyone* knew Charlie Wise,' he answered with a sneer. 'He thought he was the Godfather of bloody Peckham.'

Gaughran putted his ball closer to the hole. 'What about this 211 Club? It's come up a few times in our enquiries.'

'Oh yeah. We knew all about that place,' Arthur said.

'You ever go there?' Gaughran asked.

'Me? Joking, aren't you? Place was full of villains.'

'Fisher family were involved with the club, weren't they, Art?' Les asked as he putted his ball.

'Yeah. They were a bunch of nasty Paddies,' Arthur said as he gestured to Gaughran's ball. 'Come on, sunshine. Me and Les are getting thirsty.'

'And you're buying,' Les laughed.

Gaughran went over to his ball, lined up the shot, and sank it in the hole.

Arthur groaned. 'At last.'

Plucking his ball out, Gaughran looked over at his father. 'We've had allegations that a couple of coppers were on the take from the 211 Club?'

'What?' Arthur had a face like thunder. 'I'm gonna pretend I didn't hear that!'

Gaughran knew what Arthur and Les thought about bent coppers – they were the scum of the earth.

Gaughran shrugged. 'I'm just telling you what someone's said, Dad.'

'Yeah, well that's a load of bollocks. There were bent coppers in the West End and Soho. The fucking Flying Squad. But not down these parts. No way,' Arthur said, becoming irate.

Les laughed and clapped Arthur on the back. 'It's all right, mate. Calm down.'

Gaughran gestured to the clubhouse. 'Come on, Dad. First round's on me.'

Arthur composed himself and smiled. 'In that case, I'm having a pint and a double Jameson's.'

Les nodded as they left the final green. 'Sounds good to me.'

CHAPTER 16

Lucy stirred sugar into her coffee in the canteen at Peckham nick. She rarely had sugar in her coffee, but she hadn't slept well. The incident with the intruder the night before had rattled her. When Brooks had arrived home, he reassured her he would deal with it. He had also confirmed that the physical description Lucy had given him of the woman she had chased could have been Karen. It would be the third incident involving Karen in a week, and Lucy worried that her behaviour was becoming increasingly erratic and threatening.

'You okay, Luce?' asked a voice. It was Brooks. He put his hand reassuringly on her shoulder.

Christ, he must be worried. He's usually very careful at work.

'Not really,' Lucy sighed as she took her mug of coffee over to the till. 'We do a really difficult job, Harry. The one thing that I've always had is feeling safe in my own home ... but now I don't.'

Brooks nodded sympathetically. 'I'm sorry, Luce. Karen says that it wasn't her last night. With no evidence, there isn't anything I can do.'

'What about the bloody keys, Harry?' Lucy growled. 'Go around to the house, put the key in the front door. If it opens, you've got her bang to rights.'

'It's not as easy as that.'

'Why not? You're a bloody DCI, Harry,' Lucy said as she paid for her coffee.

'Karen has contacted me to say that she's having the locks changed this morning. She doesn't think it's acceptable that I still have access to the property.'

Lucy rolled her eyes and, with a heavy dose of sarcasm, said, 'Mmm, that's strange. It's as if she lost a set of keys last night while running away from me, and now she needs new locks and keys. But I guess that's just a coincidence.'

'I will sort it. I've spoken to a magistrate to see what we need for a restraining order,' Brooks said sheepishly. He then glanced at his watch and indicated the doors to the canteen. 'I've got to get to briefing.'

Lucy frowned as they headed towards the canteen doors. 'I know that, Harry. I work as a detective in CID, you plank! I'm in morning briefing with you every day. What's the matter with you?'

As they made their way up the back stairs, Lucy felt for Brooks' hand, held it for a second and gave it a squeeze.

'Luce,' Brooks said anxiously under his breath as he looked around.

'Your hand isn't the only thing I want to squeeze,' Lucy giggled.

Brooks laughed. 'Bloody hell, Luce. You're a nightmare!'

They arrived at the double doors that led to the CID office. Lucy turned to face Brooks and checked both ways that the coast was clear. She squeezed his crotch and winked at him. 'Give it ten seconds before you follow me in will you, lover boy?'

Brooks shook his head but smiled.

As she walked over to her desk, Ruth approached. 'You okay?' she asked Lucy under her breath.

'Fine. I'll talk to you about it later.'

Ruth pointed to Gaughran who was deep in conversation with Hassan. 'Tim's dad is coming in this morning to talk to us. Tim said he can fill us in with some background information on Charlie and Alfie Wise from way back when.'

'Sounds good. Is it me, or is Tim actually acting like a grown-up detective these days?'

Ruth sat down. 'Let's see how long it lasts, eh?'

The doors opened and Brooks strolled in. Lucy smirked to herself as she thought about what they had just been doing outside.

'Morning everyone. If we can get started as quickly as we can. We've got a lot to get through.' Brooks arrived at the scene board and pointed to a photo of Alfie Wise. 'Do we have a front runner for who shot and buried Alfie Wise yet?' The room was full of mutterings, but it was clear that opinion was divided. 'Okay. I'll take that as a no. Tim, what is the latest on Droy and Bannerman?'

Gaughran sat forward in his chair. 'They definitely have motive. And they've both admitted they were looking for Alfie to get revenge for Frank Weller's murder. But they claim they were warned off by local police officers. And they both maintain that they had been called up for National Service basic training in Kent, so they weren't even living in London the day that Alfie disappeared.'

'Anyone confirmed that yet?' Brooks asked. 'It seems convenient.'

Gaughran shook his head. 'Military records are calling me back this morning, guv.'

'Any progress on getting a DNA sample to match our remains?' Brooks asked.

Lucy shook her head. 'Not yet, guv.'

'What about the carbon dating?'

Hassan looked up. 'Should be a result in the next day or so, guv.'

Brooks nodded. 'Good. Ruth, have we got any more on Trevor Walsh?'

Ruth shook her head. 'Nothing, guv. He can't remember where he was that day, which is not surprising. We've got nothing to link him to the murder except for Droy's claim that he and Alfie were lovers and that Walsh was jealous. It's a nonstarter at the moment. He said that he got a letter from Alfie around that time telling him he was going away and wouldn't be around anymore.'

Gaughran raised an eyebrow. 'Don't suppose he's still got that letter?'

'He thinks he kept hold of it so he's going to dig it out,' Lucy explained.

Brooks pointed to a recent photo of Charlie. 'What about Sir Charles Wise? What do we think?'

Lucy took the pen out of her mouth and looked over. 'My instinct is that he didn't know for certain that his brother was dead. But whether his connections to the criminal underworld made Alfie a target is another thing.'

Ruth made eye contact with Brooks. 'I've been onto Cavendish Road Police Station in Balham, guv. They're going to dig out anything they can find on the 211 Club from the mid to late 50s. Plus, I'm getting the original missing persons file on Alfie sent up from the basement. It's taken them this long to find it.'

'Okay,' Brooks said. 'And I've arranged for some of us to go to the pub at lunchtime.'

There were a few cheers and laughs from the room.

Brooks smiled. 'Yeah, well don't get excited. Just me, Lucy and Ruth.'

Gaughran grinned. 'Guv, I'm not sure a threesome is appropriate.'

There was more laughter.

Lucy looked at Ruth and gestured to Gaughran. 'Told you. Still a prize knobhead.'

Brooks smiled. 'Thanks Tim. We're meeting a true crime journalist, Craig Sullivan. He refused to come in here and suggested The Castle. He's a bit of a hack. You know all those bloody books you see at the train station or airport. *Life Inside The Firm* or *The Godfather of London's Underworld.* All that bullshit.'

Lucy gave a wry smile. 'Why are we talking to him then, guv?'

A uniformed officer came in and approached Gaughran. He was holding a fax.

'Because he's an expert on everything that was going on in the criminal world in London in the 50s. And given that most of the people we want to talk to have either been murdered or have died of natural causes, it seemed like a good idea,' Brooks explained.

Gaughran gestured to the fax he had just been handed. 'Guv. Fax from the British Army Service Records at the National War Museum. Terry Droy and Eddie Bannerman did both complete their National Service. But because of their date of birth, they didn't do their basic training in Kent until 1957, not late 1956.'

Brooks raised an eyebrow. 'Which means they were both lying to us about having an alibi.'

CHAPTER 17

'The bloody tea doesn't get any better, does it?' Arthur Gaughran said with a sarky grin.

Ruth and Lucy laughed. They had been talking to Tim Gaughran's father for a couple of minutes in the Peckham nick canteen.

'Oh, is that why you put four sugars in it?' Lucy joked.

Arthur chortled. 'Yeah. I don't want to actually taste it.'

Ruth sipped her coffee and looked over at him. 'I'm sure that Tim has filled you in with some of the background?'

Arthur shook his head. 'I couldn't believe that you found Alfie Wise after all those years.'

'Do you remember him going missing?' Lucy asked.

'Vaguely. I was only a bobby on the beat back then. The Wise family was well known to us around here. Especially Charlie. He drove around in a big, flash American car. Thought he was a big shot.'

Ruth, who was now writing in her notebook, looked up. 'We have information that he worked at the 211 Club in Balham?'

'Yeah, that's right,' Arthur said. 'The 211 Club was the place to go in South London in the 50s if you were a face.'

'What did Charlie do at the club?' Lucy asked.

'From what I know, he worked the door for a bit. And then he helped run the club. They had a casino room on the top floor. Jack 'the Hat' McVitie virtually lived in there. Well, that was until he accused a croupier of cheating, pulled a knife on him and got banned.'

Ruth's brow creased quizzically. 'Jack the Hat? Why do I know that name?'

'Reggie Kray stabbed him to death in the 60s. They never found the body. Rumour was they went out to sea off Kent and dumped it.'

Lucy raised an eyebrow. 'Nice ... We're working on a theory that Alfie Wise was murdered because Charlie had crossed someone at the 211 Club.'

'That was the rumour in this station. No one in CID took Alfie's disappearance very seriously, though.'

Ruth frowned. 'Why not?'

Arthur shrugged. 'Without a body, there wasn't even a crime. It was just a missing persons case. And in those days, CID officers were given a bit more free rein. They were basically left to get on with the job and as long as they solved crimes and nicked people, no one interfered. There was none of this crime detection rates nonsense. Charlie Wise was a flash prick, excuse my French. If his brother had gone missing, no one was really going to bust a gut to find him.'

'But there was speculation in the station about what had actually happened to Alfie?' Lucy probed.

'Oh yeah. Lots of rumours. There was a family over in Tooting called the Fishers. Irish. Proper villains. They tried to get the 211 Club to pay them protection, which was pretty dangerous seeing as Freddie Foreman owned the club and he was in with the Krays. Apparently, Charlie laughed and told them to fuck off. If I remember correctly, in the October of

1956, Declan Fisher tried to throw a petrol bomb into the ground floor bar at the 211 Club. Charlie caught him outside, coshed him unconscious and put him into intensive care down at St George's. Gave him brain damage. No one reported it so no police ever got involved. A month later, Alfie Wise vanished.'

'So, you think the Fisher family killed Alfie in revenge?' Ruth asked.

'It was just one rumour going around at the time.'

Ruth looked down at her notepad. 'There is something else that you might be able to help us with ... although it's a bit sensitive.'

'Fire away. It's all ancient history now, isn't it?'

'We're aware of an allegation that there were detectives from the South London Murder Squad who were asking for bribes from the 211 Club? Is that possible?' Ruth asked, aware that this was a delicate subject.

Arthur paused for a few seconds as he took in the question. 'No. No way. They were decent coppers, so I'm 99% sure that's a lie.'

Lucy sipped her tea. 'Arthur, you said there were various rumours about what happened to Alfie. You told us about the Fisher family. Is there anything else, or anyone else, we should be looking at?'

Arthur nodded. 'The most obvious person to look at is Charlie Wise, or Sir Charles Wise. Christ, I couldn't believe he got a bloody knighthood after all he'd been up to. Just shows you, doesn't it?'

'Why do you think Charlie Wise would want to kill his own brother? Ruth asked.

'This is only gossip, but a grass told us that Alfie Wise had told Charlie that he wanted nothing to do with what was going on at the 211 Club or what Charlie was getting himself involved in. Rumour was that Alfie had threatened to go to the police if he didn't stop.' Arthur looked over at them. 'Charlie and Alfie got into a row about it. And Charlie shot him.'

GAUGHRAN SHIFTED FORWARD on his chair. They were back in the interview room in Wandsworth Prison with Terry Droy.

'You see, Terry, we've been onto the Army Service Records and you and Eddie didn't do the basic training for your National Service until 1957.'

'Didn't we?' Droy shrugged. He reached into his top pocket and took out a cigarette. 'I don't know. It was bloody forty years ago.'

Hassan furrowed his brow in disbelief. 'You were pretty certain the other day that when Alfie Wise went missing, you were in Kent doing basic training.'

Droy fixed Hassan with a stare. 'What's your name again?' he asked scornfully.

'DC Hassan.'

'DC Hass- what? Bloody hell,' he said with an ironic laugh.

'DC Hassan,' he said politely.

Gaughran knew Droy was having a pop at Hassan and trying to get a rise out of him. Hassan was incredibly calm when it came to morons like Droy.

Droy ignored him and looked back at Gaughran with a smirk.

Gaughran cleared his throat. 'You see, Terry, I'm certain that when you heard the news that Alfie Wise had gone missing, you would be able to remember exactly where you were. You know, like everyone knows where they were when Kennedy was shot? Bit like that. Alfie Wise had murdered your mate Frank two weeks earlier. There is no way on earth that you don't know where you were when you found out he had disappeared.'

Terry took his time lighting his cigarette. He then looked at the match before waving it until it stopped burning.

Stop all the theatrics, dickhead, Gaughran thought.

Droy shook his head again. 'Sorry, but I don't. My memory's not what it was, you know?

Gaughran gave a sigh. 'Forensics are due back tomorrow, Terry.'

Droy blew smoke across the table at them. 'Oh, that's good. Maybe it'll help you find out who killed Alfie. And then I can send them a bottle of Champagne and a thank you card.'

'Not worried about the DNA or forensic evidence that we're going to get from Alfie's body then, Terry? Hassan asked.

'Sorry?' Droy said as he stared at Hassan and pretended that he couldn't understand the question. Then he looked back at Gaughran. 'Not really as I didn't kill him. I thought I told you to go and talk to Trevor Walsh.'

'We've talked to Trevor Walsh. He seems to think you were lying to us,' Gaughran said.

Droy laughed. 'Bloody hell. He would say that. What kind of fucking coppers are you? You ask him about him and Alfie then?'

'Yes.'

'Did you find Eddie? Why don't you ask him about all this?'

'Don't worry. We did,' Hassan snapped.

'Why are you so sure that Trevor Walsh had something to do with Alfie's disappearance?' Gaughran asked.

'I'm not. I just know it wasn't me or Eddie. And Walshy was a nasty piece of work. I'm just trying to do your job for you because you two are clearly shit at it.'

'Eddie told us you were warned not to look for Alfie, is that right?' Gaughran asked.

Droy looked confused. 'Eh? Don't know what he's talking about.'

Gaughran's eyes bored into him. 'You sure? Eddie seemed to be very clear that you two had been told to stay away from Alfie Wise.'

A baffled expression appeared on Droy's face. 'What? Who by?'

'Coppers. He thought they were on the take.'

'Eh? Eddie said bent coppers told us not to look for Alfie Wise?'

Hassan looked at him. 'That's what he said.'

Droy laughed and shook his head. 'No idea what he's talking about.' He smiled mischievously. 'If you see him again, make sure you send Eddie my regards, eh? Haven't seen him in donkeys. See how he reacts when you tell him that Terry Droy said to say hello.'

Gaughran wasn't sure what Droy was getting at. It sounded like some kind of threat. Or was Droy just wasting their time and playing silly buggers?

'Why's that then, Terry?' Hassan asked.

Droy scratched his cheek and then sat forward. 'Look, I'm not a fucking grass or nothing. But I saw Eddie Bannerman every day of my life up until the day Frank got stabbed. We grew up together, went to school together. In the forty years since Frank was killed, I've seen Eddie twice. Once at Frank's funeral and once sitting in a car with Trevor Walsh.'

'Trevor Walsh?' Gaughran asked incredulously.

Droy nodded. 'Yeah, that's what I thought. It was about two months after Frank had died. I had no idea what they were doing together. Maybe Eddie was giving Walshy a blow job?'

'And you didn't say anything to them?'

'Nah. I just thought it was bloody weird, that's all.'

CHAPTER 18

Lucy, Brooks and Ruth had been in The Crown pub in Tooting with Craig Sullivan for about five minutes. Brooks brought over a round of drinks from the bar and placed them down on the table.

'Not the friendliest barman I've ever met,' Brooks said with a perplexed expression as he sat down.

Sullivan sipped an inch from his pint and sniggered. 'He can tell you lot are coppers. And in this pub, you're the enemy.'

Lucy faked a smile. 'Great. Now I feel really relaxed.'

Brooks sat back and looked around the pub. 'I've never been here. My old man told me about The Crown pub in Tooting.'

Sullivan raised an eyebrow. 'What did he say?'

Brooks laughed. 'Told me never to come in here. It's a villain's pub.'

As Lucy looked around, she could see that the walls were full of true crime memorabilia. Book covers, film posters, and old photographs. She could feel herself getting wound up. As far as she could see, it was a pub that glamourised men who had maimed and killed people, and treated them like movie stars.

'It's a bit of a Mecca for true crime junkies now, to be fair. You wouldn't get your local faces coming in anymore. But there's a lot of dark history in here,' Sullivan explained as he gestured to a long table at the back of the pub. 'That's where they planned the Great Train Robbery of '63.'

Brooks pulled out a book from the folder he was carrying. It was called *A History of London's Gangland by Craig Sullivan*. 'Actually, we wanted to pick your brains about something a few years before that, Craig.'

Craig looked pleased that Brooks had brought the book out. 'I can sign that for you, if you want?'

What a dick, Lucy thought.

Brooks smiled. 'Maybe later. What can you tell us about Charlie Wise and his brother Alfie?'

'You really are going back. Charlie and Alfie Wise were from Peckham. Charlie spent a lot of his time over this way.'

Ruth looked over. 'The 211 Club?'

Sullivan nodded. 'Yeah. If you've done any digging around, you'll know that Charlie worked there. He started by running errands for Freddie Foreman. But Charlie was smart, and after a while he was basically running the club. From what I understand, his brother Alfie was only young but he'd knock about the place. Everyone called him 'The Kid'.'

Lucy looked down at her notebook. 'What can you tell us about the Fisher family at the time?'

Sullivan shook his head and tutted. 'The Fishers were local to here. Used to run this pub in the 50s. Nasty lot. Tortured people who crossed them.'

'We're interested in an event that is meant to have taken place at the 211 Club involving Declan Fisher,' Ruth said.

'Yeah. It's one of those events that seems to have passed into criminal folklore. If you read most books, they'll tell you that Declan Fisher was asking the 211 Club for protection money.

The story goes that he went to petrol bomb the place and Charlie Wise beat him unconscious.'

Brooks leaned forward and raised his eyebrows. 'But you're saying that's not what happened?'

Sullivan cackled. 'Of course not! No villain would be stupid enough to demand protection money from the 211 Club. It was part-owned by the Krays. That would have been suicide.'

Ruth shrugged. 'So, what *did* happen?'

'Charlie Wise and Declan Fisher were planning to buy the Krays out of the 211 Club. Reggie and Ronnie were looking to expand into the West End and wanted their money out of the club. It was basically a done deal. There wasn't any animosity between Charlie and Declan. The opposite really. The only major problem they had were officers from the South London Murder Squad,' Sullivan said.

Lucy exchanged a look with Brooks and Ruth. *That doesn't sound good.*

Brooks cleared his throat. 'Why were officers from the Murder Squad a problem?'

'Everyone knew that there were coppers in the Met taking bribes to turn a blind eye or fit someone up. The Murder Squad wanted a piece of the action down here, south of the river,' Sullivan explained.

Lucy's face expressed astonishment. 'Detectives from the South London Murder Squad wanted to be paid off by the 211 Club?'

'Yes, exactly,' Sullivan replied. 'Except Declan Fisher and Charlie Wise told them to fuck off. They caught Declan Fisher round the back of the club, beat him unconscious, and then created the story that Fisher had gone there to burn down the place.'

Brooks sighed. 'Bloody hell. Do you have any evidence of this?'

Sullivan shook his head. 'Only people that spoke to me off the record.'

'What about Alfie? How does his disappearance and death fit with all this?' Lucy asked.

'Same thing. Charlie wouldn't play ball with the Murder Squad. Next thing, his brother Alfie disappears off the face of the earth,' Sullivan said, and then drained his pint. 'I heard a rumour that he was murdered by bent coppers to force Charlie to do what they wanted.'

CHAPTER 19

Gaughran and Hassan were back at Eddie Bannerman's home to find out why he had lied to them about doing National Service at the time of Alfie Wise's disappearance, and probably his murder.

The front door opened slowly. Bannerman squinted out at them.

Gaughran gave him a sarcastic grin. 'Have you missed us, Eddie?'

'Jesus! What do you want?' he groaned.

'Just a couple of things we'd like you to clear up for us. Can we come in?' Hassan said, indicating for him to open the door fully.

Bannerman shook his head. 'Do I have a choice?'

Gaughran moved towards the door. 'Not really.'

They followed Bannerman inside. The house was dark and smelled of dog food and cigarette smoke.

He led them into a small living room, and gestured for them to sit on a shabby sofa. There had been some attempt to keep the room tidy, but it was cluttered with old newspapers and books.

'What's this about? I told you everything I know about Alfie Wise,' Bannerman said as he reached for his cigarettes.

Hassan took out his notepad and pen. 'Slight problem with your dates, Eddie.' Bannerman put a cigarette into his mouth and let it hang from his lips. 'What dates?'

'Basic training for your National Service. You told us you did it in November 1956. At the time of Alfie Wise's disappearance?' Hassan said, reading from his notes.

'Yeah. That's right.' Bannerman lit his cigarette and avoided any eye contact.

Bloody hell. He's not a good liar, Gaughran thought.

Hassan tapped his notebook. 'Problem is that according to the British Army Service Records, you and Terry Droy both did your basic training down in Kent in April 1957.'

Bannerman shook his head. 'No, that can't be right.'

Gaughran gave him a scathing look. Bannerman was wasting their time. 'Don't lie to us, Eddie. We know you lied to us. Terry told us this morning.'

'So, what are you doing wasting my bloody time with all the questions?' Bannerman said angrily.

'If you weren't doing National Service, where were you when Alfie Wise went missing in November 1956?' Gaughran growled.

'I don't know. How am I meant to remember what I was doing forty years ago?'

Hassan rolled his eyes. 'Alfie Wise murdered your mate, Frank. If someone told you Alfie had gone missing, you would remember it.'

Bannerman took a long drag on his cigarette. 'I told you what happened. Me and Terry were warned to stay away from Alfie by your lot. When someone told me he'd been missing for over a week, I just assumed the obvious.'

'Which was what?' Gaughran asked.

'That the coppers had bumped him off and buried him somewhere. I wanted nothing to do with it. In those days, if you didn't do what coppers told you to do, you could be fitted up and spend the rest of your life in the nick.'

Gaughran fixed him with a stare for a few seconds. 'Terry says that a few months after Frank's death, he saw you and Trevor Walsh in a car together?'

Bannerman shifted uncomfortably in his seat and rubbed his nose. 'So what?'

Gaughran shook his head slowly and then glanced at Hassan. 'Come on. What were you doing sitting in a car with a bloke who was involved in a fight where your mate got killed?'

Bannerman rubbed his face again and tapped the ash from his cigarette. 'I can't remember.'

'Don't be a mug, Eddie,' Gaughran snorted and then looked at Hassan. 'DC Hassan, did you notice anything about the car that Eddie drives?'

Hassan smiled. They had already discussed how they could use a bit of leverage on Bannerman before the interview. 'Actually Sarge, Eddie has got a set of ladders attached to his roof.'

Gaughran nodded. 'That's right. And when I had a little look inside his car, there were sponges, a hose and various cleaning products. If you had to guess what Eddie does for a living, what would it be DC Hassan?'

'At a guess, I reckon Eddie's a window cleaner.'

Bannerman frowned and stubbed out his cigarette. 'I'm a window cleaner, so bloody what?'

'Firstly, you've lost your licence, so the DVLA will be very interested by the fact you're still driving around,' Gaughran smirked. 'And I bet you put all that cash you earn through the books and pay your taxes properly, don't you Eddie? And you wouldn't worry if HMRC took a thorough look at your accounts, would you?'

Bannerman's face dropped. Gaughran had got him. 'You can't do that!'

Hassan raised his eyebrows. 'Actually, we can, Eddie.'

Gaughran smiled at Bannerman, who now looked worried. 'You were going to tell us why you were in a car with Trevor Walsh.'

Bannerman raised an eyebrow. 'Because Walshy was a snout for the police.'

CHAPTER 20

As Brooks made his way to the centre of the CID office, he looked frustrated. Rubbing his forehead, he took a large breath and went over to the scene boards. 'The more we find out, the more confusing the investigation becomes. And as far as I can see, we just don't have a front runner for a prime suspect, do we?'

Ruth glanced around the room to see if there was any response. *Brooks is right*, she thought. *There are multiple suspects and various lines of enquiry, none of which is helped by the fact that this is a cold case over forty years old.*

'Anyone looked through the original missing persons file for Alfie Wise yet?' Brooks asked.

Hassan held it up. 'I've got it here, guv. Just had a flick through it.'

'Anything that might help us?' Brooks asked.

'Nothing much. Charlie Wise's statement reporting Alfie missing. His last known movements. Investigating officer was a DS Clive Rigby. I checked his personnel file. He retired in 1980 and died last year.'

Brooks nodded. 'Okay. No mention of any other officers working on the case?'

Hassan shook his head. 'No, guv. No one else ... There is one thing here though that doesn't tally with what we know so far. Sir Charles, or whatever we're calling him now, told us that Alfie went out on Tuesday 27th November in his car to run some errands. He then came home, dropped off the car and went out. That was the last time anyone saw Alfie ...' Hassan pulled out an old-looking piece of paper with typing on it, '... except there is a note here about an Eileen Walters. It's dated Sunday 2nd December, which is nearly a week after Alfie was reported missing. She claims to have seen Charlie and Alfie Wise in his car, late at night, on Tuesday 27th November. She was responding to some missing posters that went up in the area.'

Lucy looked over. 'That definitely contradicts what Charlie Wise told us.'

Brooks frowned. 'Are there details of any kind of follow up?'

'As far as I can see, the statement was filed, and that was that,' Hassan said.

Ruth shook her head. 'Christ, they really didn't care if they found Alfie or not.'

'Have we got a current address for her?' Brooks asked. 'If she's still alive.'

'Not yet, guv. I'll see if I can track her down,' Hassan replied.

'Good,' Brooks said.

Lucy looked up. 'Tim, you mentioned something that Bannerman said about Walsh working as a snout for the local police?'

Gaughran nodded. 'It's definitely weird that Bannerman and Walsh were spotted together in a car a few months later.

But I don't see how any of that would explain Alfie Wise's murder.'

'I agree with Tim,' Brooks said. 'I can't see a connection.' He walked over to the old black-and-white photograph of Charlie Wise. 'My gut feeling is that Alfie was murdered because of something criminal his brother was into.' He then pointed to a photograph of Declan Fisher. 'We have conflicting accounts of Charlie's relationship with the Fisher family. Tim's father was a copper here at this time. He thought the Fisher family wanted revenge on Charlie because Declan Fisher had been attacked and permanently brain-damaged outside the 211 Club. It's a theory that was corroborated by Walsh.'

Drinking from his water bottle, Brooks took a few seconds as he looked out at the room. Ruth knew what was coming next and why Brooks had paused for a second. 'Of course the other more worrying and sensitive hypothesis is that there were officers from the South London Murder Squad who were either taking or demanding payoffs from the club. This led to some kind of altercation with Charlie Wise, and Alfie was murdered as a result.'

A phone rang, and Lucy went over to answer it.

Gaughran looked puzzled. 'I thought my old man said he was certain there weren't any bent coppers down this way?'

Brooks shrugged. 'What your dad told us was very useful. But we have the same account of corrupt officers from both Bannerman and Craig Sullivan. There's nothing to connect those two. It's something we've got to look into Tim.'

Gaughran didn't look happy. Ruth knew that because he came from a long line of coppers, he found it difficult to believe that there had ever been any corruption, bribery or criminal behaviour by officers of the Met. It was admirably supportive, but very naïve.

Lucy put down the phone and caught Brooks' eye. 'That was our financial unit, guv. We pulled all our prime suspects' bank accounts. Trevor Walsh's account shows a regular payment of £500 a month from a company called Stanmore Holdings PLC. They thought it looked strange and did some digging. Turns out that Stanmore Holdings PLC is owned by Sir Charles Wise.'

Brooks had a bewildered look on his face. 'Sir Charles Wise is paying Trevor Walsh £500 pounds a month? What for?'

Lucy shrugged. 'No idea. But according to the financial search, Stanmore Holdings has been paying him for years.'

PULLING INTO THE DRIVE of Charlie Wise's home, Ruth and Lucy parked up and sat for a moment. Both cars were on the drive, which might indicate that Charlie was home.

Ruth was feeling apprehensive. They had discovered so much about his past since the last time they had met. It was going to make for a very uncomfortable conversation and she didn't know how he was going to react.

Lucy glanced over. 'Ready?'

Ruth rolled her eyes as she opened the car door and heard a dog barking inside the house. 'Not really. I hope he doesn't set the dog on us.'

They walked up the gravel drive, their shoes crunching noisily on the stones. Lucy pressed the buzzer.

'Hello?' said a female voice.

'It's DC Henry and DC Hunter to see Sir Charles Wise,' Lucy said, leaning forward to speak into the entry phone.

'Hang on a sec,' said the voice as the dog barked again at the front door.

Then everything went quiet.

Lucy raised an eyebrow. 'What do we do if she says he's not in?'

Ruth gestured to the main road. 'Park up somewhere and wait and watch.'

They need not have worried. There was the sound of keys turning in locks and then the heavy front door swung open. Charlie looked out at them and gave a half smile. 'Good afternoon, ladies. Come in, come in.'

Following him through the house, they came into the huge designer kitchen and living area where they had been a few days earlier.

Charlie motioned for them to sit down. 'Do you want something to drink? I'm going to get some sparkling mineral water?'

Ruth and Lucy nodded. The glass ceiling above them meant that the room was hot.

'Thanks,' Ruth said as she moved her chair closer to the table.

A few seconds later, Charlie returned with a bottle of Perrier and three glasses and sat down. 'Here we go.'

'Thank you,' Lucy said.

Ruth took a DNA sample kit from her pocket. 'Okay if we take a DNA swab from you today, Charlie? So we can formally identify Alfie?'

'Yeah, of course.' Pouring out the water, Charlie looked at them. 'Is that it, or was there something you need to talk to me about?'

'There's a few things we need to clarify with you, Charlie,' Ruth said. 'We came to your office yesterday but I think you were in Belfast?'

Charlie furrowed his brow. 'Belfast? No, I wasn't. I wouldn't be going to Belfast with all this hanging over me.'

'Your PA came out to talk to us,' Lucy said. 'She said you were in Belfast.'

'Oh right. She's a temp. Only just started. I'm sorry if you wasted your time.' He took a swig of his water. 'Are you any closer to finding out what happened to Alfie?'

Ruth exchanged a look with Lucy. 'There have been some developments in the investigation which is why we wanted to talk to you.'

Charlie pulled a face. 'Okay. For some reason, I sense this isn't going to be a straightforward conversation?'

'No,' Ruth said quietly.

Taking out her notepad, Lucy looked over at him. 'I think the first thing we'd like to establish is where you were working and what you were doing around the time of Alfie's disappearance?'

Charlie sipped his water and sat back in his chair. His reading glasses hung on the pocket of his navy Armani shirt. 'I think it's well documented that I was working at a club in Balham called the 211 Club. But I'm guessing you knew that already?'

Lucy nodded. 'Yeah, we did.'

Charlie gave a wry smile. 'Yeah, I'm not particularly fond of looking back to that time. But I was young and headstrong. And I guess we all make mistakes when we're young, eh?'

Ruth looked at Charlie. For the first time since they had met he looked a little rattled. 'The picture we're getting Charlie is that Alfie's disappearance was linked to your life and what was going on at the club.'

Charlie took a few seconds to think. 'Yeah, well that's always been in the back of my mind. But I have no way of knowing, do I?'

Lucy gave him a quizzical look. 'How do you mean?'

'Until three days ago, all I knew was that my brother Alfie had gone missing forty years ago. No one ever came to me and said that his disappearance was some kind of warning or revenge. I'm not going to pretend that I wasn't knocking about with some pretty unsavoury characters in those days. But I was a young man, and it was a long, long time ago.'

Ruth sipped her water and then said, 'What can you tell us about Declan Fisher?'

Charlie nodded sadly. 'Yeah, that was terrible. Declan was a lovely bloke. He didn't deserve what happened to him.'

'Do you know who attacked him?' Lucy asked.

'No ... I've no idea. Happened outside the club. As I said, there were plenty of shady blokes around at the time. Could have been any one of them.'

'And you didn't hear any rumours about what had happened?' Ruth asked.

Charlie shrugged. 'A few. But nothing that I can really remember.'

'What was the nature of your relationship with Declan Fisher?' Ruth continued.

'Declan used to come into the club. We drank together. Me and him had been looking at doing some business together. We were just a couple of Jack the lads.'

Ruth pressed him further. 'What kind of business?'

'Buying, renovating properties in the area. Converting houses into flats, that kind of thing.' Charlie sat forward. 'Declan had nothing to do with what happened to Alfie, I can tell you that for nothing. He thought the world of Alfie.'

Ruth turned the page of her notebook. 'When we spoke the other day, you didn't tell us that Trevor Walsh has been a paid employee of yours for many years.'

'Why would I?' Charlie asked. 'Does it matter?'

'What does he do?' Lucy asked.

Charlie rubbed his chin and gave an ironic laugh. 'Not a lot these days. Look, I liked Walshy. Still do. He never got over what happened to Alfie, and blamed himself for starting a fight that night. He kept in touch to see if I'd heard anything and to see if I was all right. I used him to do a bit of driving for me. Pick people up from the airport, take packages. Over the years, he ran errands for me and I bunged him a few quid every month.'

'Five hundred pounds,' Ruth said.

'It's nothing sinister. I liked having him around because he had been Alfie's best mate. And then he just became part of the furniture wherever I worked. He's a decent bloke these days and I trust him. And I don't trust many people.'

'He mentioned a letter that he had got from Alfie between the evening he killed Frank Weller and when Alfie went missing?' Lucy said.

Charlie frowned and leant forward. It looked like it was news to him. 'No. He never mentioned it to me.'

'Alfie wrote to him to say he was going away somewhere and wouldn't be in touch again,' Lucy explained.

A reflective frown crossed his face. 'I didn't think Alfie and Walshy had any contact after the night of the murder.'

Lucy turned over a page of her notebook. 'What can you tell us about officers from the South London Murder Squad at that time?

Charlie sighed and his eyes widened. 'Bloody hell. You really have been doing your homework, haven't you? What do you want to know?'

'We have several accounts that claim police officers were demanding bribes from the club or were being paid off?' Ruth said.

Charlie shook his head. 'Not really. There were a couple of young detectives from the Murder Squad. Fancied themselves. They used to come into the club, drink too much and go upstairs to the casino. One night they said they were looking for a handout. I told them to piss off. The lanky one managed to fall down the stairs and break his leg, he was so hammered. We had to call a bloody ambulance.'

'And after that?' Lucy asked.

'Never saw them again ... You think they had something to do with what happened to Alfie?'

Lucy shrugged. 'It's something that keeps cropping up in our investigation. You're sure that was the only time you had that kind of conversation with police officers?'

Charlie nodded. 'Yeah. I just thought they were drunk and trying their luck.' Then he thought of something. 'Tell a lie. I did see the lanky one again. He came in. His leg was still in plaster and he had crutches. He tried to say that I'd pushed him down the stairs that night and his leg was permanently damaged. He wanted me to pay him compensation.'

Ruth exchanged a quick look with Lucy. Was she thinking the same thing?

'What did you say to him?'

'Same thing I told him the first time. I told him to piss off!' Charlie said in an indignant tone.

'I don't suppose you remember his name, do you?' Ruth asked.

Charlie squinted as he tried to recall the officer's name. 'Irish. I'm pretty sure it was an Irish name. I remember thinking how many Paddies there were everywhere.'

Ruth looked at him. 'Gaughran?'

Charlie shrugged. 'I don't know. Could have been.'

CHAPTER 21

By the time Lucy had showered, grabbed some food and slumped down in front of the telly, it was growing dark. She was watching a BBC drama called *Ballykissangel* about an English priest who had been sent to a small parish in Ireland. It made her think about Charlie's comment about a young DC with a damaged leg and an Irish name. Arthur Gaughran had told them he was still in uniform in 1956, but that could easily be checked with records. Arthur was adamant that there was no police corruption in South London. Maybe he had good reason to say that?

Glancing at her watch, Lucy saw that it was after eight and that Brooks should be home any second now. They had hardly talked since the incident the other night when she had chased someone that had been in her garden. She didn't know what he was thinking, but he was becoming a little distant.

Suddenly, out of the corner of her eye, Lucy spotted something move in the garden.

What the bloody hell was that?

She wasn't sure if it had been a figure, but it had startled her. Her heart was thumping.

Running to the windows, she cupped her hands and peered into the garden. *No fucker is going to make me scared in my own home!* She couldn't see anything. It might have been a cat.

Pulling across the curtains angrily, Lucy took a deep breath. She marched around the ground floor, pulling all the curtains and blinds, and checking and locking the doors.

This can't go on, she thought to herself.

A minute later, she heard the sound of a key in the front door. It must be Brooks. The metallic sound continued.

Then a male voice shouted, 'Luce! I can't get in!'

She remembered she had dropped the latch, so she went to the door to let him in.

He looked concerned. 'Everything all right?'

Feeling on the verge of tears, Lucy shook her head. 'No. I thought I saw someone in the garden.'

Brooks shook his head. 'Bloody hell! Are you sure?'

'No, I'm not sure, Harry. But I've had enough. I can't live like this - worrying that someone's watching me or in my garden,' Lucy said, fighting the tremor in her voice. She wiped a tear from her eye. She was so frustrated and upset.

Brooks took her in his arms, but she could feel herself tense up. 'It's all right. I'll sort it out.'

Lucy moved away from him. 'You keep saying that, Harry. But what does that mean?'

'I spoke to a solicitor but we don't have enough evidence to apply for a restraining order.'

'Have you told her to stay the fuck away from here?' Lucy asked.

'Of course.'

Lucy shook her head in frustration. 'What's next? Am I going to come home and get attacked on my own doorstep?'

'What do you want me to do? Throw her under a bus?'

'That wouldn't be a bad idea,' Lucy replied with sarcasm.

Brooks looked at her. 'Come on.'

'No, *not* "Come on". I will *not* feel scared in my own home. And if that means you can't be in it, then that's what needs to happen.'

RUTH'S PHONE BUZZED. It was a text from Dan. It was the third one in as many hours. Having missed picking up Ella the previous day, he wanted to rearrange a time to see her. As far as she was concerned, he could go and fuck himself. In fact, she didn't want Ella to see Dan at all because when he sodded off to Australia in a few weeks it would hurt her even more.

Sitting back on the sofa, Ruth drained a large glass of wine and let out a sigh. She poured herself another glass and looked around the room. *Is this it now?* she wondered. As she looked for her cigarettes on the table, the doorbell rang. She wasn't expecting anyone.

She went to the door, put on the chain, and opened it. Shiori gave her an embarrassed smile and waved a bottle of wine at her.

'I've come to apologise,' she said with an awkward shrug.

Ruth didn't know if it was because of the wine she'd drunk, but she was glad to see Shiori. With all the resentment of recent weeks, she had forgotten quite how beautiful and sexy she was.

'Are you trying to bribe me?' she asked, opening the door.

'I miss staying up, getting drunk and smoking in the evenings, and putting the world to rights,' Shiori said. Her eyes looked a little glazed.

Ruth raised an eyebrow. 'Are you drunk?'

'No. Well, a little bit.'

Ruth could smell smoke on her clothes. 'And you've been smoking?'

Shiori laughed and put her hands up. 'Busted. Life's too short not to smoke.'

Ruth gave her a playful hit on the arm. 'You tosser. After all the crap you gave me when you quit.'

'Hey, I'm a sanctimonious control freak, but I'm trying to change.'

They looked at each other in the half light of the hallway.

'This is weird,' Ruth said in a virtual whisper after a few seconds.

Shiori pointed to the bottle of wine she was carrying. 'Shall we go and open this?'

Ruth shook her head. 'No'. She then moved forward and took Shiori's face in her hands and kissed her. Softly at first, and then more passionately. Shiori tasted of booze and cigarettes. As Ruth nuzzled and bit her neck, she could smell her sweet, musky perfume.

Taking her by the hand, Ruth led her down the hallway towards the bedroom. Putting down the bottle of wine, Shiori pulled off Ruth's t-shirt, and they tumbled onto the bed.

For the next thirty minutes, they kissed, caressed and made love.

Afterwards, Shiori placed her head on Ruth's shoulder and looked at her as she ran her fingers through her hair. 'I wasn't expecting to do that today.'

Ruth smiled with a post-coital glow. 'Neither was I.'

'What do we do now?' Shiori said quietly as she interlocked her fingers with Ruth's.

'No offence, but you can be bloody hard work,' Ruth said.

Shiori gave a self-effacing smile. 'Yeah. Unfortunately, I'm well aware of that.'

'I'm a single mum with a very challenging job. I don't have the time, energy or patience to be with someone who is bloody hard work.'

Shiori raised her eyebrows. 'I know. I'm sorry. Can we try *us* again if I promise not to be such a bitch?'

Ruth puffed out her cheeks. 'I guess. I don't know.' She indicated that she was heading for the kitchen. 'Do you want a drink?'

Shiori nodded. 'Please.'

Grabbing her thin Japanese-style kimono, Ruth went into the hallway and turned to head down to the kitchen.

There was a bang on the door.

Who the hell is that?

She put on the safety chain before opening the door six inches. Dan was standing on the doorstep.

'You're not answering my texts,' Dan said reproachfully.

'Are you fucking kidding me!' Ruth snapped as she took the chain off and opened the door aggressively.

'How am I meant to see Ella if you don't get back to me?'

Ruth exploded. 'How about you turn up to pick her up when you say you're going to, you dickhead!'

Shiori appeared in a long shirt from the bedroom and looked down at them. 'Everything all right, Ruth?'

With a confused look, Dan looked at Shiori and then back at Ruth. 'Bloody hell. Now I've seen it all.'

Ruth took a deep breath in an attempt not to punch Dan in the face. 'Don't you dare judge me! You had at least one affair. You're a pathetic excuse for a father and come to think of it, for a human being. You're a spineless, selfish wanker, Dan. And I'm going to do everything in my power to stop you seeing Ella before you run away to Australia. So, you'd better get yourself a solicitor!'

Ruth slammed the door in his face, closed her eyes and felt tears well up. Shiori came over and took her in her arms.

CHAPTER 22

It was about thirty minutes after morning briefing. Even though Lucy and Brooks had travelled to work together, they had hardly said a word since their argument the previous evening. However, Lucy knew that once they were over the threshold of Peckham nick, they were in work mode.

Glancing around, Lucy made sure that Gaughran wasn't about. She could see that Hassan was at his desk, but it was far enough away to be out of earshot. 'What are we going to do about Arthur Gaughran, guv?'

There had been no mention at the briefing of Ruth and Lucy's meeting with Arthur the previous day. They were still processing what Charlie had told them about a young DC.

Brooks swept his hand through this hair as he perched on a table. 'Check his service records for starters. We don't know it's him yet.'

At that moment, Gaughran came sweeping into CID. He was holding a folder as he looked over. 'Never asked you how you got on with my old man yesterday?'

Lucy and Ruth exchanged a look as he approached.

Lucy forced a smile. 'Very useful, thanks Tim. What a nice man, which was surprising as he's your dad.'

Gaughran laughed sarcastically. 'Funny. What did he say?'

Lucy gestured to Brooks. 'I was just getting the guv up to speed.' That was bullshit. Lucy and Ruth had talked to Brooks about it before the briefing. 'He thinks the Fishers were involved. Either that, or Alfie threatened to go to the police and Charlie killed him.'

Gaughran gestured to the piece of paper in his hand. 'I did some digging around. The only member of the Fisher family who's still alive from that time is Declan's uncle. Paddy Fisher. It turns out he's in an OAP home in Streatham. He's kicking on a bit, but I thought me and Syed should have a chat?'

Brooks nodded. 'Good idea. He's not likely to tell you that his family killed Alfie Wise. But what he might do is clarify Declan Fisher's relationship with Charlie Wise and the 211 Club.'

Hassan approached, looking at his notebook. 'Guv, I'm not sure if it's anything, but I did a quick search on Frank Weller on the PNC. There was nothing on there, but there was a hit for his sister?'

'Jackie Weller has a criminal record?' Lucy asked in disbelief.

'Convictions for theft, assault and GBH. She served time in Holloway in the 1960s.'

Ruth's eyes widened. 'Are you sure we're talking about the same Jackie Weller?'

'It's on the PNC,' said Hassan.

The phone rang on a nearby desk and Gaughran went over to answer it.

Lucy frowned. 'It's a bit of a stretch to think that Jackie Weller shot Alfie Wise and then buried him.'

Hassan shrugged. 'Unless someone helped her?'

Ruth's forehead creased. 'She must have been very young in November 1956?'

Hassan checked his notebook and nodded. 'She was fifteen, nearly sixteen.'

Brooks looked from Ruth to Lucy. 'Have another chat with her.'

Gaughran put down the phone, picked up a piece of paper he had scribbled on and approached. 'Guv, report from uniform of a possible suspicious death. They think the victim was strangled and there are signs of a struggle.'

'Got an address?' Brooks asked.

Gaughran looked down at the piece of paper. 'A flat in Catford. 68 Doggett Road.'

Lucy knew the address as she looked over at Ruth. 'Shit! Did you say 68 Doggett Road?'

Gaughran nodded. 'Yeah, why?'

'That's where Trevor Walsh lives.'

CHAPTER 23

'Thank you, Constable,' Ruth said as she put her warrant card away.

Ducking under the tape, she could see that the front of 68 Doggett Road was already sealed off with blue and white evidence tape. A young, uniformed officer stood by the open front door. He stood up straight as they approached.

It's all right, mate. We're not royalty, Ruth thought. There were some uniformed officers that acted like that when CID arrived, especially the young ones. Ruth suspected it was because they had ambitions to join CID themselves and wanted to make a good impression.

Lucy stopped by the front door. 'Were you first on the scene, Constable?'

'Yes, ma'am. Neighbour said she hadn't seen Mr Walsh last night or this morning and she was worried about him. When she mentioned she had heard raised voices late last night, we used her spare key to go in. Victim was lying on the floor.'

'And there are definitely signs of a struggle?' Ruth asked.

'Yes, ma'am.'

'Can we get some preliminary witness statements from everyone in this property and next door?' Lucy asked. 'See if anyone else saw or heard anything suspicious last night.'

The Constable nodded. 'Yes, ma'am.'

Ruth and Lucy went up the stairs to the first-floor flat where they had visited Trevor Walsh only a few days before. A couple of other residents were standing on the stairs, trying to see what was going on as they talked in hushed voices.

Ruth flashed her warrant card at them and said in an authoritative tone, 'If you can go back inside, please? An officer will come and take a statement from you and explain what's going on.'

A large woman in a floral housecoat frowned. 'I need to do my shopping this morning, dear.'

Ruth smiled at her. 'Once you've spoken to our officer and given a statement, you can leave the building. Until then, I would ask if you could go back inside and wait. Thank you for your patience.'

There were some disgruntled mutterings as the residents dispersed.

Ruth and Lucy proceeded to the first floor landing. Ruth could see a female uniformed officer standing outside Trevor Walsh's flat. Flashing their warrant cards, they went in.

There was an eerie stillness and silence inside the flat as Ruth snapped on her blue latex gloves. The flat smelled musty and damp and the air was filled with stale cigarette smoke. Lucy turned right into the living room and Ruth followed. It had been totally ransacked. Trevor Walsh's body lay at a strange angle on the floor by the window, his legs splayed.

'Bloody hell! There wasn't just a struggle in here. Someone smashed the place to pieces,' Lucy said, looking around at the mess.

'Maybe they were searching for something?'

Approaching the body, Ruth could see that Walsh's eyes were still open. The life had now gone, and they were opaque like soft stones. Ruth felt the disturbing chill that she always got in the presence of death. She looked at Walsh, who had so recently been sitting in this room chatting to them. The life had been taken from his body and it was unsettling to see.

As she crouched down, Ruth noticed that Walsh's eyes had tiny red dots on them. She knew it might be petechiae, which was one sign of strangulation. She could also see that a thick purple line of bruising was developing around his throat.

Ruth looked up at Lucy. 'He's been strangled. Looks like some kind of ligature was used.'

Lucy squatted down next to her. She took a pen from her pocket and pushed it against Walsh's skin. The pressure blanched the skin, making it appear whitish. They both knew that after about twelve hours, the blood no longer blanched as rigor mortis set in.

Turning her wrist, Lucy glanced at her watch. 'My guess is that he was killed within the last twelve hours.'

'And the neighbour mentioned raised voices late at night which would fit that timeline,' Ruth added.

Lucy stood up and inspected the room again. 'I'm guessing our killer took the ligature with them.'

'Not to speak ill of the dead, but I don't think they would be searching for cash or valuables.'

Lucy raised an eyebrow. 'No. We'd better have a look around the rest of the flat.'

'I'll get onto SOCO and get this flat established as a major crime scene.'

Glancing down at the floor, Ruth noticed a smashed photo frame. The photograph inside was of Walsh and another man with blonde hair and a moustache. They were sitting on a sun lounger together, smiling at the camera with lurid coloured cocktails in their hands. Ruth slipped the photo out from the cracked frame and turned it over. There was some scribbled writing on the back – *Me and Steve, Menorca August 1981 x.*

Lucy looked over her shoulder. 'Found something?'

Ruth shook her head. 'Not really.' She showed Lucy the photograph and the writing.

'They look so happy,' Lucy said sadly.

'I wonder what happened to Steve.'

The constable from outside entered and looked at them. 'Ma'am, neighbour from the ground-floor flat confirmed that she heard raised voices just before midnight last night. She then heard the front door close and looked out. A man came out, got into a car and drove away.'

'Can she give us a description of him?' Ruth asked.

The constable shook his head. 'She said he was big and wearing a hat or hood. But there's a streetlight outside, so she got a good look at the car. *And* she managed to scribble down the licence plate.'

Ruth looked over at Lucy. 'Nice one.'

IT WAS LATE MORNING by the time Gaughran and Hassan tracked down Eileen Walters, the eyewitness who had seen Alfie and Charlie Wise in a car late on the day that he was supposed to have disappeared. Eileen, now in her late 50s, worked in the Cancer Research shop on Peckham High Street.

As they parked up, Gaughran took his sunglasses from his shirt pocket. There was blazing sunshine outside. On the journey from Peckham nick, he had felt an element of pride that his dad had helped out with the investigation. Even though he had taken early retirement, Gaughran knew that his dad still missed the cut and thrust of daily police work. In fact, since the discovery of Alfie Wise's remains, he had seemed rejuvenated, asking him detailed questions about the case on a daily basis. Gaughran knew it must be difficult to know that your best years were behind you, so maybe a case from forty years ago was allowing his dad to relive his youth.

Hassan puffed out his cheeks. 'Bloody hell, Sarge, I swear it's getting hotter.'

'Hot, damn hot. That's nice if you're with a lady, but it ain't no good if you're in the jungle,' Gaughran said in an American accent, doing his best Robin Williams impersonation.

'Sorry, Sarge?' Hassan said blankly.

'Good Morning Vietnam?' Gaughran said in disbelief.

'No, Sarge. Never seen it.'

Gaughran shook his head and said with a wry smile, 'I don't know why I bother, Syed.'

They got out of the car, walked across the pavement and entered the Cancer Research shop. The walls were lined with second-hand clothes, books, VHS cassettes and ornaments. Gaughran could instantly smell the aroma of mothballs, which reminded him of his grandmother Flora. She was ninety-seven and lived in a home close by. He made a mental note to visit her at the weekend.

He took out his warrant card and looked at the woman behind the till, whom they assumed was Eileen. 'We're looking for Eileen Walters?'

She looked instantly flustered. 'Yes.'

Bloody hell, she looks terrified, he thought.

Gaughran gave her a reassuring smile. 'It's all right. We're investigating a historical crime and just wanted to ask you a few questions to help with our enquiries.'

Eileen nodded but the blood had drained from her face. 'Right, erm, okay.'

Hassan looked around the shop and said in a virtual whisper, 'Is there somewhere we could go and talk for a couple of minutes?'

Eileen gestured towards the door to a small office. 'Oh yes. We can go in there if you like?'

Gaughran and Hassan followed her inside. There was a low table with a few plastic chairs scattered around. On the far side, there were mountains of clothes and boxes of books that obviously still needed to be sorted.

Sitting down, Eileen forced a smile but still looked anxious.

Hassan took out his notebook and pen. 'We're investigating something that took place over forty years ago in November 1956.'

Eileen pulled a face. 'Oh right. That's many years ago. It was the only time I've ever really spoken to a policeman.'

Gaughran looked at her. 'So, you remember talking to a police officer about what you had seen on the evening of the 27th November 1956?'

'Oh yes. I had to give a statement and then sign it.'

Gaughran exchanged a look with Hassan. There had been no statement in the file on Alfie Wise's disappearance, just a note to say that Eileen had seen him.

Hassan frowned. 'You definitely gave a statement?'

'Oh yes. Definitely. I asked the policeman if I needed my father to come along as I was only seventeen. But he said I didn't.'

Gaughran gave her a kind smile. 'Could you tell us what was in that statement and what you saw that night?'

Eileen looked away as she thought back. 'I'd been out with a friend of mine. Sally, although everyone called her Sal. There had been a skiffle band playing in The Royal Oak pub. You know, all those Lonnie Donegan songs?'

Gaughran didn't really know what she was talking about.

'I don't suppose you can remember the name of the band, can you?' Hassan asked.

'I'm pretty sure they were called The Rattlesnakes. I remember thinking it was a weird name for a group. This was a few years before The Beatles, you see.'

'And when you left the pub?'

'We had a few drinks and left at closing time. We were going to get some chips on the way home,' Eileen explained. 'We waited to cross the road by the lights on Bridge Street. I saw this big American car pull up. I'd seen it before. You didn't get cars like that in Peckham.'

Hassan looked up from his notebook. 'Did you get a look at who was inside the car?'

Eileen nodded. 'There was a bloke driving who was probably in his twenties. Someone told me later that he was Charlie Wise. And this boy sitting in the passenger seat. He looked out at me. He had this black quiff. He was nice looking. Bit like Billy Fury.'

'So, you got a good look at him?' Gaughran asked.

'Oh yeah. That's why when some missing posters went up, I recognised him straight away. His name was Alfie Wise. That's when I went to the police and told them what I'd seen.'

'What about your friend, Sal? Did she talk to the police?' Hassan asked.

Eileen shook her head. 'The policeman said just one of us was enough.'

Gaughran exchanged a look with Hassan – that wasn't the correct procedure for any kind of police investigation.

Hassan tapped his pen on his notebook. 'Are you still in touch with your friend, Sal?'

'Not anymore. We lost her to cancer quite a few years ago now,' Eileen explained sadly.

'I'm sorry to hear that. But she saw exactly what you've described to us?'

Eileen shrugged. 'Actually, I think she was looking at the boy in the back of the car.'

What boy? Gaughran's jaw dropped. 'There was someone else in the car?'

Eileen nodded. 'Oh yeah. There was a boy in the back about the same age as the one in the front. Had this big curly red quiff that came down onto his forehead.'

'Red? Do you mean he had ginger hair?' Hassan asked.

Eileen smiled. 'Yeah, ginger. I think Sal thought he was dishy 'cos he smiled at her.'

Gaughran glanced at Hassan. They were thinking the same thing – it was Trevor Walsh.

CHAPTER 24

'Are you sure I can't get you some water?' Jackie Weller asked as Lucy and Ruth sat down in the living room, just as they had done a few days earlier.

Lucy gave her a kind smile. 'We're fine thanks.'

Ruth got out her notebook and made eye contact with Jackie. 'Last time we spoke, you told us that Terry Droy and Eddie Bannerman said they were going to find Alfie Wise. Is that correct?'

Jackie nodded. As she placed her hands in her lap, Lucy noticed a large circular bruise on the back of her right hand. It was about the size of a cricket ball and was a mixture of dark blue and purple. Lucy couldn't remember, but she was relatively certain that she or Ruth would have noticed it the last time they had visited. And that would mean it had appeared in the last couple of days.

Ruth flicked over the notepad. 'I know this is a very long time ago Jackie, but can you remember where you were on Tuesday 27th November 1956? It was the night that Alfie Wise went missing.'

Jackie pulled a face. 'No ... How am I meant to remember a thing like that?'

'I know. I can't remember what I had for breakfast sometimes,' Ruth said with a smile. 'Could you tell us where you were when you found out that Alfie was missing?'

'No. It was a long time ago.'

'But you did know around that time that he had gone missing?' Lucy asked.

'Of course. It was probably Terry or Eddie that told me.'

Ruth gave her a quizzical look. 'I know it's a long time ago, but you knew that Alfie had probably killed your brother Frank. I'm guessing it would have been quite an emotional thing when you found out that Alfie had gone missing.'

Jackie moved uncomfortably in her chair. Lucy could sense that she was not telling them something, and her manner was decidedly different from their last visit.

Lucy looked at her and said gently, 'I think I would have remembered something like that.'

Jackie glared at Lucy and snapped. 'Well, I can't bloody remember! I just told you that!'

For a second or two, Lucy glimpsed a very different side to Jackie's personality. There was an underlying aggression that contradicted the persona that she had been projecting.

'I'm sorry. I didn't mean to suggest that you were lying,' Lucy said calmly.

Jackie's chest was visibly rising and falling quickly. She had clearly been rattled by something they had said.

Ruth leant forward. 'You were very close to your brother Frank, weren't you, Jackie?'

Jackie's frown was now bordering on a sneer. 'Of course. He was my brother. That's a stupid question.'

As she glanced up, Lucy spotted two teacups sitting on the mantelpiece over the empty fireplace. They stood out in a room that was so tidy and clutter free. Someone had been for a friendly cup of tea, and probably earlier that day.

'Do you have many visitors here, Jackie?' Lucy asked, hoping to catch her off guard.

'No, not really. I go out to meet people. I'm a member of the local church, so I do a lot down there,' Jackie explained. 'I don't really have visitors at home.'

Lucy looked at her – she was lying for some reason, which would suggest that she didn't want them to know that someone had visited her recently.

'Jackie, you must have been furious at the person who had killed Frank?' Ruth suggested.

'Yeah, of course I was.'

'What did you think when someone told you it was Alfie Wise that had killed him?'

Jackie shrugged. 'I was upset.'

'Did you want to take the law into your own hands?' Ruth asked.

'No. Of course not.'

'You didn't want to get some kind of revenge for Frank then?'

Jackie gave Ruth a daggered look. 'I'm not like that.'

Lucy sat forward. 'That's not strictly true, Jackie. We had a look at your criminal record.'

Jackie gritted her teeth. She was furious. 'You think that because I served time in prison, that means that I could have shot Alfie Wise?'

Lucy raised her eyebrow as she glanced fleetingly at Ruth – *Shot?*

'I'm pretty sure we didn't mention that Alfie Wise had been shot,' Ruth said with certainty.

The colour drained from Jackie's face. 'It was a guess. You said he had been found dead. I assumed someone must have shot him.'

CHAPTER 25

As Lucy opened the patio doors to the garden, she breathed in a lovely smoky waft from someone barbequing nearby. Having kicked off her work shoes she was now barefoot and, as she stepped onto the patio, she could feel that the paving stones were still warm from the sun. She closed her eyes and took a long breath. It had been a hell of a day. Even though she had worked in CID for a few years now, she would never get used to seeing a dead body. It was far less of a shock these days, but it still stayed with her. Only a couple of days earlier she and Ruth had spoken to Trevor Walsh. To see him sprawled out on his floor with his eyes open, having been violently murdered, was disturbing, even for her.

Lucy remembered seeing her first dead body when she had only been a probationer in Streatham for a matter of weeks. Lucy and another young constable had been called to a report of screaming. As they arrived at the house a frantic Asian woman, who was clearly in shock, tried to speak to them. She was shaking and crying, describing to them how she had come home to find her husband hanging from the bannisters. The woman was being comforted by neighbours out on the street.

At first, all Lucy could see through the open front door were the man's legs moving in a circular motion. Knowing that she had to go in, she had braced herself. The dead man had soiled himself, so the hallway reeked. For a moment, she thought she was going to vomit, but she didn't want to lose face in front of the other PC. She knew that if she was sick, word would soon get round the station and there would be jokes at her expense. The sight of the man hanging in his hallway haunted her for weeks and appeared in her nightmares. More experienced officers assured her it was normal and she would get used to it.

The noise of children playing in a nearby garden broke her train of thought. Gazing up at the cloudless sky, the laughter and shouting of the kids reminded her of what she really wanted in life. She yearned to spend evenings like this sitting in her garden with a barbeque smoking, and watching her own children play with the same carefree abandon.

Checking her watch, she expected that Brooks would arrive any minute. They had agreed to have dinner and talk. The most pressing problem was his ex-wife Karen. He had promised to have a conversation with her, or at least deal with her behaviour, but she got the feeling that his guilty conscience was getting the better of him. Lucy wasn't prepared to put up with it, and it was Brooks' problem so he needed to sort it out. The other issue was more ambiguous. Brooks was in his 40s and there had never been any meaningful discussion of whether they wanted to have children as a couple. If Brooks was adamant that he didn't, then that would give Lucy a significant problem. She blamed herself for allowing their relationship to progress too quickly. Having tried the whole 'keeping it casual', she soon realised that she had fallen in love with him. He had moved in, but since then they just hadn't talked about it.

She walked to the kitchen, took a cold beer from the fridge and opened it. As she took a sip, the doorbell rang.

He's actually on time for once, she thought with a smile.

She strode to the door and opened it.

Standing on the doorstep was a middle-aged woman. She had been crying, and she was visibly shaken. Lucy then noticed that she had a bloody nose and cut lip.

Oh my god, poor woman, Lucy thought.

Opening the door fully, she looked at the woman. 'Are you all right? What happened?'

As the woman swept her hair back from her face, Lucy recognised her from a photograph she had seen.

It was Karen, Brooks' ex-wife.

Karen sniffed as she shook her head. 'He did this to me. Are you happy now, you bitch?'

'What?' Lucy asked in shock. 'Harry did this?'

Karen glared at her. 'Of course he did. He came around and told me to keep away from this house. We got into an argument and he did this to me.'

Lucy couldn't believe what Karen was saying to her. She had never known Brooks to be aggressive or violent. Even as a copper, he had a reputation for being calm and considerate.

'Harry hit you in the face?' Lucy asked in a tone of disbelief.

'Oh my God. Who else do you think did all this?' Karen yelled. She was starting to unravel.

At that precise second, a car drew up outside. It was Brooks.

Turning around, Karen looked at Lucy in horror. 'Don't let him attack me again, please. Don't let him come near me.'

Lucy put her hand up to calm Karen down. 'Stay there. Let me go and talk to him.'

Marching down the path, Lucy's head felt in a spin. Had Brooks really gone around to Karen's home and attacked her? She just didn't believe that he could do something like that. But Karen had clearly been attacked and injured. How did that happen if it wasn't Brooks?

'What the hell is going on?' Brooks asked, gesturing to Karen and looking anxious. 'Are you okay?'

Lucy nodded. 'I'm okay. But Karen has turned up on my doorstep. Her nose and lip are bleeding. She said you attacked her.'

'Oh my God! Are you joking?' Brooks' eyes widened in disbelief. 'I haven't seen her. I've been nowhere near her!'

Moving to one side, he looked up the path to where Karen was cowering.

'Don't come anywhere near me, Harry. I'm going to report you for what you've done to me and get you sacked,' Karen shrieked. 'You're a monster!'

Harry shook his head in bewilderment. 'Karen? What are you talking about? I haven't seen you!'

As Harry went to go up the path, Lucy put a hand on his chest. 'You need to stay here, Harry.'

He looked at Lucy in utter shock. 'You can't believe that I did this to her?'

'It doesn't matter. You need to stay here.'

Lucy watched as Karen darted across the small paved front garden and climbed over the low wall onto the pavement. She was sobbing and looking over at Harry.

'Karen? What are you doing?' Brooks said quietly.

'Stay away from me!' she screeched as she reached her car.

'This can't be happening,' Brooks said, staring into space.

The car pulled away and sped out of sight down the road.

'What the hell is going on?' Lucy asked. The last five minutes felt completely surreal.

'I really don't know. Please, you've got to believe me. I didn't attack her.'

'Then why has she got blood on her face?'

Harry shrugged. 'I don't know. I can't explain it. Unless she ...'

'You can't think that she did that to herself, Harry?'

'What else?' Brooks said and then moved as if to hug Lucy. She moved away.

'You need to go back home, Harry. Seriously,' Lucy said, feeling teary.

'Can't I come in so we can talk?'

'No,' Lucy shook her head. 'It's all too much at the moment.'

Turning on her heels, Lucy went up the path, inside the house and closed the door behind her.

AS RUTH FINISHED THE washing up, her mind turned to the developments in the Alfie Wise case and Trevor Walsh's murder. She was certain they were linked, but how? Who had a motive to kill Walsh? Why was his flat turned upside down? Did Walsh know something about Alfie Wise's death that had cost him his life?

Reaching for the tea-towel, she realised that the case was escalating and becoming more complex as the days went by. It was usually the other way around. The further along in an investigation, the simpler it became. Suspects and witnesses would be interviewed and eliminated. Evidence would be examined to rule out more suspects. Eventually they would have a prime suspect. A case would then be built focussing on that suspect so they could be charged and successfully prosecuted.

Alfie Wise had been killed over forty years ago, which created a unique set of complications.

Ruth checked her phone as she reached for a ciggie. Since Shiori had spent the night, they had exchanged a few text messages. Ruth had invited her and Koyuki over at the weekend for a 'sleepover'.

As Ruth went to grab a lighter, there was a knock at the door. For a second, she hoped it was Shiori with a bottle of wine again. It wasn't likely, as they had texted each other half an hour ago.

After wandering down the hall, Ruth checked that the security chain was on and opened the door.

It was Dan.

Ruth glared at him. 'Just fuck off, Dan!'

As she went to slam the door in his face, he put his hand up. 'Wait! Please. This is important.'

Ruth let out a loud sigh. 'What do you want?'

'Can I come in?'

'No.'

'It's about me going to Australia,' Dan said with an awkward expression.

Ruth shook her head. 'Brilliant. I've had a long, difficult day, so what I really need is to have a conversation with you about when you, and the woman you're having an affair with, are going to move to the other side of the world while I bring up our daughter on my own.'

Dan said nothing for a few seconds. 'Angela has flown to Australia without me.'

Ruth assumed that Angela had seen sense, realised that Dan was a feckless prick and dumped him.

Ruth frowned. 'Why?'

'Her dad had a stroke last night. They're not sure if he's going to make it, so she's flown home.'

Even though she hated Dan, Ruth felt a little guilty at having been so aggressive towards him. She took the security chain off, opened the door and beckoned him inside. 'You'd better come in.'

'Thanks. Sorry ...'

Ruth followed him down the hallway and into the living room.

'Ella asleep?' Dan asked.

Ruth rolled her eyes. 'It's nearly nine o'clock, Dan. Of course she's bloody asleep.'

'Right. Sorry,' Dan said as he fidgeted.

Ruth wondered what she had ever seen in him.

'I'm sorry Angela's dad's not well but you could have told me that on the phone,' Ruth grumbled.

'You haven't answered any of my last three texts or phone calls,' he said.

He has a point, Ruth thought.

'So, what do you want?' she asked.

'I want to fly out to be with Angela. Especially if anything does happen to her dad. And if I do that, then I'll be staying for good,' Dan explained.

Here we go.

'When are you going?' Ruth snapped.

'I don't know. End of the week,' he said. 'I want to see Ella before I go.'

'Why?'

Dan looked despondent. 'She's my daughter.'

'You've seen her half a dozen times since you moved out in May!'

'I've seen her seven times.'

'In four months! That's not okay, Dan.'

'Can I see her to say goodbye or not?'

'No.'

'What?'

'No. You can't see her. She's two years old. She doesn't understand why you're not here anymore. And she won't understand why you're moving to Australia. But she will be upset ... So, no.' Ruth glared at him and pointed to the door. 'I want you to go. Now.'

Dan shook his head, turned and slammed the front door as he left.

CHAPTER 26

Lucy was lost in thought at her desk when Ruth approached. She was trying to clear paperwork, but the events of the previous evening had thrown her.

Ruth handed her a coffee. 'Here you go.'

Lucy forced a smile as she took it. 'Thanks.'

Ruth flinched. 'Christ, I thought *I* had a shit evening last night. Are you okay?'

Lucy shook her head. 'Don't even ask. If I told you what happened last night, you would not believe me.'

Ruth shrugged. 'Try me.'

The doors to the CID office opened, and Brooks came marching in holding a pile of folders. For a second, he looked over at Lucy and gave her a half smile. She didn't know how to feel or what to think.

'Morning everyone. If we can get going that would be great,' Brooks said as he went over to the scene boards and prepared to take the morning briefing. 'As you all know, the direction of this investigation has changed quite radically with Trevor Walsh's murder. This is now a double murder case, which I don't think we've had in this CID for quite a few years.' He went to the board and pointed to a recent photo of Walsh. 'Unless anyone thinks otherwise, I believe that Trevor Walsh's murder is directly linked to our investigation into Alfie Wise's death. I've been a detective long enough to know that coincidences are so rare that they aren't worth considering.'

Gaughran looked up from his desk. 'Guv, do we think that whoever killed Trevor Walsh also murdered Alfie Wise?'

'I think it's likely, but I'm yet to even see the link,' Brooks answered. 'Who has motive to kill Trevor Walsh?'

Ruth sat forward in her chair. 'We know Walsh was on some kind of paid retainer from Charlie Wise. We also know that he was seen in Charlie Wise's car, with Charlie and Alfie, on or around the day that Alfie was reported missing.'

Hassan nodded in agreement. 'We also have Eddie Bannerman's allegation that Walsh was a police informant.'

Trying to avoid eye contact with Brooks, Lucy said, 'We also know that Walsh claimed to have received a letter from Alfie, just before he went missing, telling him that he was going away and that he wouldn't see him ever again.'

Brooks raised an eyebrow. 'Who knew about that letter?'

'We asked Charlie Wise about it yesterday. He said that he knew nothing about it or why Alfie would have written that in a letter.'

Brooks took a deep breath as he studied the board for a few seconds. 'Let's imagine that Charlie Wise murdered his brother. Why?'

'Alfie had threatened to go to the police about Charlie's criminal activities,' Hassan suggested.

Brooks nodded. 'That gives us motive. So, he lures Alfie into the car with his best mate, Trevor Walsh. They go for a drive, Charlie murders Alfie and he and Trevor bury the body at Dixon's Timber Yard. To keep Walsh quiet, Charlie pays him 'hush money' for forty years in exchange for his silence. Alfie's body is found and we turn up to question Charlie. Walsh tries to throw us off the scent by claiming that Alfie was killed by South London gangsters who were trying to get to Charlie. Ruth and Lucy then go and talk to Charlie and tell him we've spoken to Walsh again, and he's told us about some letter. Charlie fears Walsh might crack or tell us about what really happened to Alfie that night. He arranges for someone to murder Walsh to keep him quiet.' Brooks paused briefly and then looked at them all. 'It's a decent hypothesis, but it's not a provable one. And if we're going after a knight of the realm, then we need a watertight case or we'll end up directing traffic down by Peckham station.'

'Doesn't really explain the letter, guv,' Ruth added.

'I know. It's the best I could do off the top of my head.' Brooks looked over at Lucy and she felt her pulse quicken. 'You and Ruth went to speak to Jackie Weller yesterday, didn't you?'

Lucy felt very uncomfortable as she took out her notebook. 'Yes, guv. She said something very strange. She said, '*You think that because I served time in prison, that means that I could have shot Alfie Wise?*' We had made no mention of Alfie being shot, and it hasn't been reported in the media.'

Brooks tilted his head slightly. 'Did you confront her about it?'

'Yes, guv. She claimed it was a lucky guess, but she looked rattled.'

'What did you think, Ruth?' he asked.

Ruth cleared her throat before replying. 'Clearly Jackie Weller had plenty of motive to kill Alfie. She might even have motive to kill Trevor Walsh, as he was the one who instigated the fight that resulted in her brother's death. But she was sixteen in 1956. I know she served prison time, but do we think a sixteen-year-old girl had the wherewithal to track down Alfie, find him, shoot him in the back of the head and bury him?'

'Not without help,' Gaughran said.

Brooks went back to the board. 'Okay. What about Bannerman and Droy? Are we ruling them out?'

Gaughran shook his head. 'They lied about their alibis. And we know they were looking for Alfie and probably intended to kill him out of revenge. Again, they also might have motive to kill Walsh, although the question would be why wait until now? We don't have any evidence linking them to either murder. They both insist they were warned off and that Alfie's death was linked to Charlie's criminal activity.'

'Has anybody talked to anyone from the 211 Club from that time who might remember what was going on?' Brooks asked.

Hassan raised his hand to answer. 'Guv, we've tracked down a Michael Fisher. He's Declan Fisher's older brother and apparently used to drink with Declan and Charlie at the club.'

'Good. Let's see what he can remember,' Brooks said. 'And what about our two mystery officers from the South London Murder Squad?'

Ruth looked up. 'Charlie told us he remembered two young detectives that frequented the club. They asked for money and he told them to piss off. We've no idea if that's connected to Alfie's death.'

Lucy knew they had to withhold some of the information about what Charlie had told them. The fact that one of the officers had fallen down the stairs, walked with a stick, and had an Irish name might put Arthur Gaughran in the frame. They didn't want to alert Tim to the fact that they might be looking at his father in the investigation.

'The Coroner's asking about a DNA sample so we can formally identify Alfie's body,' Brooks said.

Lucy nodded. 'We got a sample from Charlie yesterday. Results will be back within twenty-four hours.'

'Any word on the carbon dating of the bones as a backup?' Brooks asked.

'I'm chasing it today, guv,' Hassan replied.

Brooks looked out at the CID team. 'Is there anything else?'

Gaughran gestured to an old paper. 'Guv. Our eye witness, Eileen Walters, claimed to have seen Charlie and Alfie Wise, and possibly Trevor Walsh on the 27th November 1956. She and a friend had seen a band called The Rattlesnakes play in Peckham that night. So I eventually tracked down a number for the lead singer of The Rattlesnakes. Apparently they still play the odd gig even now. He remembered the gig because 27th November 1956 was also his 21st birthday. And that strongly suggests that Charlie, Alfie and Walsh were in a car ten hours after Charlie had reported Alfie missing.'

Brooks nodded as he rubbed his hand over his head. 'Brilliant. That's great work, Tim.'

RUTH AND LUCY WERE making their way across South London towards Charlie's house in Wimbledon where they had agreed to meet him. They had explained that there were a couple more things that they needed to check with him. He'd told them he wasn't prepared to attend a voluntary interview at Peckham Police Station and that he would have his brief present.

Ruth heard the car's cigarette lighter click. She pulled it out and felt the glowing red heat on her face as she lit her cigarette and took a deep drag.

'You haven't told me why your evening was shit last night,' Ruth said as she blew a long plume of smoke out of the window and watched as the wind snatched it away.

Lucy pulled a face. 'Karen, Harry's ex, turned up on my doorstep with her face bashed in. Cut lip, bloody nose.'

'Christ! What happened?'

'She told me that Harry had gone round to see her and told her to leave us alone. They got into an argument and he attacked her,' Lucy explained.

Ruth's eyes widened. She couldn't believe what Lucy had just told her. 'Harry attacked her? Are you sure?'

Lucy shook her head. 'No, I'm not. I've never seen Harry lose his temper. He can be grumpy when he's tired, but punching a woman in the face ...'

'I know that Karen's behaviour has been very strange and scary recently, but I just don't believe he'd punch her,' Ruth said. She had never seen Harry remotely aggressive or confrontational even at work. There were plenty of coppers with a short fuse, and she'd even seen some of them arguing and coming to blows. But Harry wasn't one of them.

Lucy shrugged. 'My instinct says that he didn't attack her. But that means she was crazy enough to do it to herself to set Harry up.'

'Yeah, and that is bonkers,' Ruth said. 'But you've been a copper long enough to know that people do some very bizarre things. Harry left her and maybe she just can't get over it?'

'Bloody hell! Why can't she get a new haircut, live in the gym, drink too much wine and go on a crash diet like every other middle-aged woman whose husband leaves them?' Lucy spat.

'What are you going to do?'

Lucy shook her head. 'I just don't know. We can't carry on like this. I'm scared when I go home. What's next? Is she going to be waiting for me with a carving knife?'

Ruth raised an eyebrow. 'Restraining order?'

'We don't have any evidence that she's done anything wrong.'

TEN MINUTES LATER, Lucy and Ruth pulled into the drive at Charlie's mansion and got out of their car. They pressed the door buzzer and were shown through to the kitchen.

Charlie barely acknowledged them when they entered. Instead, he was having a long conversation with his solicitor, a serious-looking woman in a dark suit and glasses who was sitting next to him taking notes.

Ruth smiled as she sat down, but Charlie's demeanour had changed. The happy-go-lucky, cheeky chappie attitude had gone. It had been replaced by a steely and distinctly unfriendly manner.

Ruth pulled her chair close to the table and cleared her throat. 'We just have a few more things we'd like to clarify with you, Charlie.'

Charlie gave a sarcastic smile. 'I'm sure you do.'

'I take it you know that Trevor Walsh was murdered the day before yesterday?' Ruth asked.

Charlie nodded. 'Yes. I hadn't seen him in a while, but I was really sad to hear about that.'

'Could you tell us where you were on Tuesday evening between 8 pm and midnight?' Ruth asked.

Charlie whispered to his solicitor and then looked at Ruth. 'I was having dinner in the Chelsea Arts Club. There were probably about eight of us. I was there all evening.'

'Thank you,' Ruth said. 'And they'll confirm that, will they?'

Charlie shrugged. 'I don't see why they wouldn't.'

'And you say that you haven't seen Trevor in some time?'

'That's right. It's got to be about six months.'

'In which time you had paid him three thousand pounds?' Lucy interjected quickly.

Charlie frowned, snorted, and looked over at his solicitor. 'I wasn't aware that was a crime, were you?'

The solicitor raised an eyebrow. 'It isn't.'

Lucy flicked over a page of her notebook. 'If I can take you back to the time that Alfie went missing ... We have the file on his disappearance, which states that you came into Peckham Police Station to report that Alfie was missing on the 27th of November.'

The solicitor leant over and said something to Charlie.

'Sounds about right but I can't confirm it,' he said.

Lucy peered down at her notes. 'We have an eyewitness who saw you, Alfie and Trevor Walsh in your car on that evening at the traffic lights on Bridge Street, Peckham. Could you explain that to us?'

Charlie spoke again to his solicitor, this time in more depth and for longer. He nodded a few times before turning back to them. 'I'm sorry. My recollection of that time is pretty hazy. I could have been in a car with Alfie and Walshy. I used to give them lifts all over the place. But I've no idea about the date that you're asking me about. But if I came in to report Alfie missing, how could I be in the car with him later that day? That makes no sense, does it?'

Lucy looked at him. 'Which is why we're asking you about it.'

Charlie shrugged. 'I don't know what to tell you. Someone has made a mistake somewhere down the line.'

'Actually, our eye-witness is very clear because she had seen a band playing in Peckham that night. We have evidence which shows they only played on the night of the 27th November. Could you explain that to us, please?' Ruth asked.

Looking at his watch, Charlie was clearly flustered as he leaned in and spoke to his solicitor again.

The solicitor put down her pen. 'My client is a very busy man, and this is a voluntary interview at his convenience. However, I am advising him not to answer any more questions today. And if you would like to speak to him again, then it will have to be under caution.'

Ruth glanced at Lucy – Charlie was definitely rattled.

CHAPTER 27

Gaughran and Hassan rang the doorbell to the small flat where Michael Fisher lived. It was part of a 1930s Deco-styled block that was sheltered housing for pensioners.

After a few seconds, Fisher came to the door. He was well into his 70s and clearly out of breath from the effort of walking.

He squinted at them and raised his bushy white eyebrows. 'Can I help?'

Gaughran noticed that he still had a faint Irish accent. 'We're looking for a Michael Fisher?'

Fisher looked guarded. 'Yeah?'

Gaughran and Hassan showed him their warrant cards. 'We're from Peckham CID. I wonder if we could ask you a few questions about an ongoing investigation, Mr Fisher?'

Fisher shrugged tetchily, opened the door and gestured. 'I suppose so ... You'd better come in.'

They followed him inside into the living room. Despite the heat of the day, Fisher was dressed in a large burgundy cardigan. He went over to a faded, patterned armchair and sat down. There was a small canister of oxygen on a trolley. He leant down, took the mask that was attached to the oxygen, placed it to his nose and mouth and took three deep breaths.

Glancing around, Gaughran saw that the room was neat and tidy. There was a bookshelf stacked high with non-fiction and a table that was full of old photos in frames, most of which were black and white.

'I saw you'd found Alfie Wise's body on the news. Poor bastard,' Fisher said as he sat back and eventually got his breath back. 'Do you know what happened to him?'

Gaughran shook his head. 'Not yet. We're hoping you might be able to help us with that.'

Fisher looked puzzled. 'It wasn't me, if that's what you're thinking.'

Hassan ignored his comment and took out his notepad. 'I know it might be difficult to remember that far back, Mr Fisher ...'

'Michael,' he said.

Hassan nodded. 'Michael. We'd like to talk to you about Declan and anything you can remember about Alfie and Charlie Wise, especially towards the end of 1956.'

Fisher coughed for a few seconds and then composed himself. 'What d'you want to know?'

'Have you any idea who attacked Declan?' Gaughran asked. As the investigation had progressed, Gaughran had become pretty sure that whoever had attacked and given him brain damage was the same person, or persons, who had also shot and killed Alfie Wise. He was certain the two were linked.

Fisher glared at them. 'You've got some bollocks asking me that.'

Gaughran knew from his response what Fisher was going to say, but he needed him to say it. 'Why's that, Michael?'

'It was one of your lot, wasn't it?'

Gaughran peered over at him and said gently, 'Could you elaborate on that?'

Fisher shook his head and huffed. 'Declan and Charlie were in business together. They ran everything out of the 211 Club in Balham. Then a couple of bent coppers decided they wanted a regular backhander to leave them alone.'

It was what Gaughran had feared Fisher was going to tell them.

Hassan frowned. 'Which means there was some kind of criminal activity going on?'

Fisher pulled a face. 'Nothing heavy. After hours gambling, scrubbers.'

'Drugs?' Hassan asked.

'Grass, speed,' Fisher said.

'What happened?' Gaughran asked.

Fisher coughed again and cleared his throat. 'Charlie and Declan paid these coppers off for a while. Then they got greedy and asked for more, so Charlie and Declan told them to fuck off. There was some kind of a fight one night. A few days later, Declan was attacked round the back of the club. They put him in a coma and he never came out of it.'

Gaughran could see that Fisher was getting upset. 'You think it was these police officers that attacked your brother?'

'Of course it was,' he snapped. 'They wanted to show Charlie that they weren't fucking about. It wasn't too long after that Alfie Wise went missing. We all knew what had happened.'

'Did you ever see or meet these police officers?' Gaughran asked.

Fisher shrugged. 'Couple of times.'

Hassan looked up from his notepad. 'Do you remember their names?'

He shook his head. 'Not really. I think one of them was called Clive, but I couldn't swear to it.'

'Could you describe them?' Gaughran asked.

Fisher thought for a few seconds. 'One of them was tall, lanky and young. The other one was big. Not fat, just really big.'

Hassan scribbled in his notebook. 'Anything else that might help us?'

As he sat forward in his chair, Fisher wiped his mouth with a handkerchief. 'Tell you what. I've got a photograph.' He looked at Hassan and pointed to a framed, black-and-white photograph at one end of the table. 'Pass me that, would you?'

Hassan stood, retrieved the photograph, and then handed it to Fisher. He turned it around. It showed two young men in smart suits and pencil ties, arm in arm, smiling at the camera. From what Gaughran could see, it had been taken inside a nightclub – the 211 Club he presumed.

'It's the only photo I've got of me and Declan together,' Fisher said. He then pointed to a table in the background of the image where two men were having a drink. 'You can't really see very well, but these two blokes here are the coppers I'm talking about. They must have been drinking in there that night. You can't see the big bloke very well, but you can see the lanky one.'

Fisher leaned forward and handed the photo to Gaughran. He turned the frame around to inspect the photograph with the image of the two detectives.

The lanky copper's face was clearly visible. His heart dropped.

It was his father, Arthur Gaughran.

CHAPTER 28

Ruth and Lucy marched down the deserted hospital corridor of St George's towards the mortuary, as they had done many times before. Their shoes echoed loudly and the air smelled of cooked hospital food and disinfectant. Ruth could feel her stomach tense a little. She still couldn't quite get used to strolling into the mortuary and looking at a dead body.

Trying to distract herself, she glanced over at Lucy. 'Dan came round last night.'

Lucy frowned. 'I thought you told him to only contact you through a solicitor?'

'There's been a change of plan ...' Ruth shrugged.

Lucy rolled her eyes and groaned sarcastically. 'Dan and a change of plan. Now there's a shock.'

'I know,' Ruth sighed. 'Angela's dad is at death's door, so she's flown back to Australia. He wants to follow her out there in a few days. So, he wants to say goodbye to Ella this week.'

Lucy shook her head. 'What did you tell him?'

'I told him to piss off and that he couldn't see her.'

'Good for you!'

'I'm not sure that's the right thing to do though,' Ruth said pensively.

Lucy raised an eyebrow. 'Why not? He's a useless dad and it will just confuse and upset Ella!'

'I know that. But I'm allowing my feelings towards Dan to interfere with her saying goodbye to him.'

'You're just protecting her.'

'Maybe saying goodbye would make it clear that he's going, rather than me trying to explain it to her. I just don't know.'

'Well for what it's worth, I think that the sooner he's in Australia, the better,' Lucy growled.

Ruth reached the double doors to the mortuary and opened them. 'I'm not going to argue with you there.'

The icy stillness inside the examination room made Ruth feel a little anxious. The buzz of fans and the air conditioning added to the unnatural atmosphere. Smells of sterile clinical disinfectants and other cleaning fluids masked the odour of the gases and the beginnings of rot and decay.

The hospital's Chief Pathologist, Professor Sofia Deneuve, looked over and smiled a hello. She was tall and thin, with a professional manner that could sometimes be intimidating.

Lucy and Ruth arrived at the metal autopsy table where Trevor Walsh's body was laid out. Ruth shivered as she glanced up at the intense lights that shone down from the ceiling. Mortuaries were just too quiet, too sterile and too lifeless for her liking. Walsh's bluish corpse was spread out clinically in front of her.

She looked up and down his skinny body. The essence of life, of personality, was gone.

'Good morning, detectives,' Professor Deneuve said quietly without looking up as she continued to examine Walsh's body that had been cut open from the throat down to the stomach.

'Morning,' Lucy said.

'Morning ... Do we have a more accurate time of death?' Ruth asked, cutting to the chase. She didn't want to spend any more time staring at the insides of a person than she had to.

'Given the lividity, I would narrow it down to between midnight and two am,' she said.

'Are we definitely looking at murder?' Lucy asked.

'Yes. Cause of death was asphyxiation. I can see evidence of compression of the neck structures that would have led to asphyxia and neuronal death.'

Ruth nodded as if she knew exactly what that meant. 'Anything that might give us a clue who our killer might be?'

The pathologist looked at them. 'You're looking for someone who is incredibly strong. The injuries that your victim suffered were caused manually, but they were what I would expect to see from a suicide by hanging. There is a spinal fracture, spinal trauma, and spinal shock that has caused priapism. The carotid intimal is completely ruptured.'

Ruth and Lucy looked at each other – *what does that mean?*

Professor Deneuve gave them a withering look. 'In layman's terms, whoever strangled your victim did it with such force that he nearly took his head off.'

Bloody hell. That's horrific, Ruth thought as she felt a little queasy.

Dressed in pastel-blue surgical scrubs, the professor adjusted her black rubber apron and pointed to various grey patches within the body. 'Were you aware that your victim was incredibly ill?'

Ruth shook her head. 'No, we had no idea.'

Professor Deneuve indicated the grey patches again. 'Your victim was riddled with cancer. These are all tumours. It would have been very painful. And it explains the extreme weight loss.'

'Are you saying that the victim was dying?' Lucy asked.

'Yes. I'm saying that if someone hadn't strangled him, he would have been dead in a matter of weeks.'

AS SOON AS RUTH AND Lucy got back to CID, Brooks called an impromptu briefing of all CID officers that were currently in Peckham nick. It was the middle of the day, and the fans that had finally arrived did very little but blow hot air around the office.

Going to the board, Lucy noticed that Brooks' tie was loosened by about four inches. She was still trying to process what had happened the previous evening. In her heart, she knew that Brooks didn't have it in him to punch Karen in the face and cause those injuries. And if Karen had injured herself to turn everyone against Brooks, then she was a very unwell woman. It also meant that Lucy hadn't trusted Brooks when he had denied the attack. She wondered what that meant for their long-term future. Could they get past the events of the last few days? All she knew was that when she looked at Brooks as he stood by the crime scene board, with his handsome, chiselled face and shirt sleeves rolled up, she was madly in love with him.

'Right everyone. Ruth and Lucy have just returned from the post mortem. Ruth?' Brooks gestured for Ruth to feed-back.

Maybe he just doesn't want to look my way? Lucy thought.

'Guv. The post mortem confirmed that Trevor Walsh was asphyxiated. Professor Deneuve also noted that there was very serious damage to his spine and neck, which indicated that whoever strangled him was incredibly strong. The other puzzling thing was that Walsh had terminal cancer. In fact, had he not been murdered, it's likely he would have died from the disease within a few weeks.'

Brooks looked over to Gaughran. 'You all right, Tim? I've never known you so quiet.'

Lucy smiled. 'Don't complain, guv!'

There was laughter from some detectives. Gaughran gave them a sarcastic smile, but Lucy could see that he wasn't his usual feisty self.

Brooks glanced over at Gaughran again. 'Tim, what did Michael Fisher have to say?'

'He didn't tell us very much that we didn't already know, guv. He confirmed that Charlie Wise and Declan Fisher were mates and probably ran businesses out of the 211 Club.'

Brooks frowned. 'Did he specify what type of businesses exactly?'

Gaughran looked up. 'He said it was nothing heavy. Prostitutes, Class B drugs and a bit of after-hours gambling.'

Hassan pulled a face and said, 'Unfortunately, he confirmed that two young detectives from the South London Murder Squad were being paid off by Charlie Wise on a regular basis. Trouble started when they wanted more and there was some kind of altercation. The next thing, Declan Fisher is beaten unconscious and Alfie Wise vanishes.'

'And presumably Fisher thought that these police officers were responsible for both crimes?' Brooks asked in a solemn tone.

Gaughran nodded despondently. 'Probably, guv.'

Lucy could see that this information had really got to him.

Hassan looked over. 'He gave a description of the two detectives but no names. *But* he gave us a photograph taken at the 211 Club of Declan and Michael Fisher. In the background, you can just about make out the two officers he was talking about.'

'Yeah,' Gaughran said. 'I've left the photo in the car but I'll go and grab it in a second.'

Brooks took all this in and rubbed his chin. 'Do we think two police officers committed a vicious assault and a murder because a club owner refused to pay them bribes?'

Ruth shrugged. 'We know there were plenty of officers in the Met on the take in the 50s, guv.'

'And Operation Countryman was only twenty years ago,' Lucy said.

'Operation Countryman' was an investigation into police corruption in London's Met in the late 70s. There had been allegations that the Met's Flying Squad were receiving bribes from armed gangs in return for tip-offs and details of investigations, raids or arrests. It was also alleged that detectives had manipulated evidence to prevent criminals being convicted, as well as fabricating evidence against innocent men. Two hundred and fifty Met officers were forced to resign and many ended up facing criminal charges. When the report was published, it was seen by many as one of the darkest days in the Met's history.

'Okay, let's get that photograph enlarged,' Brooks said. 'I then want anyone we can find who worked in this nick, or any other South London nick in the 50s, to have a look at it. Let's see if we can get names for these two officers.'

As the fax machine whirred, Ruth got up from her seat and went over to it.

'Guv, I can show it to my old man,' Gaughran suggested.

Brooks nodded. 'Thanks Tim. What about Charlie Wise?'

'He's not going to talk to us now until we charge him with something,' Lucy said. 'But there is definitely something dodgy about him, Alfie, and Trevor Walsh being in that car.'

Ruth came over with a fax in her hand. 'Guv, we got a hit for the car that was seen driving away from Trevor Walsh's address. It's a hire car but came as a package through the Kensington Place Hotel. And we've now got a name. Daniel Keane. He's staying at the hotel and hasn't yet checked out.'

'Ah ... at last,' Brooks said.

Ruth and Lucy grabbed their jackets as they went to leave.

Brooks looked at Ruth and then directly at Lucy. 'Just be careful, will you?'

CHAPTER 29

Ruth and Lucy walked into the plush reception area of the Kensington Place Hotel. It was fully air-conditioned and Lucy could feel the cold air on her face and in her nostrils. It was a pleasant relief from the heat outside.

They wandered over to the busy reception desk where affluent guests were checking in and out. Taking out her warrant card, Lucy approached a young man at the end of the counter. 'I wonder if you can help? We just spoke to the rental car company that you use in your Executive Package ...'

He nodded. 'Prestige Cars?'

'That's it,' Lucy said. 'We're looking for a guest by the name of Daniel Keane?'

The young man went over to a large ledger and ran his finger down the list of guests and rooms. He looked up at them. 'Room 25. Second floor. Mr Keane has a taxi booked for Heathrow airport in half an hour.'

'I don't suppose you know where he's flying to, do you?' Lucy asked.

He paused thoughtfully. 'I'm pretty sure it's Belfast. He had BFS on his luggage when he arrived.'

'So, Mr Keane should still be in his room?' Ruth asked.

'I suppose so. I could ring his room and tell him you're here?'

Lucy smiled. 'It's okay. We'll just go and knock. Thanks.'

As they walked over to the lifts, Lucy gazed around at the high ceilings, the tasteful ornaments, and the oil paintings that hung on the walls. It would be lovely to stay in a hotel like this. For a second, her mind turned to Brooks. She had no idea what she was going to do, but the situation between them was distracting her from her work. And when you were a police officer, that could prove dangerous.

'You and Brooks okay today?' Ruth asked as they got into the lift, which smelled of expensive perfume.

'It's work,' Lucy said. 'We've always been pretty good at separating the two.'

The lift arrived at the second floor and they got out and headed for Room 25.

'What do we think Keane's connection is to Walsh?' Ruth asked.

'He flies in from Belfast. He's staying at a five-star hotel with an expensive hire car. He goes and murders a virtual nobody. And then he flies back to Belfast,' Lucy said, raising her eyebrow. 'What do you think?'

'My guess is that somebody paid him to come over and kill Walsh,' Ruth said as they arrived at Room 25.

Lucy pulled a face and said quietly, 'Which means that Mr Keane might be an Irish hitman.'

Ruth gave a sarcastic smile. 'Oh good. I can't wait to meet him.'

Lucy knocked on the door and waited.

After a few seconds, there was the sound of the door being unlocked. An enormous man with black hair and piercing blue eyes peered out at them. 'Hello?' He had a thick Northern Irish accent.

Oh God. He looks scary.

'Mr Keane?' Ruth said as she pulled out her warrant card.

Keane frowned. 'Yeah?'

'I wonder if we could ask you a few questions regarding an ongoing police investigation?' she asked in a light, breezy tone.

Keane didn't look impressed. 'Do I have a choice? I've got a flight to catch.'

Lucy smiled. 'It won't take more than a few minutes.'

He opened the door and beckoned for them to come in. The room was large, neat, and stylishly decorated and furnished. It smelled of a mixture of shower gel and musky aftershave.

Keane went over to the window and casually looked outside and down at the road below.

Is he checking to see if we've got backup down there? Lucy wondered.

'How can I help?' he asked brusquely.

'Does the name Trevor Walsh mean anything to you, Mr Keane?' Ruth asked.

He shook his head. 'No. I've never heard that name before.'

Ruth took something from her jacket pocket. It was a small photograph of Trevor Walsh that they had retrieved from his flat. 'Could you have a look at this and tell us if you recognise this man?'

Keane came over, took the photograph and peered at it. 'No. Never seen him before.'

'Can you confirm you used a rental car that was provided by this hotel?' Lucy asked.

His eyes darted around the room as he thought about the question. 'Why are you asking me all this stuff?'

Lucy locked eyes with him. 'Could you just answer the question, please?'

Keane huffed and glanced at his watch. 'Yes, I used a hire car. So what?'

Ruth glared at him. 'We have reason to believe that the hire car you used was parked outside a property in Peckham where Trevor Walsh was murdered two nights ago.'

Keane didn't say anything and scratched his chin.

Suddenly, he shoved Ruth with both hands so forcibly that she fell back onto the bed. He then shoulder-barged Lucy, knocking her to the floor.

He raced to the door, opened it and ran out.

'Bloody hell!' Lucy shouted as she got up. Keane had knocked the wind out of her.

Ruth was already on her feet and heading for the door. 'You okay?'

Lucy steadied herself. 'Fine. Let's go ...'

They sprang out into the corridor and looked both ways.

Nothing. Keane was gone.

Lucy gestured to a fire exit door which was slowly closing. 'He's using the stairs!'

Flinging open the escape door, she could hear the clatter of footsteps from below.

Lucy and Ruth gave chase, running down the stairs behind Keane.

Still dizzy from being knocked over, Lucy concentrated on the steps, trying not to lose her footing.

As they reached the ground floor, they could still hear footsteps below them.

He's heading for the basement and underground car park.

Holding the cold metal handrail for balance, Lucy spotted a dark green door marked *Guest Car Parking.*

Ruth threw the door open and Lucy followed her into a dim, concrete underground car park.

Before they had time to see where Keane had gone, they heard the piercing sound of screaming. It was coming from the top of a nearby ramp that led to the exit.

What the hell is going on?

As she sprinted up the concrete ramp, Lucy immediately saw that Keane had dragged a middle-aged woman from a Range Rover and was getting into the driver's seat.

'Help me! Please help me!' the woman cried desperately.

'Shit!' Lucy muttered as she and Ruth dashed towards them. 'Stop! Police!'

'No! No!' the woman screamed hysterically as she tried to stop him.

Keane slammed the car door and sped away with the tyres squealing and the smell of burning rubber in the air.

The woman screamed again as they approached, 'My baby's in there! She's in the back of the car!'

'Oh my God,' Lucy said under her breath.

Ruth raced to the woman and put a reassuring hand on her shoulder. 'We're police officers. We're going to get her back safely. I promise.'

'My baby!' The woman's eyes were wild with panic. 'Please. Oh my god, he's got my daughter ...'

'Stay here,' Lucy said. 'We're going to get her.'

As they sprinted after the car, Ruth clicked her radio. 'Alpha zero to Control. We are in pursuit of a suspect, a Daniel Keane. Driving a black Range Rover. Licence plate papa, five,

five, tango, yankee, foxtrot. He has kidnapped a baby that is on board the vehicle, over.'

'Alpha zero from Control, received. Stand by.'

As the Range Rover smashed through the exit barriers, Lucy and Ruth continued to sprint to where their car was parked in the street.

Lucy was now breathing heavily as she unlocked the car, jumped into the driver's seat and started the ignition.

'What a wanker!' Ruth muttered as they screeched away and reached Kensington High Street a few seconds later.

'Where is he?' Glancing both ways frantically, Lucy couldn't see the car. 'Which way? Which way?'

There was heavy traffic going right into the centre of London.

Ruth gestured. 'It's got to be left.'

Lucy narrowly missed a bus as she pulled the car out onto Kensington High Street. 'Get out of my way!' she growled. Her heart was thumping in her chest.

Ruth hit the blues and twos and clicked the radio. 'Alpha zero to Control, we're in pursuit of the black Range Rover, heading west on Kensington High Street. There is a kidnapped baby on board the vehicle. No visual as of yet, over.'

The radio crackled. 'Alpha zero, received. Stand by.'

Weaving in and out of the traffic, which was now moving out of the way because of the flashing blue lights and two-tone siren, Lucy spotted the Range Rover up ahead. 'He's there.'

'Control from Alpha zero, we now have visual on suspect driving the stolen black Range Rover. Heading west. Passing Kensington High Street underground station on our left, over.'

'Alpha zero, received. We have two local patrol cars en route, eta five minutes, over.'

Up ahead, Lucy spotted the brake lights of the Range Rover which had been forced to a stop by the sheer weight of traffic. Throwing the steering wheel right, she pulled out and headed against the traffic coming the other way, forcing cars to pull over.

'Out of the way!' she yelled.

Glancing over, Lucy could see that Ruth was holding on for dear life. She knew she wasn't a fan of high-speed pursuits. 'You okay?'

Ruth shook her head. 'We've got to get her back safely.'

'Don't worry. I'm not letting him get away,' Lucy said, aware that as she was breathing in there was now a sharp pain across her rib cage.

Just as they reached the Range Rover, it pulled left down the Earl's Court Road.

'Bloody hell, he's hammering it,' Lucy said as she saw they had reached 55 mph on the clear stretch of road.

'He's going to kill someone,' Ruth growled.

From out of the corner of her eye, Lucy spotted the blue flashing lights of a marked police car which was filtering in from the right. 'Here comes the cavalry!'

It zipped out of the waiting traffic and into the path of the Range Rover, trying to slow it down. The Range Rover swerved violently left and then right.

Out of nowhere, a double-decker bus pulled out across the road from a bus stop.

Lucy held her breath as the Range Rover clipped the back of the bus and went momentarily onto two wheels before dropping back onto the road and skidding.

'Oh my God, no!' Ruth gasped.

It continued to skid and then smashed heavily into the back of an open-backed lorry carrying building materials.

Lucy pulled their car to a hard stop about thirty yards away. The patrol car, and another that had just joined it, manoeuvred to block the whole of the Earl's Court Road.

Ruth and Lucy jumped out and raced towards the smashed Range Rover which was obscured by a vast cloud of dust and sand.

'Please God, no,' Lucy muttered under her breath.

As she reached the car, Lucy could see that Keane was laying against the driver's window, face covered in blood and unconscious.

Reaching for the back door, she opened it and saw that the baby girl was still safely in her car seat looking frightened and confused. 'Thank God, thank God. Come here, darling.'

The baby cried as Lucy unclipped her harness and lifted her from the car. 'Here we go.'

'Is she okay?' Ruth asked frantically.

Lucy checked her over and she didn't appear to be hurt, just shocked. 'I don't think she's even got a scratch.'

Ruth puffed out her cheeks. 'Jesus, I thought something terrible had happened to her!'

'Me too,' Lucy said as she held the crying baby in her arms.

Ruth clicked her radio. 'Alpha zero to control. We have a major RTA involving suspect vehicle. Intersection of Earl's

Court Road and Pembroke Road. We need ambulances and the fire service, over.'

CHAPTER 30

Sitting at his desk in CID, Gaughran could feel that his stomach was knotted tightly. In fact, his anxiety was making him feel sick. He kept thinking of the image of his father, sitting with his partner in the 211 Club. The man that Michael Fisher had identified as one of the bent coppers that he suspected not only of taking bribes from the club, but of being involved in both Declan Fisher and Alfie Wise's deaths. How was that even possible? He had known his dad bend the law a little for traffic offences, or had spoken to a uniformed officer when his cousin had got in a pub brawl. But this was major corruption and murder.

He looked down at the file in front of him and hesitated before opening it. It was labelled *Arthur William Gaughran – Police Service Record – 1954-1989*. Taking a breath, he opened it and flicked through to find the date when his father had moved from being a uniformed 'bobby on the beat' in Peckham, to joining the South London Murder Squad as a young DC.

After a few seconds, he saw what he had feared he would see. His father became a DC at the beginning of 1956. Gaughran knew from a couple of passing conversations that his dad had told Ruth and Lucy that he was still in uniform when Alfie Wise had gone missing. Why had he lied? He could only conclude that it was because he was involved.

With his brain whirring, Gaughran looked down at the photo of his father that Michael Fisher had given. He knew what he had to do, but he couldn't believe it was actually happening.

Getting up from his desk, he took the photo and made his way out of the main CID area. A few seconds later, he arrived at Brooks' office and knocked on the open door. Brooks, who was in the middle of a mountain of paperwork, looked up at him.

'Tim?' he said, making it clear that he was eager to get back to his work.

Gaughran could feel that his palms were sweaty and his pulse was thudding. He took a deep breath. 'Can I have a word, guv?'

Brooks sat back in his seat. 'Fire away. Anything to distract me from doing all this.'

Gaughran hesitated and then said, 'It's a bit ... sensitive.'

Brooks' expression changed as he gestured to the door. 'Come in and sit down ... What's going on?'

That's what Gaughran admired about Brooks. He didn't suffer fools, but he looked after his officers like they were part of his family. And Gaughran knew that, in the past, some of his immature and inflammatory behaviour had annoyed Brooks.

He showed the photo to Brooks. 'This is the photo we took from Michael Fisher.' He then pointed to the two figures in the background. 'And these are the two officers that he alleges were taking bribes and were somehow involved in the attack on Declan Fisher, and Alfie Wise's murder.'

'That's great.' Brooks nodded. 'So these are the officers that Charlie Wise also told us about?'

'The officer sitting here is, or was, Clive Rigby,' Gaughran said. 'He died about ten years ago.'

'How do you know that?' he asked.

Gaughran moved the photograph closer for Brooks to look at. 'Because this officer here is my dad, and Rigby was his partner in CID.'

'What?' Brooks' eyes widened. 'That's your dad? Are you sure?'

Gaughran nodded. 'Yeah, I'm sure.'

Brooks feigned shock. 'When did you know your dad might be involved in all this, Tim?'

Gaughran lowered his head as he spoke. 'Not until I saw this photo this morning. I didn't know anything about it, I swear, guv.'

'So, your dad came in the other day to see if he could move our investigation in a different direction?'

'Unfortunately, that's what it looks like.'

'Do you think he's capable of something like murdering Alfie Wise?'

Gaughran shook his head. 'Hand on heart, guv, no. Not a cold-blooded murder like that. Shot to the head and buried. As for taking a few quid to look the other way, or even giving a little scrote like Declan Fisher a kicking, maybe. I really hope not, but I don't know.'

'We've got to bring him in, Tim,' Brooks said remorsefully.

'I know. I realise it's not appropriate, but let me go and talk to him. And then I'll bring him in.'

Brooks pursed his lips and his eyes narrowed. 'If he 'magically' disappears, then we'll both lose our jobs, you do know that?'

Gaughran smoothed his hand over his face. 'I haven't worked this hard to throw my career as a copper away, guv. If my old man has committed a crime, he needs to face justice just like anyone else. I wouldn't have it any other way. But I do want to have the chance to talk to him and bring him in myself.'

Brooks glanced down at his watch. 'I'll give you until first thing tomorrow to sort it, Tim.'

Gaughran stared vacantly at Brooks. He just couldn't believe they were having this conversation. It felt surreal. 'Thanks, guv. I know you're sticking your neck out here.'

'Just bring him in.'

As he got up from his chair, Gaughran realised that he now faced the most difficult few hours of his life. 'See you tomorrow, guv,' he said quietly, fighting the tremor in his voice.

Brooks looked at him. 'Tim?'

'Yes, guv.'

'I'm sorry this has happened. But you're a good copper, so don't do anything to jeopardise that.'

CHAPTER 31

Lucy and Ruth were waiting in the ICU area of the Chelsea and Westminster Hospital on the Fulham Road. Keane had been rushed in by ambulance and was still unconscious when he arrived.

Ruth ended her radio call and cast a glance at Lucy. 'Right, we've got a firearms officer arriving to guard Keane while he's here.'

A nurse approached and handed them a clear plastic bag containing Keane's personal belongings. 'Can you sign for these, please?'

Ruth watched as Lucy scribbled her name on the appropriate form and asked, 'Any idea how he is?'

The nurse appeared irritated. 'He's badly injured but you'll have to talk to the doctor if you need any more information.'

She's a bit spiky, Ruth thought to herself.

As the nurse walked away, Ruth delved into the bag, pulling out a wallet and a Motorola mobile phone. 'I wonder if the tech boys can get anything off this?'

'What about the wallet?' Lucy asked.

As she opened it, Ruth saw that there was a large wad of money tucked inside. There were also half a dozen credit cards and bank cards. She pulled one out and read it, 'Mr D O'Connell.'

A look of confusion crossed Lucy's face. 'What?'

Ruth held up another card and read out, 'Damian P O'Connell.' And then another card, with the same name – Damian P O'Connell.

Pulling out some receipts, she noticed that several of them were purchases of food from shops, and an Italian restaurant in Portrush. 'Where's Portrush? It's got a postcode BT56?'

'Northern Ireland, isn't it? I think it's on the coast,' Lucy replied as she then clicked her radio, 'Alpha zero to Control. I need a full PNC check on a Damian P O'Connell. Home address might be Portrush, Northern Ireland, over.'

'Control from alpha zero, received. Stand by.'

Ruth spotted a figure arriving at the nurses' station. It was Brooks. She couldn't help but think about what Lucy had told her about Karen and her injuries. She just couldn't see Brooks doing that to his ex-wife. But the job had also taught her that in a moment of utter fury, seemingly sane, ordinary people do horrible things to each other.

As Lucy moved away and took notes from the PNC check, Brooks approached.

'How is our Mr Keane?' he asked.

'Still waiting for the doctor to come and talk to us,' Ruth explained. 'It doesn't sound good though.'

Brooks looked at her. 'But you two are okay?'

'I think Lucy might have a cracked rib but essentially we're okay. And it appears that our Mr Keane might well be a Damian O'Connell from Portrush in Northern Ireland.'

'He's a long way from home.' Brooks nodded thoughtfully. 'It's sounding more and more like Trevor Walsh's murder was a paid hit.'

THE RAZOR GANG MURDER   219

'I agree, but who wanted him dead enough to hire someone to do it?' Ruth added.

Lucy approached and looked down at her notepad. Ruth noticed she didn't make eye contact with Brooks. 'I've got the PNC check on a Damian Peter O'Connell. Lives in Portrush. Date of birth is 3rd July 1956.'

'Sounds about right in terms of age,' Ruth said.

'He's got form,' Lucy continued. 'String of offences dating back to 1970. Assault, GBH, possession of a firearm, extortion. There are notes to say that it's likely he was affiliated to the Ulster Volunteer Force from the late 70s onwards.

'Sounds like a lovely bloke,' Brooks said, raising his eyebrow. 'What the hell was a man like that doing at the Kensington Place Hotel?'

Ruth watched as a young doctor approached them. He looked concerned. 'Hi there. Are you the police officers that came in with Daniel Keane?'

This doesn't look good, Ruth thought to herself.

'Yes. Any idea when we might be able to talk to him?' Lucy asked.

'I'm afraid Daniel didn't make it. I'm sorry. We did everything we could.'

GAUGHRAN PULLED UP outside his parents' home and noticed that his father's car wasn't on the drive. Part of him was relieved. There was a ball of knotted nerves in his stomach and his breathing was shallow. He wondered where his father was. Playing golf, most likely. Despite walking with a stick, he managed two or three rounds of golf a week at the Dulwich and Sydenham Hill Golf Club.

As Gaughran got out of the car, he could see that the beautiful blue sky was scarred by a band of darkening clouds to the south. His parents lived in a four-bedroom detached house in the affluent part of Peckham, close to the park and on the border with East Dulwich. He wondered if he was about to ruin everything his parents had ever worked for. He didn't have a choice. He knew that CID officers were closing in on the two bent coppers who had taken bribes from the 211 Club. Hassan had seen the photograph that Michael Fisher had given them, and it wouldn't have been long before someone at Peckham nick recognised him. Combined with his father's lies about his service record, Gaughran knew he'd had no choice but to talk to Brooks. It didn't make him a grass. The game was already up. He just didn't know the extent of the crimes that his father had committed forty years earlier.

Walking up the pathway, Gaughran thought about how many times he had ambled up to the house before. They had moved here in the early 80s when he was about twelve. The times he had come home drunk in the early hours, forgotten his keys, and thrown stones up at his parents' window. His dad would come down, roll his eyes and let him in. Sometimes, he would sit with his dad and have a whiskey and a chat before heading up to bed.

Since seeing the photograph, and his father's service records, Gaughran had started to question everything about his family. How did they afford to live in a large, detached house? His mum had never worked. His dad had told her it was far more important that she was there for Gaughran and his brother Steve. There were holidays to Spain or Portugal every year and nice cars. Gaughran knew his dad had been on the relatively decent salary of a DI by the time he took retirement, but were the house, holidays and cars a sign of something darker?

He tried to compose himself as he knocked on the door. He didn't want to alarm his mum, Celia. She worried about everything at the best of times.

The front door opened, and she looked out at him and smiled. 'Bloody hell, what you doing here?'

He forced a smile and gave her a hug and kiss. 'That's nice, Mum.'

Her face was filled with concern. 'Why aren't you working? What's wrong?'

Gaughran followed her in. 'Nothing Mum. Nothing's wrong. I just had a bit of time off and I wanted to talk to dad about this case I'm working on.'

As he followed her into the spotless kitchen, Gaughran felt a sense of calm and security. There were photos of the four of them on various holidays in frames on the walls, along with a photo of Steve on his wedding day.

Celia went over to the kettle and clicked it on. 'You'll stay for a cuppa, won't you?'

Gaughran nodded. It wasn't a question. 'Where's Dad then?'

'He's up the golf club with your Uncle Les. Might as well live up at that bloody place,' his mum groaned.

'Better than having him under your feet here all day.'

Celia laughed. 'You're right there. Messy bugger.' Celia looked at him and frowned. 'You all right? You look a bit peaky. Do you want something to eat? I can make you a sandwich if you like.'

Gaughran forced a smile and shook his head. 'It's all right, Mum. I'm fine, honest.'

'When are you gonna bring that Michelle round here for us to meet?' she asked with an indignant look. 'Anyone would think you were ashamed of us.'

Gaughran sighed. 'I told you, Mum. I'm not seeing her anymore.'

'Oh, that's a shame. She sounded nice. Wasn't she the one whose dad was a headmaster?'

'Yeah, that's right.' Gaughran looked over at her. He wasn't sure how to broach the subject. 'Mum, you know when we were kids?'

Celia looked over at him as she made two mugs of tea. 'Eh? What about when you were kids?'

'You know this house, the holidays, season tickets at Chelsea, new cars. Did you ever wonder where all the money came from?' Gaughran asked.

'What are you talking about? Your dad worked round the clock. And in those days he got bloody good money for doing overtime,' Celia explained. 'What's all this about?'

'Nothing. Don't worry,' Gaughran said. He could feel his anxiety rising. 'Look, I've got to go and talk to Dad right now.'

'I've just made you a tea,' Celia protested.

'Sorry,' Gaughran said as he turned and headed for the door. 'I'll pop back later. Promise.'

He needed to get this over and done with.

CHAPTER 32

It was evening, and Brooks had followed Lucy back to her house to have a 'summit' about the events of the week, Karen's allegations, and their relationship. They both agreed that it was getting in the way at work and so there needed to be some kind of resolution either way.

Pulling up outside her house, Lucy looked at herself in the rear-view mirror. *Bloody hell, I look tired!* She remembered a phrase that her father used to say – *You've got more luggage under there than Heathrow airport.*

She climbed out, closed the car door and sighed. What she really needed was a stiff drink, a hot bath, and an early night. Watching Brooks park his car nearby, she stood and waited for him by the path leading up to her front door. For a few seconds, she gazed at him as he walked towards her. She still fancied the pants off him, but that wasn't going to be enough if they couldn't resolve all the other stuff.

Taking off his jacket, Brooks looked at her. 'I've no idea why I'm wearing this jacket.' She could see he was nervous and for a moment he looked like a lost little boy.

'Come on then. We can sit out on the patio,' Lucy said, but as she turned to walk up the path, she noticed that something wasn't quite right.

The gate to the side entrance was open by about a foot.

'You all right, Luce? You look like you've just seen a ghost.'

'The side gate is open.'

'Sure you shut it properly?' he asked.

'Don't be a twat, Harry. After what I've been through this week I've checked it every day. There are two bolts on the inside.'

Brooks marched up the path determinedly. 'Stay there.'

'Sod that! I'm coming with you,' Lucy snapped – she was a DC and didn't need to be patronised, thank you very much.

They went cautiously through the open gate and down the dark, cool passageway at the side of the house.

Moving slowly towards the back garden, Lucy couldn't hear anything. If she was going to make a guess, then she thought that Karen might have something to do with the gate being open.

Lucy and Brooks came out onto the patio at the rear of the house.

There was someone sitting in one of the garden chairs, wrapped in a blanket, facing them.

It was Karen.

Lucy shot Brooks a look – *Are you kidding me?*

'Karen, what the hell are you doing?' Brooks asked.

Lucy was immediately on her guard. Karen's behaviour had been strange and erratic enough to warrant extreme caution. She was half-expecting her to bring out a knife and go for them both.

Karen gave a strange smile. She looked tired, grey, and very unwell. 'I've come to talk to the both of you. I need to apologise for everything.'

Her voice was slurred, and Lucy assumed she was drunk. As she tried to stand up, they could see that she was very unsteady on her feet. 'Lucy, if you knew Harry as well as I do, then you'd know that he would never hit a woman. He's a gentle giant, aren't you, Harry? He wouldn't harm a fly ...'

As Karen tried to maintain her balance, the blanket fell from her and onto the ground.

Lucy gasped as she saw that below her waist Karen was completely soaked in blood. There was a deep gash on either wrist.

Oh my God. She's bleeding to death!

Brooks rushed over to her as she fell back down on the chair. 'Jesus Christ, Karen. What have you done?'

'I'm so sorry ...' Karen burbled as she wept. 'I'm so, so sorry ...'

Lucy pulled out her phone and dialled 999. 'Ambulance please. As quickly as possible.'

THE SKY WAS A GUNMETAL grey by the time Gaughran pulled into the car park at the golf club. As the first drops of rain fell, he looked around for his father's BMW. He spotted his Uncle Les' black Mercedes at the far end, so he was definitely somewhere out on the course.

After a quick look around the clubhouse bar and restaurant, Gaughran tried to ring both their mobile phones. He wasn't surprised to find that they were switched off. He knew they took their golf seriously, and the joy of the game was to get away from everything and find a bit of peace and quiet.

Standing by the main entrance to the clubhouse, Gaughran saw that the sky was full of rain and could feel that the temperature had dropped. He didn't fancy traipsing around a hundred-acre course and getting soaked. He walked over to the reception area and looked at the young man behind the desk.

'I'm trying to find Arthur and Les Gaughran. I don't suppose you know what time they teed off?' he asked.

The man shrugged. 'Sorry. I saw them arrive, but I didn't see what time they started.'

A middle-aged man in golfing gear looked over. 'If you're looking for Les, he's on the driving range.'

'Thanks.' Gaughran turned and jogged towards the driving range as the rain began to fall. He soon spotted his Uncle Les in a bright yellow jumper smashing a ball with a golf club.

'Les?' Gaughran shouted as he approached.

Les frowned and looked at his watch. 'What are you doing here, Tim?'

'Looking for dad.'

Les pulled a face. 'Everything all right?'

'Sort of. I just need to have a chat with him about something.'

'Sounds ominous,' Les said.

'I thought you two were playing golf today?'

'Yeah. We decided to come to the driving range instead. Then he got a phone call and said he had to go. To be honest, he was acting strange.'

Gaughran shook his head. 'I've been home, and he's not there, so where did he go?'

'He told me the phone call was from your mum. She wanted a few days away, so they were going to jump in the car this afternoon and head down to the caravan.'

Gaughran immediately knew that was bullshit. His mum would have mentioned it. 'What's he talking about? I've just seen mum.'

Les looked worried and put his club back in his bag. 'Yeah, I knew he was lying. What's going on?'

He had known Les all his life and trusted him implicitly. But Les had worked as a copper for thirty-five years before retiring. Like his father, Les wouldn't have a bad word said against any police officer and had made some inflammatory comments about the Stephen Lawrence case.

'There's some stuff about that old case I'm working on. It might be to do with that,' Gaughran said, unwilling to reveal much more.

'He didn't mention it. And you know your dad, he tells me everything.' Les snorted. 'Sometimes I wish he wouldn't.'

'Did he ever mention anything about the 211 Club over in Balham when he first worked as a DC?'

'Bloody hell, Tim. We talked about that the other day. That's over forty years ago. Your dad had only just started to shave. You got a suspect yet?'

'No. Do you remember it? Alfie Wise going missing?' Gaughran asked.

Les shook his head. 'Not really. I was still at school. I remember that kid he killed down on Balham station. That was all over the papers.' Les looked directly at him. 'If I were you, I would leave all that well alone.'

Gaughran frowned. 'What does that mean, Les?'

'You might wanna encourage the investigation not to look too hard at any police involvement. The Met's taken enough of a bashing over that fucking Lawrence case.'

'Are you telling me that dad was involved in something?'

Les looked at him. 'I'm not saying anything, son. What I *am* saying to you is that you've only got one dad, so you'd better remember that.'

CHAPTER 33

Even though it was only dawn, most of the CID officers were in and working. Taking a sip of her hot coffee, Ruth was looking through a paper trail of faxes and documents, some of which she had requested be sent over from Companies House the previous day.

Lucy, who was holding a pile of papers, came over and sat down next to her. She had already told Ruth about the events with Karen last night.

'You okay?' Ruth asked kindly. Lucy looked tired and Ruth was worried about the amount of stress she had been under in recent days.

'Yeah, fine. The hospital where they took Karen rang to speak to Harry just now. They've sectioned her and sent her over to Springfield Hospital,' Lucy explained.

'That's awful. But not surprising after what's happened this week. How do you feel?' Ruth asked.

'Relieved, actually. She clearly needs help and now she's in the best place to get it. Harry seems to be blaming himself.'

'Now this has happened, maybe you and Harry can sort things out?' Ruth suggested.

Lucy forced a smile. 'Yeah. I'm sure we can.'

Hassan approached them looking slightly troubled. 'Anyone seen Tim this morning?'

Ruth shook her head. 'Not yet. He doesn't really blend into the background, so I would have noticed if he'd been in.'

'I can't find him anywhere.'

'You all right, Syed? You look very worried,' Lucy said, her voice full of concern.

Hassan held up a folder to show them. 'This is Arthur Gaughran's police service record.'

Ruth could see how anxious he was. 'What's the problem?'

He glanced around to make sure that no one else was in earshot. 'Arthur Gaughran joined CID in January 1956 and was a DC in the South London Murder Squad by April 1956.'

Ruth and Lucy looked at each other – *he was lying to us!*

'What? But he told us he was just a bobby on the beat back then,' Ruth exclaimed – she was feeling very uneasy about what Hassan had just told them.

'And why would he lie to you unless he had something to hide?' Hassan asked. 'There's no way he would have forgotten something like that.'

'Have you told Brooks?' Lucy asked.

Hassan shook his head. 'No. I wanted to give Tim the heads-up first, but I can't find him.'

'You need to take this to Brooks right now,' Ruth said with urgency. It wasn't something that they could sit on for any length of time.

'Yeah, I know.' Hassan nodded. 'The only thing is, I'm pretty certain that I saw Tim looking at this file last night. And now he's not come in.'

Brooks came into CID and, when he saw Ruth, Lucy and Hassan together, he approached them.

Ruth said in a low voice, 'Guv, we need to talk to you about something.'

Brooks looked at the file that Hassan was holding. 'Is that Arthur Gaughran's service record?'

Hassan nodded. 'Yeah. That's what we need to talk to you about, guv.'

'I know all about it and so does Tim,' Brooks said. 'I'm dealing with it right now.'

Lucy could see the stress in his eyes. 'We need to pull Arthur Gaughran in here this morning.'

Brooks smoothed his hand over his chin, looking angry. 'I know that, Luce. You need to let me deal with it in the right way. It's all in hand.'

Hassan frowned. 'Is that why Tim isn't in this morning, guv?'

Brooks didn't say anything.

AS GAUGHRAN SHIFTED on the back seat of his car, he opened his eyes and realised it was dawn. He sat up, rubbed his face and stretched, remembering that he was now in the Fairlight Caravan Park, just south of Hastings on the East Sussex coast.

Having arrived just after midnight, he had spotted his father's car parked up outside their caravan and banged on the door. There had been no answer. Gaughran knew his father was naturally a light sleeper and sometimes took sleeping pills so it might be difficult to wake him. There had been little option but to sleep in the car until the morning.

Gaughran had spent much of the journey down wondering who had phoned his father at the golf course and why he had then headed to Hastings on his own. As far as Gaughran knew, he'd never been to the caravan without his mother. Did his father have some inkling that they were looking at his service records or that they had spoken to Michael Fisher and now had an incriminating photograph? Is that what the phone call was about? Had someone inside Peckham nick rung to warn him he was under investigation, after which he'd disappeared down to Hastings?

Opening the car door, Gaughran got out and blinked in the early morning light. He glanced over at the luxury static caravan, and was alarmed to see that his father's car had gone.

Bollocks!

What concerned him even more was that Gaughran had deliberately parked his car directly outside the caravan. There was no way his father could have left without spotting his son's car.

Where the hell has he gone and why didn't he wake me? The thought made Gaughran feel very uneasy.

He went to the door of the caravan and peered through the glass.

'You looking for Arthur?' came a voice. It was an elderly man walking a dog.

'Yeah, he's my dad.'

'You must be Tim. He talks about you a lot,' the man said with a smile.

Gaughran pointed to the car parking space at the side of the caravan. 'His car's not there so he must have gone out.'

'Yeah. He sometimes drives down the coast to walk the dog.'

'Do you know where?' Gaughran asked.

'He likes walking over the cliffs at Seven Sisters – you could try there,' the man said.

Gaughran nodded as he got back in his car. 'Thanks.'

He knew exactly where the cliffs at Seven Sisters were. He'd been there a few times with his dad when he was younger. They were spectacular white chalk cliffs that were five hundred feet above the sea.

However, they were also only a mile from the cliffs at Beachy Head, the most notorious suicide spot in Britain.

CHAPTER 34

'I've got something!' Ruth said loudly as she circled the words *Cavendish Travel* on the document in front of her.

Lucy grinned as she came over. 'Oh God, well don't come near me, I don't want to catch it.'

Ruth rolled her eyes. 'You're hilarious.'

'Thanks.' Lucy pointed to her notepad. 'By the way, the manager from the Chelsea Arts Club rang. Charlie Wise was in there until well after midnight.'

'Not a big surprise. If he had anything to do with Walsh's murder, he's bound to have a watertight alibi.'

Lucy indicated Ruth's paperwork. 'So, what have you got?'

Ruth looked at her. 'Guess who owns Cavendish Travel?'

Lucy frowned. 'How many guesses do I get?'

Ruth ignored her and tapped the company documents that were in front of her with her finger. 'Right, so Cavendish Travel is owned by an offshore parent company called Hanover Leisure. However, with a bit of digging, it turns out that Hanover Leisure is a subsidiary of Stanmore Holdings.'

Lucy's eyes widened. 'Which is owned by Charlie Wise.'

'I rang the London branch that we went to the other day, and it also turns out that Cavendish Travel has eight more branches throughout the UK.'

'Okay, I know you're going somewhere with this but at the moment I'm not sure where.'

'Guess where else they have a branch?'

Lucy rolled her eyes. 'What is this, CID quiz night? I don't know.'

'It was a rhetorical guess.'

Lucy smiled. 'I don't think you can have a rhetorical guess. Rhetorical question, yes. Rhetorical guess, no.'

'Lucy?'

'Yes.'

'Shut up.' Ruth pointed to her pad. 'Belfast. Cavendish Travel has a branch in Belfast.'

'Right. And you're wondering whether they were involved in arranging Damian O'Connell's travel from Belfast to London?'

Ruth nodded. 'I rang them already. They're looking for any bookings for a Damian O'Connell or a Daniel Keane. They're going to fax me if they find anything.'

'You think Charlie arranged for Walsh to be murdered? Why?'

'Walsh was seen in the car with Charlie and Alfie on the day that Alfie was supposed to have gone missing,' Ruth said. 'And so Walsh might have been present if anything had happened to Alfie that night.'

Lucy nodded. 'He might have even helped Charlie.'

'We know Charlie paid Walsh a retainer every month. He said it was for odd jobs like driving. What if it was just hush money? Walsh knew that Charlie killed Alfie and was being paid for the last forty years to keep quiet,' Ruth explained.

'Why did Charlie kill Alfie?'

Ruth shrugged. 'He threatened to go to the police if his brother didn't go straight. Maybe he was worried that his big brother was going to end up in prison or dead?'

Lucy frowned. 'So he just shot and buried Alfie? I'm not sure I buy that.'

Their attention was distracted as Brooks marched into CID and came over. 'Anything on O'Connell?'

'We could have a lead on the company that might have booked his travel. There's a paper trail that shows Cavendish Travel is technically owned by Charlie Wise.'

Brooks' eyes widened. 'Jesus.'

'They're going to fax over anything of interest,' Ruth said.

Putting down the phone, Hassan looked over. 'Guv, the tech boys gave me a list of numbers dialled from the mobile phone that we found on Damian O'Connell.'

Brooks raised an eyebrow. 'Anything interesting?'

Hassan nodded. 'Yes, guv. O'Connell rang the same mobile phone number twenty three times in the week leading up to Trevor Walsh's murder.'

'And you've got that number?' Lucy asked.

Hassan smiled. 'Better than that. The phone is registered to an Emma Maddocks. Home address in Fulham. She set the phone up with a standing order so I was able to trace her bank account. It seems that she has a monthly salary paid by Stanmore Holdings ...'

'... which we know is owned by Charlie Wise,' Brooks added.

Ruth and Lucy locked eyes.

Hassan continued, 'It gets even better! Turns out that Emma Maddocks is Charles Wise's PA.'

As the fax whirred nearby, Brooks looked at them all. 'Right, we now have a direct link between Charlie Wise and the man who probably murdered Trevor Walsh.'

Ruth went over to collect the incoming fax and saw that it was from Cavendish Travel in Belfast. 'Guv, this is what I was waiting for.'

Taking it from the machine, Ruth read it and looked over at them all. 'This is it. Cavendish Travel arranged flights, a hotel, and a rental car for a Daniel Keane. He flew from Belfast to Heathrow the night before Trevor Walsh's death.'

Brooks was suddenly energised as he looked around the CID office. 'Right, everyone, listen up! I'll go upstairs and get an arrest warrant signed off. Then I'll talk to the CPS. Syed, see if you can get a Section 18 Search Warrant for Charlie Wise's home and offices ... Lucy and Ruth, I want him arrested and brought here as soon as you can.'

CHAPTER 35

E ven though the sun was burning away the early morning clouds, the wind that lashed across the tops of the Seven Sisters clifftops was icy and biting. Gaughran pulled his jacket around him, but he was still chilled to the bone. He had been walking for about fifteen minutes and there was still no sign of his father, or his car.

The ink-blue English Channel stretched away to his left. It was less than sixty miles across the water to the French mainland. Gulls swooped and squawked with a relentless urgency, which only added to Gaughran's anxiety. He had no idea if his father had come for a bracing morning walk with the dog, or for a much darker purpose. There was no mobile signal, so there was no way of contacting him.

For a moment, he was reminded of the cold windy days playing football for East Peckham United when he was a kid. His father rarely missed a match and would shout encouragement from the touchline. Some of the other fathers would swear and berate their sons for their mistakes, but his father was always encouraging and positive. He remembered winning a Man of the Match trophy and his dad taking him to McDonalds to celebrate. The thought of it brought a lump to his throat.

Marching on against the wind, Gaughran spotted a lone figure up ahead, close to the cliff's edge. At that distance, he couldn't make out much more than it was a man. Moving closer, he joined a muddy pathway that led along the clifftops. He could see the vast white cliff faces reflected in the shallow water and the jagged rocks below.

As the wind grew stronger, it howled unnervingly. He squinted to see ahead as a dark cloud moved across the sun, throwing an inky shadow across the clifftops. As he got closer to the man, Gaughran saw a dog running back and to. It was Jack, his father's German Shepherd.

And so the man on the cliff's edge was his father.

Picking up speed, he couldn't tell if his father was merely peering out to sea or on the verge of throwing himself into a dark oblivion.

'Dad!' He shouted at the top of his voice, but it was lost in the roaring moan of the wind. 'Dad!'

His father moved closer to the cliff edge and looked down.

Oh, God! Please don't jump!

Gaughran began to run. 'Dad! Dad! he yelled.

Even though he was only thirty yards away, his father didn't react. Either he didn't hear him or he was ignoring his shouts.

His father was now only two feet from the cliff edge.

Pumping his arms as he ran, Gaughran sprinted until he was only ten yards away. 'Dad!' he screamed breathlessly. 'What the hell are you doing?'

Arthur averted his eyes. 'You found me then?'

'What are you doing here, Dad?' Gaughran asked as he came beside him.

'Good question.'

'I need to talk to you about something.'

'Yeah, I know.'

'How do you know?' he asked with a confused expression. 'Someone tip you off from our nick?'

For a few seconds, Arthur just gazed down at the waves that were rolling onto the rocks five hundred feet below. 'You remember when I brought you and Steve up here to fly your kites?'

Gaughran nodded. 'Yeah. Steve let his go and it flew down into the sea. I thought you were going to go mental, but you didn't. You just bought him a new one.'

Arthur turned slowly and looked directly in his eyes. 'Yeah. Someone down in records gave me a bell. At least someone had my back.'

'What's that supposed to mean?'

'You know what I'm talking about.'

'You need to tell me what happened, Dad.'

Arthur looked over to where Jack was sitting and panting with his tongue hanging out. 'Yeah. Well, that's easier said than done. And you could lose your job.'

'My gaffer knows I'm here,' Gaughran said.

Arthur looked disappointed. 'You went to him first?'

'What did you expect me to do?'

'What do you think you know?'

'We went to see Michael Fisher.'

'I thought you might. What did he tell you?'

'He gave us a photograph. You and Clive Rigby in the 211 Club together. The club you said you'd never been to.'

Arthur shrugged. 'Doesn't prove very much except we were having a drink there once.'

'Fucking hell, Dad. This isn't about what anyone can prove. There are people out there, and in Peckham CID, who are going to think you murdered Alfie Wise,' Gaughran said angrily.

Arthur looked directly at him. 'It wasn't us. I can promise you that.'

'Then who killed him?' Gaughran asked.

'I dunno. I've no idea. He just vanished one day.'

Gaughran looked into his eyes. He didn't know what to believe. 'What about the backhanders?'

Arthur looked at the ground and shook his head. 'No.'

'That's bollocks, Dad, and you know it!' Gaughran snapped as he glared at his father. 'We've got multiple descriptions of a tall, thin, young DC in the South London Murder Squad, who walked with a limp, being paid off by Charlie Wise.'

Arthur took a deep breath and said, 'You don't understand, Tim. It was a different time. Everyone was at it. It was no different to giving a tip to your barber or a cabbie.'

'Fuck off. It's completely different!' Gaughran bellowed, his anger spiked. 'It's corruption, Dad, and you know it.'

'I don't expect you to understand. Back in those days, a DC's salary was a pittance.'

'You can't justify it. I just don't understand. You've always told me you hated bent coppers?'

'I wasn't talking about taking a few quid forty years ago. Don't be so bloody naïve, Tim.'

Gaughran stared coldly at his father. 'What about Declan Fisher?'

'That was Rigby. I gave Fisher a clip but Rigby took it too far.'

'But you didn't stop him?'

'No. Like I said, it was a different time.' Arthur said nothing for a few seconds. 'Clubs like the 211 expected to pay us something so punters could drink and gamble after hours. It was just part of the deal. Same with snouts. You'd bung them a few quid for some information or give them a clip if they stepped out of line.'

'What about Trevor Walsh?' Gaughran asked.

'Never heard of him.'

'You sure? We heard he was working as a snout for you lot. He was murdered three days ago.'

'And you think I had something to do with it?'

'Bloody hell, Dad. I don't know what to believe right now.'

'So, now what?'

'I've got to take you in. You need to come to the station with me and tell us what you know.'

'I'm not going to prison. It would kill your mother.'

Gaughran nodded. 'I know that, Dad. But they were coming for you anyway. I just asked my gaffer if I could be the one to bring you in.'

Arthur looked at him. 'And if I don't come with you?'

'Why, what are you going to do? Jump off a fucking cliff instead?'

'Wouldn't be a bad idea.'

'You're a selfish bastard, you know that?' Gaughran took a breath and blinked away the wetness from his eyes. 'You were my bloody hero, Dad. I worshipped the ground you walked on. I became a copper because I wanted to be like you.'

'Yeah, well I'm sorry about that.'

Gaughran gritted his teeth as he felt the tears well up. He refused to bloody cry. 'Is that it?'

'I don't know what else to say. What's done is done.' Arthur whistled to the dog and put him on his lead. 'You'd better take me in then, hadn't you?'

CHAPTER 36

Having established that Charlie Wise was not at his Wimbledon home, Ruth and Lucy headed for the Southbank offices of Stanmore Holdings. The traffic was heavy as they passed Waterloo Station.

As Ruth buzzed down the window, she could see that the blue skies were now giving way to dark, low clouds that seemed to suck the light and colour from the London streets. Reaching for a cigarette, she glanced over at Lucy.

'You know, Charlie had me fooled from day one,' Ruth admitted.

'Me too.'

'He was so convincing when we told him we had found Alfie's remains.'

'And when he saw the signet ring.'

Ruth shook her head. 'Maybe I'm losing my touch but I really liked him.'

Lucy shrugged. 'I've met some very charming killers in my time.'

They headed around the roundabout at the foot of Waterloo Bridge and went east along Stamford Street, before cutting right and passing the back of the National Theatre.

'Christ, I haven't been to the theatre in years,' Ruth said.

Lucy nodded. 'I went with my mum to see Miss Saigon a couple of years ago.'

'Miss Saigon isn't the theatre, darling,' Ruth said in an exaggerated upper-class voice.

'Isn't it? Do you mean boring, long plays about posh people?' Lucy asked.

'I suppose I do.' Ruth pointed to the National Theatre building. 'I've been there once. On a school trip to see 'King Lear' because we were doing it for A-level.'

Lucy frowned. 'You did A-levels?'

'Oh thanks. I'm not a complete thicko,' Ruth laughed. 'Anthony Hopkins was playing King Lear. And in the storm scene, he took all his clothes off. And I mean *all* his clothes.'

Lucy's eyes widened. 'You went on a school trip and ended up seeing Hannibal Lecter's todger live on stage? How's that okay? Your teacher should have been sacked.'

Ruth laughed. 'Actually I thought it was great.'

'Anthony Hopkins' tackle?'

'No, stupid. The play. It was very dramatic.'

Lucy rolled her eyes. 'Yeah, it bloody sounds it.'

'Here we go,' Ruth said, pulling the car over and parking in a space just outside the enormous tower block that housed Stanmore Holdings' offices.

Turning off the ignition, Ruth took a deep breath as she thought of the prospect of arresting Sir Charles Wise, a knight of the realm and minor celebrity, for conspiracy to murder.

'Ready to go?' Lucy asked as she got out.

Ruth noticed that the sky was almost black, and it had started to rain. 'Yes, let's do this.'

As she glanced down the road, Ruth noted that Hassan and a marked patrol car had also parked. A few seconds later, Hassan and two uniformed officers joined them as they began to walk up the stone steps and into the reception area.

Ruth approached the security guard and flashed her warrant card. 'DC Hunter, Peckham CID. We're going up to the 17th floor.'

He ushered them through to the lifts.

A few minutes later, the doors opened and Ruth, Lucy, Hassan and the two officers came out into the seated reception area of Stanmore Holdings.

Ruth and Lucy marched over to the receptionist, whom they recognised from before. She looked a little startled by their arrival and because there were five of them.

'Erm, are you looking for Sir Charles?' she asked, clearly flustered.

Hassan stepped forward and showed her the warrant. 'We have a Section 18 Search Warrant for these premises. Someone should alert your staff that we will be taking statements and removing anything we feel is relevant to our investigation.'

Without waiting for a response, Hassan took out his warrant card and, with the two uniformed officers in tow, marched through the doors and into the central office.

Lucy pointed to where Charlie's office was located. 'Is Sir Charles in? This is very delicate, but it's very important that we see him right this second.'

'Erm, I don't think he's in,' the receptionist replied as her eyes blinked nervously. 'Let me try the line.'

Ruth gave her a smile. 'It's all right, we know the way.'

Lucy and Ruth strode through the doors and headed left across the open plan office to Charlie's corner office. The staff looked confused by the sudden appearance of police officers.

As they arrived at the office door, Ruth could see through the glass that no one was inside.

'Can I help?' asked an approaching PA with a forced smile.

'Are you Emma Maddocks?' Ruth asked.

The PA shook her head. 'No. Emma's not in today.'

Lucy pointed to the empty office and asked brusquely, 'Where is he?'

The PA pulled a face. 'Are you looking for Sir Charles?'

'We need to see him immediately,' Ruth said sternly.

'Oh, he's not available, I'm afraid,' the PA said with a haughty look.

Lucy looked at Ruth as if to say, *This woman is getting right up my nose.*

'We have to see him now. So, you need to tell us where he is,' snapped Lucy.

The PA raised her shoulders. 'I can't possibly reveal Sir Charles' itinerary.'

Lucy glared at her. 'What's your name?'

Here we go, thought Ruth.

The PA looked concerned. 'Penny, why?'

Lucy let out an audible sigh. 'Listen *Penny*, we are working on a double murder investigation. We have an arrest warrant with us. If you obstruct us executing that warrant, then I am also going to arrest *you* under Section 68 of the Criminal Justice and Public Order Act. I'm then going to put you in a piss-ridden cell in Peckham Police Station where you can sit for the rest of the day until I decide to interview you. And if I'm really fucked off, you can stay there overnight.'

Penny looked terrified. 'You can't do that!'

Lucy reached for the handcuffs on her belt. 'Watch me.'

Penny put a hand up and mumbled, 'Sir Charles is going to the airport.'

'Which airport?' Ruth asked.

'Heathrow.'

'Where's he flying to?'

'Spain. Malaga.'

'When?'

'One thirty.'

'Thank you. And I assume he's travelling with Lesley Harlow?' Ruth asked. She was the business associate that they had learned about on their visit to Cavendish Travel.

The PA nodded. 'I think that was the plan.'

Lucy patted the PA on the arm with a smile. 'You see? That wasn't difficult, was it?'

Ruth glanced at her watch. It was just gone eleven. 'Two and a half hours before he flies.'

Lucy gestured to the doors. 'Better get our skates on then.'

CHAPTER 37

Having left his father down in Peckham nick's custody suite, Gaughran made his way up to CID and headed for Brooks' office. The journey back from East Sussex had been made in virtual silence. Gaughran was desperate to believe that his father hadn't been involved in Alfie Wise's murder. He knew that there was a vast gulf between taking backhanders from a club and giving a local villain a bit of a kicking, to the cold-blooded assassination of a teenager.

Taking a breath to steady himself, Gaughran looked in at Brooks, who was sitting at his desk. He knocked on the open door.

Brooks looked up at him and said quietly, 'Come in and close the door, Tim.'

As Gaughran took a step inside the office, Hassan walked past. 'Where the hell have you been?' he asked in a light-hearted tone.

'Long story, mate. I need to talk to the guv,' Gaughran said as he began to close the door.

'Come and find me when you're done,' Hassan said.

Gaughran went over to Brooks' desk and sat down. He was so tired that he couldn't think straight.

'You okay?' Brooks asked.

Gaughran was all over the place. 'Yes, guv.'

'Is he with you?'

'Yeah. He's waiting down in the custody suite.'

'What did he say?'

'He and Rigby had nothing to do with Alfie Wise's murder,' Gaughran said. 'He admitted off the record that they had taken backhanders from the 211 Club and that it was Rigby who put Declan Fisher in a coma.'

'And you believe him?' Brooks asked.

Gaughran nodded slowly. 'I have to.'

Brooks looked directly at him. 'There's been a significant development. We've just issued a warrant for Sir Charles Wise's arrest.'

Gaughran's eyes widened. 'Bloody hell! What's the charge?'

'Conspiracy to murder,' Brooks said. 'We can link him to Damian O'Connell, the man who likely killed Trevor Walsh.'

Gaughran was taken aback for a moment. And then he realised the implication of this. 'That means we think Wise murdered his brother?'

'Yes ... I think the night Charlie Wise, Alfie, and Walsh were spotted in the car by our eyewitness, was also the night that Alfie was murdered,' Brooks said. 'Walsh was there and probably helped Wise to bury his body. It explains why Wise paid him off for years to keep him quiet.'

'And you think Wise was scared that Walsh was going to crack now that Alfie's body has been found?'

'Walsh only had weeks to live. He had nothing to lose by getting the truth off his chest. Wise must have guessed that Walsh was going to eventually tell us what really happened to Alfie. So, he paid someone to fly in and shut him up.'

Gaughran nodded. 'And that puts my old man in the clear on that count.'

'Yeah. The allegations against him aren't going to be relevant to our investigation. I'm going to have to hand it over to the ghost squad and they'll contact him.' The ghost squad was slang for Scotland Yard's Anti-Corruption Unit.

Gaughran blew out his cheeks. 'Do you think he'll do time?'

Brooks shook his head. 'No. He can put his lie to us about the timing of his entry into CID as a lapse of memory. All the allegations against him and Rigby are unsubstantiated. Basically, they're just hearsay. There's no evidence that they took bribes.'

'But we know he was bent,' Gaughran said sourly.

'Yeah. And I'm sorry. It must be hard to find that out?'

Gaughran took a few seconds. It still didn't feel real. He'd spent the past twenty five years believing that his father was a brave, honourable copper with an impeccable service record in the Met. 'He was my hero. It's going to be tough to get my head round this.'

Brooks gave him a sympathetic look. 'You think you two will get past it?'

'I don't know,' Gaughran said. 'He's a stubborn, unforgiving bastard.'

'You've done nothing wrong, Tim. We were going to bring him in anyway,' Brooks said. 'Your dad took bribes to look the other way. And he stood by while another man was beaten into a coma. *You've* got nothing to be ashamed of.'

'Yeah. I hope my family see it like that,' Gaughran said.

Brooks picked up the phone. 'Do you want me to ring down to the custody suite and release him now?'

Gaughran nodded as he stood up. 'Thanks, guv. I'd rather not see him again today.'

As Gaughran went to the door, Brooks looked at him. 'Tim?'

'Yes, guv.'

'You did the right thing. Don't let there be any confusion in your mind about that.'

'Thanks, guv,' he said as he went out of the door and watched as Brooks rang down to the custody suite.

Walking away from Brooks' office, Gaughran felt numb. He reached the end of the corridor and stood in the stairwell. A couple of CID officers from the Drugs Squad smiled hello as they came up the stairs and passed him.

In that moment, Gaughran realised that his entire belief system, everything he thought he knew and trusted, had been taken away. His entire body shook as he leant on the railings and gazed out of the large window that overlooked the station's car park. He felt sick.

Out of the corner of his eye, he spotted a figure coming down the short flight of stone steps that led out of the back entrance.

It was his father.

Gaughran watched him, hoping to see a flicker of contrition or shame.

There was nothing.

His father strolled across the car park as if he owned the place and didn't have a care in the world.

What a prick.

As if somehow aware that Gaughran was watching him, his father turned and looked in his direction.

Their eyes met for a second.

His father's face was expressionless as he turned back and walked away across the car park.

CHAPTER 38

Ruth and Lucy had been searching Heathrow Airport for over twenty minutes but had seen no sign yet of Charlie Wise or his female companion, Lesley Harlow. They had no idea if she was a business associate or a romantic companion. They scoured the huge seating area and bars close to the check-in desks. They were still waiting for Heathrow Security to check their passenger lists for all flights to Malaga that day. There were seven, so it was going to take a while.

Ruth's mobile phone rang, and she answered it. 'DC Hunter?'

'It's Kevin Abbott again at Heathrow Security.'

Ruth had spoken to Kevin twice on the journey to the airport to advise him who they were looking for and to explain the serious nature of the investigation.

'Hi Kevin. Any luck tracking them down?' Ruth asked hopefully.

'Sorry. I've checked all the flights to Malaga today. None of them have first or business class,' Kevin explained. 'I've had Security do a sweep through the first class and business lounges but there's no one matching the description of your suspects.'

'Thanks Kevin. I'm guessing they must be out here somewhere. What about the passenger lists?'

'We've checked five out of seven and your passengers aren't on them. I'm chasing the other two.'

'Thanks Kevin. Call me as soon as you've got them.' Ruth ended the phone call. She then looked at Lucy and said, 'Looks like Sir Charles Wise and his lady friend are going to have to slum it in economy.'

'Poor them,' Lucy said sarcastically and then gestured to the escalators. 'Come on, they've got to be in here somewhere.'

Taking the escalators to the first floor shopping precinct, Ruth scanned the busy concourse. It was August, which was holiday season, so the airport was rammed. There were 100,000 passengers flying out of Heathrow that day.

Ruth gave Lucy a frustrated look. 'Make a sentence out of haystack and needle.'

Lucy went over to the central concourse. 'We've been everywhere, haven't we?'

By now, Ruth was wondering if they were wasting their time.

'Where would you go if you wanted to keep out of sight at an airport?' Ruth asked.

Lucy pointed over to a large but dimly-lit pub. 'I'd hide in a dark bar in the corner out of the way.'

'As good a place as any,' Ruth agreed.

They turned and headed for the pub entrance where guests in fancy dress at a rowdy stag do were chanting a football song.

Moving forward into the darkened pub, Ruth scanned the customers. It was busy, noisy, and a little difficult to see much.

They gradually made their way towards the back.

Suddenly, two figures rose from their seats on the other side and headed towards the nearest exit.

It was Charlie and his companion, Lesley. They were wearing baseball caps and sunglasses.

'Over there!' Ruth yelled, tapping Lucy's shoulder.

Got you, you bastards!

They broke into a run across the pub, barging past customers at the bar.

'Police, out of the way!'

Following Charlie out of the exit, they looked left and then right.

Nothing.

'Where are they?' Lucy growled.

Ruth spotted Charlie heading back towards the escalators, with Lesley Harlow close behind.

'There!' she said, and they set off again.

Ruth watched as Charlie pushed people aside and ran down the escalators to the ground floor.

'Police! Move out of the way!' Ruth yelled as she and Lucy zig-zagged down the moving escalator.

By the time they reached the bottom, Charlie and Lesley had disappeared again.

'Down this way!' Lucy urged, as she took over the lead and they headed towards passport control.

Now out of breath, they arrived at the entrance to passport control. Glancing around, there was no sign of them.

Ruth took out her warrant card as she jogged through security to check the queues of passengers who were waiting to get through to the departure lounges on the other side.

Frantically scanning to the right and the left, she couldn't see Charlie or Lesley anywhere.

Lucy shook her head. 'How can they have vanished?'

With her pulse still racing, Ruth shrugged. 'I don't bloody know.'

HASSAN AND GAUGHRAN were sitting at their desks when Brooks came into the CID office. Gaughran had been distracted by the events with his father. He couldn't remember ever feeling this anxious or disturbed before. His train of thought was broken as Brooks approached.

'Ruth and Lucy have spotted Charlie Wise at Heathrow Airport. I'm liaising with SO18 so we can make sure that he doesn't leave the country,' Brooks said. SO18 was the Aviation Security Operational Command Unit, which was essentially Met police officers at the airport.

Hassan looked over. 'Have they narrowed down which flight he's supposed to be on yet?'

Brooks shook his head. 'No, Heathrow are dragging their poxy feet.'

Gaughran gestured to a file that he was looking at. 'Guv, I've found a record of Trevor Walsh working as an informant for CID in this nick in the 1970s. Looks like Bannerman was right.'

Brooks frowned as he took this information in. 'We're still looking for a clear motive for Charlie Wise to have organised for Walsh to be murdered.'

Gaughran nodded. 'Yes, guv. You think it was connected to Walsh being a snout?'

Brooks shrugged. 'What if Charlie was paying Walsh to feed information back to CID officers?

'That makes sense,' Gaughran said. 'If Walsh was being paid, Charlie could keep one step ahead of CID as well as feed them false information.'

'Although it poses the question why would he choose to kill Walsh now?' Brooks wondered aloud.

'Wise knew we would be talking to Walsh about the discovery of Alfie's body. He knows Walsh has a terminal diagnosis and panics that he's going to tell us about his involvement in Alfie's murder, and being paid to provide false intelligence while working as a police informant?' Gaughran proposed.

'That's two motives for Wise to have Walsh killed,' Brooks agreed.

Hassan came back from the fax machine with a quizzical look on his face. 'Guv?'

'Syed? What have you got?' Brooks asked.

Hassan held up the fax as he approached. 'Forensics stuff back from the lab.'

'Is it the DNA test on the remains?' Gaughran asked.

Hassan nodded. 'Yeah. Although it says it's only a partial match with Charlie Wise's DNA and an 0.05% variable.'

Brooks frowned. 'What does that mean?'

'No idea, guv. We'll have to ring them to get an explanation,' Hassan said as he pointed to another part of the text. 'They've had the carbon dating for the remains back which I don't understand.'

'What do you mean?' Brooks asked.

Hassan arrived at the desk and handed it to him. Gaughran could see that he was looking thoroughly perplexed. 'I think you'd better have a look at this yourself.'

CHAPTER 39

Having made their way through passport control and baggage checks, Lucy was scanning the passengers for signs of Charlie Wise and his companion while Ruth answered a call from Kevin Abbott at Heathrow Security.

Hanging up her phone, Ruth looked at Lucy. 'Right, we've got the flight number and the departure gate.'

'Great!' Lucy said as they broke into a run. 'Where are we going?'

'Gate 23,' Ruth said, pointing left. 'Flight 274 to Malaga.'

'What time does it go?'

'One thirty.'

Lucy glanced at her watch. 'It's one ten.'

'Yeah. I know,' Ruth said as they picked up speed. 'They're already boarding.'

'Can't they prevent them from boarding?'

Ruth shrugged. 'They said they'd try!'

'That's helpful.'

As they weaved in and out of passengers, Ruth was getting out of breath. She knocked into a woman who walked straight into her path.

'Sorry!'

Glancing left, she saw they had reached Gate 18.

Running full pelt, Ruth was desperate to get to Charlie Wise before he boarded the plane or they closed the gate.

They passed Gate 20.

Feeling a buzz in her pocket, Ruth pulled out her phone as she ran. Someone from Peckham nick was calling her. *They'll have to bloody wait. I'm a bit busy.*

Gate 23 loomed into view as Ruth and Lucy slowed.

To her relief, there was a long line of passengers who were waiting to have their boarding passes checked.

'Just in time,' Lucy gasped.

Ruth's phone rang again. Someone was trying to get hold of her, so she answered it as she and Lucy scanned the waiting passengers for Charlie Wise and Lesley Harlow.

'DC Hunter?'

'Ruth, it's Brooks ...'

Ruth interrupted him. 'Guv, I'm a bit busy at the moment. Can I call you back?'

'No. Not really.'

Suddenly, Ruth spotted Charlie Wise and another figure waiting in the queue. They were still wearing baseball caps and sunglasses, but she could tell it was Wise.

'Guv, I'm about to nick Charlie Wise in about five seconds, so can it wait?' Ruth said, tapping Lucy on the shoulder and pointing out Wise to her.

'The body we found at Dixon's Timber Yard isn't Alfie Wise.'

Ruth thought she had misheard Brooks. 'Say again, guv.'

'It wasn't Alfie Wise in there. Those weren't his remains.'

'Who was it then?'

'No idea.'

'Are you sure?' Ruth was now utterly confused.

'Fairly sure, Ruth. The bones in that hole were over three hundred years old,' he said.

'What? I don't understand.'

Ruth tried to take in what Brooks had just told her as she and Lucy approached Charlie Wise. They were only about ten yards away.

Ruth tried to catch her breath. 'I don't ... that doesn't make any sense.'

'I know. So, when you nick him, you might wanna ask him what the hell is going on.'

'Yes, guv. I'll call you back when we have him in custody,' Ruth said breathlessly as she ended the call.

'Everything all right?' Lucy asked.

'Not really but let's get this done now.'

Taking a few steps forward, Ruth and Lucy were beside Charlie Wise in the queue.

'Charlie?' Ruth said.

Charlie spun, saw them and looked as if he was going to run.

'Come on, Charlie. Let's not make this a big drama. It's over,' Lucy said grabbing his arm. 'You're not going anywhere.'

'There's no law against me travelling to Spain, is there?' he asked.

For a second, the figure next to him went to run, but Ruth grabbed them. 'Hey! Where do you think you're going?'

Except, the figure she had stopped wasn't a woman but a man in his 60s.

'Who are you?' Lucy asked.

'Leslie Harlow,' the man grumbled in an annoyed voice as he handed over his passport. Lucy looked at it to confirm that was his identity.

Bloody hell. Leslie - the male name!

'Okay, but you're both going to have to come with us,' Ruth said. As she spoke, an idea was forming very quickly in her mind based on what Brooks had just told her.

Moving them to one side, Lucy cuffed Charlie. 'Charlie Wise, you're under arrest for conspiracy to murder. You do not have to say anything, but anything you do say may be taken down and used in a court of law.'

'You know who my brief is. And you do know that I'll be walking out of your station after twenty minutes and then suing you for wrongful arrest?'

'That's all very interesting,' Lucy said. 'Come on.'

Harlow looked at them. 'You can't stop me from flying. I haven't done anything.'

Having taken a very close look at Leslie Harlow, Ruth gestured to him. 'Mr Harlow, can you take off your sunglasses and hat please?'

Harlow sneered. 'Why?'

Ruth looked at him. 'Just do it, please.'

As Harlow removed his baseball cap and sunglasses, Ruth realised she wasn't looking at Leslie Harlow.

Ruth looked at Charlie. 'I can see the family resemblance, Charlie.'

Charlie frowned. 'I don't know what you're talking about.'

Taking out her cuffs, Ruth looked at the man in front of her. 'Alfie Wise, I'm arresting you for perverting the cause of justice.'

CHAPTER 40

Three hours later, Ruth and Lucy were in Interview Room 1 with Charlie Wise and his solicitor, who had been present at the interview they had conducted at Charlie's home two days earlier.

Pressing the button on the recording equipment, Ruth moved her chair forward. 'Interview with Sir Charles Wise, Peckham Police Station, 29th August 1997. Present are DC Hunter, DC Henry, Sir Charles Wise and his legal representative, Ms Barbara Lister.' Ruth looked at her watch. 'Interview commencing at 3.18 pm.'

Lucy reached into a folder that was placed on the table. 'Sir Charles Wise, can I just remind you that you are still currently under caution. I want to take you back to the 27th November 1956. Could you tell us, in your own words, what happened that day?'

He and his solicitor had a hushed conversation.

'No comment,' Charlie said with no sign of emotion.

'Let me tell you what I think happened and then you can tell me if I'm wrong. You, your brother Alfie, and Trevor Walsh travelled to Dixon's Timber Yard in the evening. You had obtained human remains, presumably from one of the nearby cemeteries, which you buried along with Alfie's signet ring and your car key. Somewhere along the line, you may have fired a bullet into the back of the skull that you had stolen,' Lucy said.

'You presumed these remains would be found a few months or even a couple of years later. The key would be traced back to you, and you would identify the signet ring as belonging to Alfie. Alfie would then be declared dead and would therefore be safe. This is a long time before anyone had ever heard of DNA or carbon dating. How am I doing?'

Charlie shrugged. 'No comment.'

'We've checked the passport that Alfie was carrying. Leslie David Harlow was born on 12th October 1939. However, Leslie David Harlow died three days later and is buried in Guildford cemetery,' Lucy explained. 'Could you explain that to us, Charlie?'

'No comment.'

Ruth then put some papers down on the table. 'Checking the electoral register, it also appears that Leslie David Harlow has been a resident of Walton-on-Thames since December 1956. We've also checked UK passport control. Leslie Harlow has accompanied you on trips to Spain for the last forty years. Could you explain that to us, Charlie?'

'No comment.'

'My guess is that you felt Alfie was in great danger. Either from Terry Droy and Eddie Bannerman, who wanted revenge for Frank Weller's death, or from something that happened at the 211 Club. You faked Alfie's death and created a new identity for him to live in safety in Surrey for the last forty years. Is that correct?' Ruth asked.

'No comment.'

'The only person who knew that Alfie was alive and probably also knew where he lived was Trevor Walsh. To keep him quiet, you paid Trevor Walsh on a monthly basis for his silence.

Except something changed all that. The discovery of Alfie's fake remains meant we interviewed Trevor Walsh. But instead of keeping quiet, he told us about a letter that Alfie had written to him. Walsh had only weeks to live, and you knew that. You were worried that he didn't want to take what he knew about Alfie to his grave. You couldn't take the risk of Walsh blowing Alfie's cover, so you used a contact in Belfast to find someone who would fly in and kill him to keep him quiet. Is that correct?'

'No comment.'

Charlie and his solicitor exchanged a few words.

'I have advised my client to make no comment until he is officially charged with a criminal offence. If you are not going to charge my client, then I would ask that you release him,' the solicitor said.

Lucy looked at her watch. 'As you are well aware, we have a full twenty-four hours within which to make a charge. Charlie can return to a holding cell until we need to speak to him later.'

'You can't expect me to stay the night here,' Charlie protested.

'I know it's not the Kensington Place Hotel, Charlie, but it's the best we can do at the moment,' Ruth said. 'I'm sure they will give you a blanket if you ask nicely.'

CHAPTER 41

I t was the next day as Ruth stretched out her legs and rolled over in bed, becoming aware there was someone else in the bed. Blinking open her eyes, she saw Ella's beautiful face on the pillow. She must have crept into her bed during the night, but now she was fast asleep. Reaching over, Ruth moved a strand of her hair from her face and then traced her finger over Ella's hand.

As Ella stirred and turned a little, the early morning light shimmered on her face. *God, she really looks like Dan,* Ruth thought. *Her nose, lips and chin are identical to his.* She remembered being in this bed with Ella in between her and Dan when she was first born. How had it all gone so wrong? They had been so happy then, hadn't they? Taking Ella in her pram up to Clapham Common, or wandering along Abbeville Road and getting takeaway coffees. She remembered being so happy that she didn't want days like that to ever end.

Taking her phone from her bedside table, Ruth clicked it open and then hesitated. She knew in her heart that allowing Dan to say goodbye to Ella was the right thing to do. Despite all that he had done, he deserved to see his daughter before he left, didn't he? Denying him that felt cruel.

Tapping the keys on her phone, Ruth composed a text – *Hi there. I'd like you to meet me and Ella up by the swings on*

Clapham Common this afternoon. Let's say 2 pm. Please don't let her down. Ruth.

She sent it and, before she had even put the phone back down, a new text arrived – *I'll be there, Dan.*

Ruth reached for the remote control and switched on the early morning news. It was a weather report, and she was pleased to see that it was going to be 82 degrees with bright sunshine in London.

The news anchor looked at the camera and said, *'And the headlines this morning.'*

A photograph of Charlie Wise appeared on the screen.

'Business tycoon and political advisor Sir Charles Wise has been arrested and kept overnight at a South London police station. A police spokesperson said that Sir Charles was helping them with their enquiries. It comes only a week after the remains of a body, thought to be that of his brother Alfie Wise, were discovered, also in South London.'

Ruth's phone rang. It was Brooks. As she answered the phone, she muted the television.

'Guv?'

'Sorry to call you early on a Saturday, Ruth.'

'No problem. I'm watching the news. Charlie Wise is the lead story.'

'Well, it's about to get even bigger.'

'Why's that?'

'The CPS has looked through the evidence overnight and we're going to charge him with conspiracy to murder, as well as perverting the course of justice. It's going to trial.'

'After what happened to Trevor Walsh it somehow doesn't feel enough, if you know what I mean, guv?'

'He can still get a life sentence if we have a decent judge.'

'What about Alfie?'

'He's going to prison too. Perverting the course of justice. They looked at Arthur Gaughran, but there's not enough to charge him with anything. He's not a serving officer so he won't even have to talk to the ghost squad.'

'Okay. I guess Tim will be relieved in one way. Thanks for letting me know, guv.'

'No problem. Have a good weekend, Ruth. You deserve it,' Brooks said.

GAUGHRAN SAT IN HIS car down the road from his parents' house. Having checked that his father's car was on the drive, he knew it was likely that he was home. Brooks had called him an hour earlier to say that the CPS were not going to pursue any historic charges against his father. It was a huge relief, but Gaughran now wondered where he stood with him. When he had driven to Hastings to bring him in, his father seemed to have seen it as an act of betrayal rather than a compassionate act of support. He had no idea why. He hadn't instigated the investigation, and the allegations of police bribery and involvement in Declan Fisher and Alfie Wise's death had been a mere by-product of the initial enquiry.

Unclipping his seatbelt, Gaughran got out of the car. The air was full of the smell of freshly-cut grass as their next-door neighbour, Dave, cut his front lawn. As Gaughran walked past him towards his parent's house, Dave gave him a friendly wave. He had known him most of his life. He had even been out with

Dave's daughter Anna when they were about fifteen, until she dumped him for Matty Henshaw who everyone said looked like John Taylor from Duran Duran.

He opened the metal gate and heard the reassuring whine of the rusty hinges. Taking a breath, he stepped slowly towards the front door and knocked. His heart was thumping in his chest and his palms were sweaty.

There was the familiar sound of a key being turned, and the door opened. His mum, Celia, peered out and gave him a sombre look.

'Hi Tim,' she said in a subdued tone.

'Dad in?' Gaughran asked casually. He had no idea what his mum knew, or whether she had an inkling about what had happened in the past forty-eight hours.

'He doesn't want to see you,' she said.

'What? Why not?' Gaughran asked. Her answer had taken the wind out of his sails.

Celia shook her head and looked a little tearful. 'I don't know what's happened between the two of you, or what happened in Hastings, but he's adamant he doesn't want you in the house.'

'He hasn't told you anything?'

She shook her head. 'Nope. He said I wouldn't understand.'

'You know I haven't done anything wrong, don't you?'

'If that's the case, why's he not talking to you?'

'I really don't know, Mum.' Gaughran felt a lump in his throat. 'But I can't sort it out if he won't speak to me, can I?'

Celia shrugged. 'It's his house, love. There's nothing I can do.'

Gaughran took a few seconds to process what had been said. 'Listen, can you tell him that I forgive him?'

Celia frowned. 'I don't think that's going to go down very well.'

'No, but can you tell him anyway? Please?'

'Yeah.' Celia looked directly at him. 'Just give him a bit of time, eh? I'm sure whatever it is, he'll come round.'

Gaughran nodded sadly. 'Yeah ... I suppose I'd better go then.'

Celia sniffed and then blinked. He could see the tears forming in her eyes. 'It's all right, mum. Don't worry.'

Gaughran turned to go, and took a few steps down the path.

'Love you, Tim,' she said in a virtual whisper.

He turned and looked at her. 'Love you mum.'

He opened the gate and made his way back to his car.

CHAPTER 42

Lucy pushed her sunglasses up the bridge of her nose as she sat relaxing on the patio. Paul Weller's album *Heavy Soul* was playing inside, and she was on her third glass of wine already. It had been a very demanding week, but they had got a result, however surprising it had turned out to be.

'Here we go,' Brooks said as he appeared with a huge china dish full of food. 'Tricolore salad. Actually, I've added some figs and basil.'

'Bloody hell, Harry. Who are you? Bleedin' Marco Van Basten?' Lucy giggled as he set down the food.

Brooks laughed. 'Marco Pierre White.'

'What?'

'If you're talking about the poncy French chef, then it's Marco Pierre White.'

'What did I say?'

'Marco Van Basten.'

'Who's he then?'

'He's a Dutch footballer with a very questionable haircut,' Harry explained.

Lucy snorted and then gestured to the food. 'What have I done to deserve all this then?'

Brooks peered over his sunglasses at her as he sat down. 'You've had quite a tough week to say the least.'

'What a treat,' she said as she took a plate and helped herself to the food.

As she sat back to eat, the music from inside stopped as the album came to an end. For the next few seconds, all she could hear was the sound of children playing in a nearby garden – laughing and then excited screams.

She looked at Harry and smiled. 'I love that sound, don't you?'

'Screaming kids? Yeah, brilliant,' Brooks joked as he swigged his beer.

'Don't be a twat, Harry. I mean it. The sound of happy children playing ...'

Brooks gave her a quizzical look. 'DC Henry, it almost sounds like you're broody?'

Lucy shrugged with an anxious twinge. 'What if I am?'

'Broody?'

'Yeah. What if I was broody? We've never talked about it, have we? And I don't know why.'

'You mean kids?'

'Christ, for a top London detective, you can be very slow on the uptake.'

Brooks shrugged. 'I love kids. They're great.'

Lucy sighed. 'What about your own?'

Brooks took a few agonising seconds to respond. 'I've always wanted my own kids. Karen couldn't have them.'

'So? What do you think?'

'Think?' Brooks smiled. He was teasing her.

'Don't be a dickhead,' Lucy said shaking her head. 'Read my lips. Harry Brooks, would you like to have a baby with me?'

Brooks tried to look nonchalant but couldn't help breaking into a beaming smile. 'Why not?'

BY THE TIME RUTH AND Ella arrived at the swings on Clapham Common, Dan was waiting on a bench nearby. The Common was heaving with groups of friends picnicking, playing frisbee and football, or just lazing in the sun. The playground was a chaotic frenzy of small children running, jumping and climbing.

As Ruth drew closer to the swings, she pushed her sunglasses up onto her head and looked at Dan. It was so surreal to think that she might not see him again for years, or ever. He had been an integral part of her life for the past seven years. She wasn't naïve. The anger and bitterness from his affair and walking out on her and Ella was still there. She had no desire to be with him or for him to be in her life anymore. But the finality of Ella saying goodbye to her father was a poignant end to a significant chapter in her life.

Leaning down and unclipping her from her pushchair, Ruth looked at Ella. 'Go and say hello to Daddy, sweetheart.'

For a moment, Ella looked a little confused.

Dan squatted down and smiled at her. 'Hello, Ella.'

As recognition dawned, Ella began to walk towards him and then broke into a run. Dan hugged her. 'Hey, you look so pretty in your dress.'

'Thank you,' Ella said sounding pleased.

Taking her in his arms, Dan stood up and twirled her around as she giggled.

'Is Daddy going to take you to the swings?' Ruth asked.

'YEAH!' Ella yelled.

Sitting down on the bench, Ruth looked up at Dan. 'It's okay. I'll watch from here. And don't push her too high because she gets scared.'

Dan smiled uncertainly. 'Yeah, I remember ... I'll see you in a bit then?'

Ruth put her sunglasses back on and took out her cigarettes.

Turning back, Dan looked at her. 'Ruth?'

'Yeah?'

Dan gave her a meaningful look. 'Thank you.'

Ruth lit a cigarette and watched them as they walked away, hand in hand, towards the playground.

And then her tears came ...

AMAZON REVIEW

If you enjoyed this book, *please* leave me
a short review on Amazon. I really
does make all the difference.
Many thanks.

Enjoy this book?
Get the first book in the
DI Ruth Hunter Snowdonia series
https://www.amazon.co.uk/dp/B08268L6L8
https://www.amazon.com/dp/B08268L6L8

AUTHOR'S NOTE

Although this book is very much a work of fiction, it is located in Snowdonia, a spectacular area of North Wales. It is steeped in history and folklore that spans over two thousand years. It is worth mentioning that Llancastell is a fictional town on the eastern edges of Snowdonia. I have made liberal use of artistic licence, names and places have been changed to enhance the pace and substance of the story.

Acknowledgements

I will always be indebted to the people who have made this novel possible.

My mum, Pam, and my stronger half, Nicola, whose initial reaction, ideas and notes on my work I trust implicitly. And Dad, for his overwhelming enthusiasm and valuable background information on South London in the 1950s.

Thanks also to Barry Asmus, former South London CID detective, for checking my work and explaining the complicated world of police procedure and investigation. Carole Kendal for her acerbic humour, copy editing and meticulous proofreading. My designer Stuart Bache for the incredible cover design. And my superb agent, Millie Hoskins at United Agents.

Your FREE book is waiting for you now

Get your FREE copy of the prequel to
the DI Ruth Hunter Series NOW
at www.simonmccleave.com[1]
and join my VIP Email Club

---

1. http://www.simonmccleave.com

1 Don't know why you changed this bit ... but you made a typo!!!!

2 Making consistent with previous.

3 Capitalised to make consistent with the other two later in the story.

4 Missed one of these above, so added 'again'.

5 In the bit you added in Chapter 11, Walsh said he got the letter "... just *before* he went missing." Come on Simon, get a grip ...!

6 I've put this in full 'cos the only other time it appeared in the book so far was when Brooks said "This man has lunch with the PM." Saves possible confusion for readers.

7 Just realised they still think this is the female version.

Printed in Great Britain
by Amazon

31667475R00159